T0390782

THE PREMONITIONS CLUB

THE
PREMONITIONS
CLUB

GWENDOLYN WOMACK

CamCat
Books

CamCat Books
2810 Coliseum Centre Drive, Suite 300
Charlotte, NC 28217-4574

Hardcover ISBN 9780744311266
Paperback ISBN 9780744311273
eBook ISBN 9780744311297

Library of Congress Control Number: 2024944539

Book and cover design by Maryann Appel

Interior artwork by Desifoto, Ekaterina, Lazarev, LOVE A Stock, Rikirennes

5   3   2   4

To my dear friend,
Beth Szymkowski

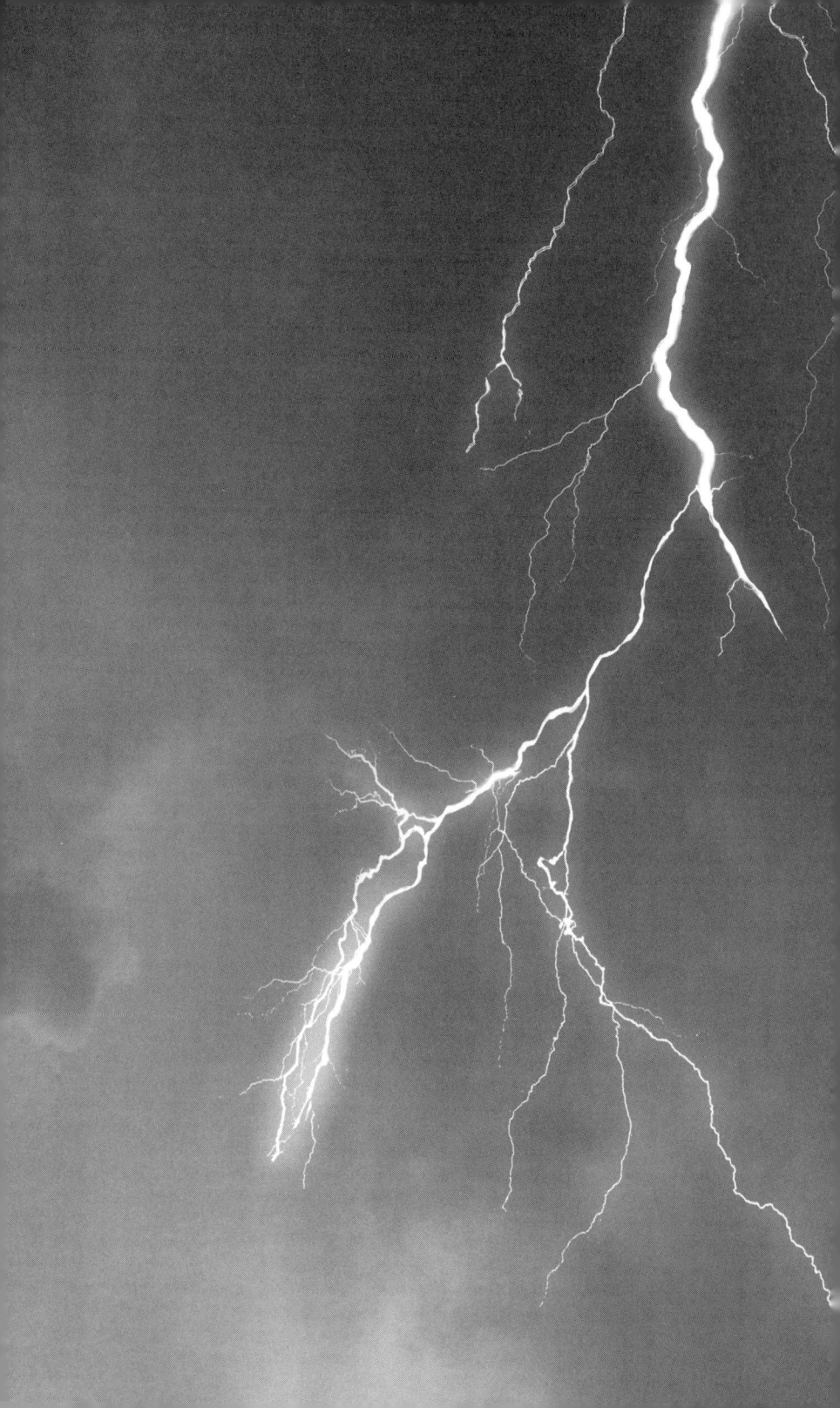

In 1968, the Premonitions Bureau formed,
inviting people to mail in letters with predictions.
Some of those predictions came true.
With the rise of the Internet,
the Bureau finally closed its doors in the 1990s.
But where did all the letters go?

1993

GRAYSON HAD NEVER TRIED TO SEE so far into the future before.

The possibility of what he'd seen weighed on him like a heavy stone, still waiting to be cast into the rippling water.

This would have to be his last letter. Hopefully, it would never need to be read by the person he was writing it for. He thought about all the things he could say and then what he should say. With a deep breath, he put his pen to paper.

PRESENT DAY

1

LIV

premonition:
a strong feeling something is about to happen

LIV HALL DIDN'T BELIEVE IN KNOWING the future before it happened. If she did, maybe she would have sensed her stepdad had been cheating on her mom all year. Or maybe she would have known he would abandon them to go live with his new girlfriend. Or maybe she'd have known she and her mom—who was busy having a nervous breakdown—would pack up and leave New York City to go live with her grandfather in Hyde Park. And definitely she would have known she'd be forced to finish out her junior year, all two and half months of it, at Roosevelt High School as the new girl. "That girl from Manhattan" with the funky jewelry and silver armband. And maybe, just maybe, she would have had the inkling to know her grandfather would pass away peacefully in his sleep two months later, leaving her mom the house and everything in it.

But life hadn't been predictable. It had come at them full speed, an eighty-mile-an-hour chain of disasters. During the worst of it, Liv would hide out in her room making jewelry, her longtime hobby. She'd stay up late, bent over her worktable with a soldering iron as if she could somehow weld her life back together again.

Her favorite piece she'd made was a silver armband that looked like braided rope, when really it was a chain of triskelions, an ancient Celtic symbol of three spirals joined together. She'd found the symbol in a design book and making the armband had gotten her though that last horrid month of the divorce. Now she never took it off. The only other thing keeping her from completely losing it over the dumpster fire of her life was that at least she had one friend in town—Winnie—the daughter of her mom's oldest friend. She and Winnie had spent summers together as kids and fortunately stayed in touch over the years.

After her grandfather's funeral, Liv's mom fell apart. She basically locked herself in her room to power through Kleenex and watch Netflix all day. It didn't help that the house suddenly had become one big ghost of her grandfather's memory. He had lived there forever and amassed enough stuff to prove it.

Liv was planning to go through his things over the summer and organize the house for her mom, but her grandfather's estate attorney kept calling and leaving messages about coming to sort her grandfather's things right away. Liv asked her mom to stall them because she wanted to go through everything before strangers did.

She decided to start with the attic and work down. The house was a two-story Victorian-style riddled with nooks and crannies. The attic was huge, the kind that could be turned into a spare bedroom or a loft. It had a pitched-roof ceiling with enough room to stand, and an old-timey circular window looked down onto the street. The space was crammed with a smorgasbord of keepsakes, knickknacks, and junk waiting for a flea market. Countless boxes, storage chests, cast-off furniture, luggage, and her grandfather's golf clubs filled the space.

Liv had convinced Winnie (more like begged and pleaded) to come over to help, even bribing her with fresh cinnamon rolls and mochas from the local bakery. They spent all Sunday morning in the attic listening to music while sorting and opening boxes.

"I think there's more stuff behind this thing." Liv stood on a step stool and tried to peer over the stack of wood panels draped with a black tarp.

"Sorry. I draw the line with heavy lifting." Winnie fanned herself, beginning to look wilted. She was *not* in let's-go-through-the-attic attire. She always wore black pencil skirts, no matter what, and dressed in vintage clothes. Her hair was the star, a 1920s pageboy, blunt cut and dyed jet black with the edges ringed in sapphire blue. The dramatic style framed perfect black eyeliner, siren-red lipstick, and cat-eyed glasses. She was sitting on an old blanket like a queen, and Liv had brought up a fan for her an hour ago when it got warm.

"Come on, please?"

"And destroy my manicure?" Winnie flashed her nails. They were painted silver with purple stars and moons stenciled on them. "Maybe Matty can help. He should be off work soon."

Liv raised her eyebrows without comment. Matty was Winnie's best friend. He was even shorter and skinnier than she was. He also liked to dress like a fashion designer from *Next In Fashion* and had already told them he refused to touch anything dusty today. Liv sighed and twisted her long hair back up into its clip. "Who knows when he'll get here? I want to move it now."

"Good luck," Winnie teased. She reached into her purse, pulled out the Tarot cards she always kept with her, and drew a card.

She flashed it playfully to Liv. The image on the card was an old man walking alone with a lantern and said *The Hermit*.

"See? You're on your own."

Liv rolled her eyes. Winnie loved to use her Tarot cards to make a point.

She drew another card. the *Ten of Pentacles*. "But I do see buried treasure up here." Winnie showed her a card filled with gold coins.

"Yeah, it's behind this wood if you help me," Liv shot back. She tried on her own to get it to budge and put her hands on her hips in frustration.

Winnie pulled a third card, *Death*, and held it up with dramatic flair. "Or maybe the wood's not meant to be moved."

Liv stared at the Death card and tried to shake off the sudden unease it gave her. Winnie had taught herself Tarot over a year ago and gotten good at it. She'd even done a reading for Liv last summer when Liv was in town visiting. At the time, everything Winnie told Liv sounded so far-fetched. Over a spread of cards, she said Liv's parents would get divorced and Liv would leave New York City. Now it'd all come true.

Liv asked her, only half joking, "Should I be worried?"

"Yeah, if I don't get a break soon." Winnie put the cards away and stood up to fix her skirt. "I vote we grab lunch."

Liv looked out the window. Her neighbor across the street was washing his car, an old Ford Mustang, in the driveway. He was wearing board shorts, a workout tank, and flip-flops. The tank showed off every muscle on his tanned arms.

"I bet he could he move it." Liv nodded to him.

Winnie joined her at the window, her eyes going round. "No. Way. You live across the street from Forester Torres? How did I not know this?"

Forester went to their school, but Liv had never talked to him. He was the football team's quarterback and the most popular guy at school. Looks-wise he reminded Liv a little bit of her stepdad with his thick, wavy black hair tied back. Maybe that's why she was feeling so fearless and started opening the window.

"Wait! What are you doing?" Winnie gripped her arm in alarm.

"Asking for help. He looks like the Hulk down there. He can totally move this thing."

"Have you completely lost it?" Winnie tried to stop her. "You can't ask Forester Torres to come move your furniture."

"Why not? It's not like either of us like him." Only one guy at school was the object of Liv's fantasies, and he was *not* Forester Torres. "Seriously, Win. Who cares?"

"I care! It'll look weird. What if he says something to his friends?"

Liv turned to Winnie in surprise. "I thought you didn't buy into all that social clique crap."

"I don't. I'm not. But you haven't lived your whole life going to school with these people."

At school, Winnie was a loner and sometimes hung out with the Drama Club with Matty. Liv didn't know where she fit into the scheme of cliques and cool status at school, and right now she was beyond caring. All she wanted to do was move this stupid wall of wood.

"Win, come on. What if he's really nice? And like you said, *I* need help." Liv cranked the window open with the handle before Winnie could stop her and called out, "Hey! Hello down there!"

Forester looked up, and Winnie ducked down to hide.

Liv laughed and yelled down, "I'm your new neighbor and clearing out the attic with my friend and we need help moving some wood panels. Think you can come over for a minute?"

Winnie was laughing now too. "Oh my God. I can't believe you're doing this." She put her face in her hands. "What's he saying?" she whispered.

"He nodded and put down the hose."

"You're kidding me."

"No, he's coming over." Liv grinned and closed the window back up. "See? That was easy."

"I hate you." Winnie picked up the electric fan and blasted her face to cool off. The doorbell rang and Liv ran downstairs, knowing her mom was still asleep. She whipped open the door, a little harder than she intended.

Forester took a step back and put a friendly hand up. "Whoa there."

"Sorry, hi." Liv smiled, trying to play it cool even though she was sure she looked wrecked. She was wearing frayed cutoff jeans she'd chopped off herself and an old tank top that showed off her armband. Her hair was up in a messy bun with a clip that liked to slip off every hour.

Forester towered over her. He was huge, well over six feet. She stared up at him, wondering if this was really a good idea. But it was too late now. "Thanks for coming over. I'm Liv."

"I know. The new girl." He gave her an easy grin.

"Yeah, that's me." Liv grimaced. "I really appreciate the help."

"No prob. Let's do it." He shrugged off the thanks and followed her up the stairs.

When they got to the attic, he gave Winnie a friendly salute. "Yo yo."

Winnie raised her eyebrows in surprise. "Yo yo yourself."

He teased them, "So ladies, what are we moving today?"

"Um . . . these wood panels." Liv pointed. "There might be stuff behind it I need to go through."

Forester circled around the chaos. "No prob. Why don't you guys take one end, and we can angle it over this way?"

"Sorry team," Winnie announced, shaking her head regretfully. "I gotta sit this one out. My nails." She wiggled them for effect.

"It's fine, Win." Liv rolled her eyes with an exasperated smile. She and Forester each took a side and tried to lift it together.

They made several failed attempts until Forester finally said, "I think we need more muscle." He pulled out his cell and speed dialed someone.

Liv looked at Winnie in alarm. *What* was he doing?

Whoever he called picked up on the first ring. "Yo, dude." Forester walked over to the window and stared out. "You still stopping by? I'm at the house across the street from mine. We need help moving some wood. It'll just take a sec. Think you can come over?"

Winnie was looking at Liv in alarm too, frantically signally. *Who is he calling?*

Forester hesitated, listening to whatever the person was saying. His back to the girls, he dropped his voice. "Seriously? She is? Whatever, man. I don't care. She can come." He sounded annoyed.

Winnie made several more frantic gestures: *Who is she and what is happening?*

Liv threw up her hands with an *I don't know!* Just as stressed.

Forester hung up and turned back around, and they dropped their hands. "Jax can help. He'll be here in five minutes with Nebony." He said it casually when it was anything but.

Liv turned back to Winnie, her expression one of absolute horror.

Jaxon Coleson and Nebony Price were coming over here?

To her house?

Even Liv, in her new girl bubble, knew who they were. Nebony was *the* most popular girl. Alpha head cheerleader and social media superstar, she had a gazillion followers online from all her cheerleading posts, not to mention she was a physically perfect goddess. Nebony and Forester had been a hot item for two years until they broke up over spring break. No one knew who had pulled the plug. Rumor was Nebony had moved on, with—gasp—Forester's best friend.

Jaxon Coleson.

The star of every romantic fantasy Liv had had in the past two months.

Beginning on her first day of school.

She and Winnie had pulled into the parking lot in Winnie's car. Jaxon had been standing near a Jeep with friends. The moment Liv saw him, a visceral reaction hit her full force and she had to wrench her eyes away and keep on walking. She couldn't tell if he noticed her or not. He was standing still, his eyes hidden by reflective shades, his brown hair more gold in the sun.

When she crossed the parking lot, she could have sworn he *was* watching her—but when she glanced back he was looking away. She quickly discovered he was not in any of her classes. Every day she found herself looking for him. In the parking lot. At lunch. On the field. She rarely saw him, only the taillights of his Jeep zipping in and out of the school lot with the top down. Sometimes Nebony was in the car with him, her long black hair flying in the wind. Liv never told Winnie about her secret crush. It was more like an obsession, really. She dreamed of him practically every night—and not just normal dreams; they were IMAX 4D versions where she came to his house and hung out in his room. It wasn't exactly stalking. She couldn't help what she did when she went to sleep. A lot of people had vivid dreams and overactive imaginations. That's all it was—at least she kept telling herself that.

And now he was on his way over to move her granddad's old stuff?

This was a nightmare. She tried to do damage control. "You guys don't have to help. Really. My mom will get someone to do it. Why don't you call him back?"

She did *not* want Jaxon Coleson here—or Nebony Price. Today was supposed to have been a mellow Sunday. She couldn't even remember if she'd brushed her teeth this morning.

"Relax, it's no biggie." Forester waved off her concern, already heading down the stairs. "Got anything to drink while we wait for them?"

"Uh . . . sure." Liv had no idea what to do. "I have lemonade?"

"Awesome sauce," Forester shot back, heading to the kitchen. Winnie and Liv hung back and followed more slowly so they could talk.

Winnie whispered, "Did he just say awesome sauce?"

Liv grabbed Winnie's arm and gave her a little shake, whispering, "Jaxon Coleson and Nebony Price are coming over here! What do we do?"

"Roll with it. You're the one that started this, *dude*."

Liv tried not to laugh, but her heart was now racing out of control. The impulse to call out to Forester from the window was having an unforeseen ripple effect. The enormity of which she had yet to realize.

2

WINNIE

predestined:
determined in advance by fate

WINNIE FELT THE MANIC URGE TO laugh. She wasn't sure if this was hysterically funny or about to become one of those days you looked back on and cringed. The star quarterback of the school was standing in Liv's kitchen, and his ex-girlfriend and Mr. Popular were on their way over. Things were about to get surreal.

Forester leaned back against the counter with a laid-back air, and Winnie couldn't help but stare at him and wonder . . . She squinted her eyes, focusing hard, and waited for her vision to adjust. Whenever she stared at someone long enough, she could see their aura. The energy field emanated from them like a halo of light.

Liv gave her a silent signal to stop, knowing Winnie was seconds away from looking cross-eyed, but Winnie ignored her. Right now, she was concentrating on Forester with extreme focus until the space around him began to come alive in a vibrant swirl of color.

What she saw didn't surprise her. Usually someone's aura favored one or two colors, like the palette of their personality. Forester's aura was mostly red with a little bit of yellow. Reds were passionate, goal-oriented, extremely competitive, energetic, and forceful. They were also temperamental and stubborn.

Winnie was focused so hard on seeing it, she was sure her right eye was beginning to cross. Matty always said she looked disturbing when it did.

Liv purposefully stepped in front of her to block her view.

"So what are you up to this summer?" Liv asked, diverting Forester's attention. "Just hanging out?"

Winnie caught Forester giving her a perplexed look before shifting his focus to Liv. "I'll be working at the River Connection doing kayaking expeditions. Right now I work weekends." He grinned. "You should try it sometime. On the house."

Winnie stopped aura-gazing to shoot Liv a look. Was he flirting with her? Probably. Liv was seriously pretty without having to try. Even with no makeup and her hair in a messy twist, she still looked beautiful. Liv's aura was usually vibrant green with a swirl of blue. Greens were nurturing, generous, and compassionate. The problem was, Liv's aura had dimmed and gotten mottled since she'd moved here—even more after her grandfather died. The muddy hues signaled confusion, sadness, and a lack of confidence. It was why Winnie had given up her entire Sunday to come help her clean out the attic and forced Matty to come too.

Liv glossed over Forester's open invitation with an awkward "Thanks" and opened the fridge. "We've got boysenberry ginger-mint lemonade." She poured him a glass. "My mom's a food reporter. She gets samples of new stuff to try."

"No way." Forester leaned forward to study the label. "That's rad."

"Yeah, real rad," Winnie agreed flatly, still staring at him, and Liv shot her a look.

When the doorbell rang, Forester tensed up, and Liv hurried to answer it. Winnie hovered in the kitchen doorway to watch because this was going to be good.

Jaxon Coleson and Nebony Price were here. Matty was going to flip out.

Liv opened the front door, and Jaxon's eyes widened in surprise. Nebony cocked an eyebrow at Liv and said to no one in particular, "The new girl's the neighbor?"

"The name's Liv. Nice to meet you." Liv sounded nervous, but then, Nebony was intimidating to most people. It was just one of the reasons Winnie couldn't stand her. Miss Look At Me I'm Head Cheerleader with a Gazillion Followers. Nebony's clique had made fun of her for years. Maybe Nebony hadn't said anything rude herself, but she'd been there with a condescending smirk on her face.

Today, Nebony was looking very sports glam in a running outfit that showed off every perfect curve. Her long jet-black hair was streaked with coppery highlights and accentuated by dramatic bangs. She and Jaxon made a striking couple. Jaxon was almost as tall as Forester and dressed in black cargo pants and a T-shirt. His reserved air made him seem older, like a college guy.

In her periphery, Winnie caught Liv's aura flooding with pink. The pink quickly bloomed into a full-on Barbie Dreamhouse love cloud and Winnie let out a surprised laugh. Liv had a thing for Jaxon Coleson?

Everyone turned to look at her. Winnie shook her head with a grin. "Don't mind me."

Jaxon cleared his throat, his eyes back on Liv. "Forester said you needed help?"

"Yeah, thanks." Liv opened the door wide, now staring at the floor.

Nebony breezed past Winnie and greeted Forester with a "Hey you." There was an edge to her voice. "Long time no see. What have you been up to?" Mirroring his nonchalant pose, she leaned back against the kitchen counter across from him.

"Not much. Just being a good neighbor." Forester raised his glass in a snarky toast. Gone was the laid-back friendly guy who'd been smiling a few minutes ago.

Nebony stared at him a long moment and said, "I guess you're good at a lot of things."

"I guess I am."

The tension between them was hard to ignore. No one said anything for an awkward moment. Winnie wished she could tune into the aura fireworks sure to be erupting between them but didn't want to make things weirder.

Jaxon was staring at Liv but glanced over to Winnie. "Hey."

"Hey." She nodded and then offered a reluctant "Hey" to Nebony who replied with the same. "Hey" was all anyone had to say to each other. It was downright painful. Liv hovered in the doorway looking ready to bail.

Jaxon asked her, "So what needs moving?"

Liv's face turned pinker than her aura, in an obvious I'm-blushing-badly way. "Some wood." Then she added, "in the attic," and abruptly turned to lead the way.

On the way up the stairs, Forester teased Jaxon, "Think those arms can handle one end?"

"Yeah. I'm used to taking up your slack," Jaxon shot back, sounding irritated.

Winnie wondered if it was for being dragged over here. Or maybe since he was together with Nebony, now there was bad blood with Forester. Matty would know. He knew all the gossip.

While the boys got busy figuring out how to maneuver the wood to the other corner, Nebony sauntered over to the window and pulled a neon-orange mini Polaroid camera from her purse. She took a selfie with it and lazily fanned the photo to help it develop. Then she started streaming music on her phone. She twirled around, doing some effortless dance moves.

She caught Winnie watching her and said breezily, "Party in the attic."

Winnie couldn't tell if that was sarcasm or a diss. She tried to think of a comeback, but her mind went blank. Before she could recover, she heard the front door open downstairs and Matty called up.

"Oh yooooo-hooooo! I'm here! Sorry I'm late. Hey, whose Jeep is that outside?" Matty kept talking in a steady stream, Matty-style, his voice getting progressively louder as he bounded up the stairs. "Did you guys find anything amazing to warrant my being here?"

Winnie watched Matty come to a full stop at the door and his mouth drop open when he took in the scene:

Forester and Jaxon were seriously flexing as they competed against each other in a studfest *let's move the wood* competition. Liv stood nearby, suddenly the shyest girl on the planet, looking like she was trying hard to become invisible. Winnie seriously needed to talk to her when this was over.

Matty slid up and whispered furiously in her ear, "What. Is. Happening?" His eyes darted around the room.

Winnie nodded to Nebony, who was still dancing. "We're having a party in the attic."

Nebony saw Matty and called to him. "Hey, I know you! It's Macbeth!" she said, recognizing him from the school's spring play. "Come dance with me, Macbeth!"

Without hesitating, Matty joined her in the corner and launched into his goofy breakdance robot moves.

Nebony and Winnie both laughed at the same time and their eyes met. Then Nebony surprised her by launching into her own robot. Of course she was good at it too. Winnie rolled her eyes to herself and turned away to the boys just as they finished clearing the wood panels. The pile fell to the floor with a loud bang.

Winnie startled. She and Liv could both only gape at what had been hidden behind it.

Over a dozen boxes stood stacked against the wall. Written across them in black marker were the same three words in all caps:

DO NOT OPEN
DO NOT OPEN
DO NOT OPEN

The writing had an unsettling frantic vibe, as if it'd been written in a hurry. Winnie suddenly felt like she was staring at a crime scene. All that was missing was the yellow tape. She came closer to read the shipping labels. The boxes were all addressed to Liv's house to someone named Grayson Spencer.

She gasped when she saw who the boxes were from.

The Premonitions Bureau.

3

LIV

psychography:
foretelling the future through the written word

LIV STARED AT THE BOXES, READY to die of embarrassment. What in the world was the Premonitions Bureau? Why were so many of their boxes up here?

And why were they addressed to Grayson Spencer of all people?

"What's the Premonitions Bureau?" Jaxon came to stand beside her.

Liv shook her head, at the moment unable to formulate a coherent thought. Even Jaxon was taking second place to the tumult of questions whirling in her head.

Winnie was the one who answered. "It's really wild. I read about it. They were paranormal researchers who put out ads across the country for people to mail in predictions to see if they came true or not."

"For real?" Jaxon asked, crossing his arms.

Winnie nodded and put her hand on one of the boxes. "Liv, how is your grandfather connected to the Premonitions Bureau?"

"I have no idea." Liv racked her brain for a logical answer and said the first thing that came to mind, "He was a psychiatrist before he retired. Maybe he worked with them and patients . . . ?"

"To see if they were psychic?" Nebony sounded skeptical.

It did sound like a stretch.

"Can we open one?" Winnie was practically jumping up and down. "Please please please?"

"I guess." It wasn't like her grandfather was there to mind. Liv grabbed the utility knife but then hesitated. "Or maybe we shouldn't." *Do Not Open* was written all over them for a reason.

Winnie pointed out, "Your grandfather left you and your mom everything in the house. So technically these boxes are yours. You can't just throw them away without knowing what's inside."

Liv agreed, but still she hesitated.

"I vote you open it," Forester said. He was intently checking all the boxes' return addresses as if he suddenly worked for UPS.

"I second!" Matty hovered nearby.

"I vote no." Jaxon shook his head. "It says, do not open, for a reason."

Only Nebony seemed like she couldn't care less. She was busy taking another Polaroid selfie in front of the boxes.

Liv *did* want to know what was inside. She grabbed the knife again and sliced one open.

Old, stamped envelopes spilled out. They were all addressed to the Premonitions Bureau, and the letters had been opened.

"No way," Winnie said in hushed excitement as she bent down to take a closer look. "It must be all the predictions people mailed in! Can we read them?"

"Do we want to?" Liv shivered, suddenly feeling as if they'd just let a ghost into the room. She caught Jaxon glance at her with a frown.

"Are you kidding?" Winnie took a letter from the top of the stack and slipped it from the envelope. "This is awesome. I told you there was treasure up here."

But as Winnie began to read, her smile quickly faded.

"What is it?" Liv asked, her voice barely a whisper.

"Yeah, what does it say?" Matty spoke up. "Read it out loud."

Winnie cleared her throat. "'Dear Madam or Sir, I keep having a dream of a car crashing. The car explodes and there's a girl trapped inside. I don't know who she is, but I can see her face through the glass as she pounds on the window, trying to get out. I feel the desperate need to save her, but I never can. Is this a premonition or a dream, and how can I tell the difference? Please help me, Beverly Wicks.'"

No one said a word. Silence had descended on them like a vise.

Until Jaxon turned to Forester and asked him, "Is this some kind of joke?"

"What?" Forester blinked, looking taken aback.

Jaxon ran his hand through his hair. "Seriously. Did you put them up to this?"

"No man—I would never, Jax, I swear." Forester lowered his voice, as if the group couldn't hear them. "Why would you even think that? Are you tweaking, bro?"

Liv glanced from Forester to Jaxon. She had no idea what they were talking about.

"This letter's postmarked 1989," Winnie pointed out to Jaxon. She flipped to the back page. "And look, guys. There's an analysis attached!" She read it. "'Unable to verify premonition. Most likely a dream, psychological in nature.'"

"I want to read one!" Matty announced and made a big deal out of choosing his. "Eenie-meenie-miney-mo." He plucked a letter from the bunch. "Dear Premonitions Bureau, a girl is going to be kidnapped," he hesitated at the letter's chilling opening, "in Brooklyn on the morning of December tenth. The kidnapper is alone, driving an old brown Lincoln Town Car with out-of-state plates. I can't make out the license number. He lures the girl to his window, asking for directions, and grabs her.'"

The play-by-play account was unnerving. Nebony posed in front of the box and snapped a Polaroid selfie with an over-the-top horrified expression on her face.

Winnie shot her an annoyed look.

Matty read on, now somber. "The girl's name is Carrie. I don't know her last name. She's in fifth grade and has brown hair. The kidnapper is going to take her to an old boathouse. I believe it is Hammonds Cove Marina in the Bronx. Please help. This will happen, but there is still time to save her. Sincerely, Jerald Peterson."

Winnie snatched the letter from Matty and flipped it over to read the investigator's notes aloud. "Verified. Interviewed Jerald Peterson and contacted NYPD. A copy of the letter was forwarded to them. Carrie Williams was kidnapped on the morning of December 10, 1989. Premonition determined to be authentic." Winnie put down the letter. "Holy shit. Guys, this is a real prediction!"

"Did they save the girl?" Nebony said, actually sounding concerned.

"I don't know." Winnie flipped the letter over.

Forester said, frowning, "Hopefully the police acted on it."

Matty took the letter from Winnie to read the back of it too.

Liv stared at the boxes, appalled. Were they all filled with letters like these? Predicting death, fires, and kidnappings? Was her grandfather's house secretly Doomsday Central?

Forester asked her, "So your granddad was some kind of psychic investigator?"

"No." Though Liv wasn't sure how to justify the mountain of boxes. "I mean . . . I don't think so."

"But all these letters are to the Premonitions Bureau." Forester examined a stack of letters like evidence.

Liv didn't know what to say. She took a letter too and studied it closely. "He was a psychiatrist, helping people with standard shrink stuff like depression and divorce." She felt the need to point out, "I'm sure this isn't his handwriting on the analysis." She glanced at Jaxon, who had his arms crossed and was staring at the open box of premonitions like it was full of poison.

They locked eyes and he gave her an unfathomable look. She was standing close enough to see his eyes were a startling blue with brown at the center, as if amber were trapped inside.

"Then why does he have them?" he asked her.

She swallowed, unable to look away, and her heart raced into a gallop again. He was waiting for an answer when—

Bang! Something crashed hard into the attic window. Everyone jumped, and Nebony screamed.

Liv whirled toward the sound to find a crack now splintering the glass.

She rushed over and looked down to see a black bird hopping and cawing angrily in the yard, its wing broken.

Winnie came to stand beside her. "Oh my God! It just flew right into the window!"

Matty peered over their shoulders. "'Ominous bird of yore. Take thy beak from out my heart,'" he said, getting into full thespian mode.

Winnie laughed at him. "Is that Poe?"

"Of course. It's *a raven* and it's creepy."

Nebony joined them, asking, "What's a poe?"

Winnie gave her a look, and Matty explained it was Edgar Allan Poe and lines from his poem "The Raven."

The bird kept cawing. Liv tried to calm her racing pulse and gently ran her finger down the deep fissure in the center of the window. Fortunately, it hadn't shattered.

Jaxon backed away toward the door, looking unnerved, as if the attic were an Escape Room and he needed to get out.

"Liv?" Her mom called up from the kitchen. "Honey? Are you home?"

Her mother's voice broke the spell on everyone.

Liv hurried to the stairs, and Jaxon shifted to make room, standing behind her. She called out, "I'm in the attic! Be down in a sec."

Her hair fell again. Jaxon caught the clip before it landed on the floor. Liv whirled around, startled. "Oh! Thank you."

Instead of giving it back, he turned it over and over in his hand, staring at it as if it were some kind of puzzle. Then his eyes shot up to hers and her breath hitched.

For a moment, she was sure he knew she secretly dreamed of him at night. She grabbed the clip out of his hand with a thanks and hastily twisted her hair back up while he leaned against the wall, watching her.

Liv turned to the group with an overly bright smile. "Thanks for the help guys!" The subtext was clear: *we're all done here*. She could not wait for this disaster to be over.

Forester teased her, "Anytime, neighbor. I'm right across the street. Day or night." He was clearly flirting.

Liv caught Jaxon frown and she glanced over at Nebony whose face had become a storm cloud.

Nebony sauntered over to Jaxon and laced her arm possessively in his. "Let's go, Jaxy. We've got fun to do."

Jaxy? Liv met Winnie's eyes.

Nebony blew a kiss to the group, "Ciao," and was the first one down the stairs with Jaxon right behind her. Liv brought up the rear.

Outside, she risked a glance at Jaxon to find him studying her. He asked, "Are you going to go through the letters?"

Winnie was the one who answered. "Heck yeah! It's gonna be a prediction party." She hooked her arm around Liv's shoulder. "We're reading all the letters."

Liv couldn't help but grimace. At least one person was excited about the letters. She didn't know what to think.

Jaxon's eyes shifted from Liv to Winnie and back again. "Or maybe don't," he suggested, his voice soft. "See you." He put on his sunglasses and headed to his Jeep where Nebony was already perched in the passenger seat, watching Forester cross the street to his house.

"Well that was fantastically weird," Winnie announced as Jaxon drove off.

"In more ways than one," Matty chimed in, looking at his phone as they headed back inside. "Nebony just followed me on Instagram."

"Seriously?" Winnie grabbed his phone to look.

"Liv?" Liv's mom called again from the kitchen.

"I'll meet you guys upstairs in my room," Liv told them and headed to the kitchen.

Her mom was busy making coffee. Liv's first feeling when she saw her was relief her mom didn't look like she had been crying all night, but she still looked disheveled. *Who wore a bathrobe in the afternoon?* Before the breakup, her mom had always looked good. Sometimes she could pass as Liv's older sister. Today, her mom looked her full forty-five years with serious bed head and no makeup. She looked more than that—she looked defeated.

Her mom nodded to the kitchen window where she must have seen Jaxon's Jeep. "Sweetie, I'm glad you're making friends, but I'm not exactly dressed for company."

"Sorry. Those guys coming over wasn't planned."

"Well, give me some warning next time."

"I would have texted you if I had a phone."

Her mom turned to her with her hand on her hip. "You've lost three phones since the move. I refuse to get you another one until your next birthday."

"Mom, seriously I don't know how—"

Her mom cut her off. "We've been over this a hundred times. I don't want to discuss it anymore, sweetie. I understand this has been a rough time for us both and things have been chaotic and you're scatterbrained. But three times? You need to learn responsibility to keep track of your things or pay the consequences."

Liv sighed, knowing it was an argument she couldn't win. The problem was her mom had every right to be mad. After the second time she lost the phone, the cell insurance wouldn't replace it and her mom had paid out of pocket. Liv felt horrible about it, which was why she let the discussion go.

Liv opened the pantry, eying the eclectic assortment of gourmet snacks from companies wanting a review from her mom. Right now, it was the only food in the house. She grabbed a bag of jerky made out of shitake mushrooms. "Can we eat these?"

"Sure." Her mom turned to her. "Oh, your grandfather's estate attorney's office called again. They want to come over this week to go through things, and we need to be in Manhattan on Wednesday to read the will."

Liv shook her head. "Can you ask them to wait? I still need time." She'd just started on the attic and now had thousands of predictions to deal with. "Do you know if granddad was ever involved in psychic investigations?"

Her mom blinked in surprise. "Psychic investigations?"

"Like researching premonitions, that kind of thing."

"Not that I know of. Why?"

Now she had her mom's full attention. Liv tried to downplay it. The last thing she needed was her mom up in the attic in her bathrobe going through boxes. "I found some old letters in the attic addressed to the Premonitions Bureau and didn't know what they were."

"The Premonitions Bureau? That doesn't sound like something your granddad would be into."

Liv thought so too. Her grandfather didn't seem like the kind of person who kept secrets, but hiding boxes of premonitions in the attic was a big one.

But what if it wasn't his secret?

The boxes hadn't been addressed to him.

They'd been addressed to Grayson Spencer, a name she hadn't heard in years. Her real father. The man who'd abandoned her and her mother when she was born.

Which was the only reason Liv agreed with Winnie. She planned to open all the boxes and find out why her father had hidden thousands of old premonitions in this house—and why he'd wanted no one to read them.

<ENCRYPTED TRANSMISSION>
<DEFENSE INTELLIGENCE AGENCY SERVER>

<From: MIRIAM>
<Priority: HIGH>

The Premonitions Bureau mentioned online.

Posted by @nebonycheergoddess:

Reading a spooky old letter from the
Premonitions Bureau.
😷 😷 😷 😷
😷 😷 😷 😷
#mystery #premonition #psychic

Cannot confirm authenticity of the letter
or where Polaroid photo was taken.

@nebonycheergoddess is located in
Hyde Park, New York.

Will monitor and decide next course
of action.

4

MATTY

oracle:
a priest or priestess in antiquity who foretold prophecies

MATTY HAD NEVER BEEN IN LIV'S room before. He roamed around snooping—not that there was much to snoop. Liv's room was extremely underwhelming, just like her. She didn't have any posters or artwork on the wall, only sketches of jewelry designs tacked up on a bulletin board. A jewelry-making table sat in the corner that looked more like an Etsy store headquarters. It was a full-on worktable cluttered with boxes of metal, beads, and drafting tools. Next to it was a shelf with machinery and protective eyewear. He picked up what he thought was a soldering iron and gently put it back down.

He wandered over to her bedside table to check out the books: *The Dream Almanac, The Dreamer's Interpretation Handbook.* He picked up the last one and laughed out loud. *The Dream Dictionary for Dummies.*

"They made a Dummy book for that?" He fanned through it. "Oh my God, she even highlighted it."

Winnie glanced up from reading her phone on Liv's bed. "Hey, don't make fun."

"I'm not," he said innocently, and put it back down. "But you have to admit it's weird." Matty had thought there was something strange about Liv when he first met her.

Ever since she came to town in March, Winnie had foisted her childhood friend on him and included Liv in everything they did together. As if Liv didn't know how to make friends. He'd been a good sport about it, but he and Liv had nothing in common except he wanted to live in New York City and she had just left it. The only cool thing about her was her jewelry, which he'd been stunned to find out she made herself.

So today had been an all-around surprise, getting to hang out with Forester, Nebony, and Jaxon, the coolest trifecta at school. And to think he almost hadn't come. He originally had been roped in today by Winnie to help "poor Liv." "Her aura is bleak," were Winnie's exact words. He had retorted, "Her personality is bleak," and earned a playful swat on the arm.

He spied a journal next to the dream books and couldn't resist picking it up. "She has a dream journal? Who has a dream journal? Someone without a life?"

"M, stop," Winnie warned him, though she knew he was just joking in his own snarky way.

The journal had cheesy blue and white clouds on the cover and *Dream Journal* embossed across the top in gold lettering. Like that made it official. The pages were loaded with Liv's writing. Matty nudged it open, and the book automatically flipped to her last entry, separating the written-on pages from the pristine ones.

Last night I was flying again.

The first line caught his eye, and he couldn't resist reading the rest.

Like a bird soaring over a dark highway with no path in sight. Not many cars were on the road, just a few lone headlights. I was searching for my father again. Headlight after headlight, I passed the cars. Rain fell around me fast and hard, but I couldn't feel it. Time blurred, until I finally found him driving alone. I slipped inside the car like a wraith and sat beside him. He was ignoring me like he always did, like I didn't exist. Words failed me, or maybe I couldn't talk in the dream. Instead, I looked out the window, trying to see past the shadows. The rain beat hard against the windshield, the sound a rhythmic drone in the air. The wipers were going full speed but unable to make a difference. My father continued to ignore me, his eyes fixed on the road. Then I saw a sign pass us saying Welcome to Centre Island.

It felt as real as my dreams with Jaxon—

"Hey! What are you doing?" Liv demanded from the doorway.

Matty looked up with a gasp and dropped the journal. "I'm so sorry! I didn't mean to read it."

Technically he had—oops—but still not cool.

Liv glared at him. For the first time since he'd met her, she looked pissed. Winnie glanced up from her scrolling, realizing what was happening. "Matty! What the hell? You're reading her diary?"

"It's a dream journal." He showed her the cover as proof.

Liv dumped the snacks on the bed.

"I just read half an entry and you're a good writer." He tried to compliment her, not commenting how sad the dream was with her father ignoring her like that. He didn't have a great relationship with his dad either. On second thought, it was a diary—which is why he could not help the question from slipping out. "So you dream about Jaxon?"

"Oh my God!" Liv raced forward and snatched the journal from his hands.

"*What?*" Winnie exploded, sitting up. "I knew it! I saw your aura going all pinkadoodle."

"I don't want to talk about it." She leveled her journal at Matty. "This is *private*."

"Yeah!" Winnie was back to glaring at him in disappointment.

He put his hand on his heart and rushed to say, "Please accept my apology. I'll never do it again. Cross my heart and hope to . . ." He left out *die* because he hated that word.

Liv sighed and mumbled "Whatever" under her breath. Matty tried to ignore the tension now in the room and studied the snacks she'd brought. Shitake mushroom jerky, cayenne caramels, and guava sticks. *Okay.*

"Well these are fun!" he enthused, attempting to lighten the mood. He tried a cayenne caramel first, and his eyes began to water. He kept talking, his mouth now on fire. "Your mom being a food writer is so cool. Unlike my mom, who's the principal of the school and can literally give me detention. Believe me, no one wants to date the principal's kid." Matty knew he was starting to ramble, but he couldn't stop. Anything to fill the awkward silence. He swallowed the sticky blob of peppery caramel before the saliva in his mouth spontaneously combusted and kept on talking. "Not that I have time right now for a love life. I've got Drama Club, the LGBTQ Alliance and the yearbook and school paper." OMG *shut up already.* Liv didn't even look like she was listening to him. She was staring at her journal as if he had defiled it, making him feel worse. He shouldn't have read it. "Ooooh mushroom jerky!" He pretended to be fascinated by the bag.

Winnie rescued him by changing the subject. "Did you ask your mom about the Premonitions Bureau?"

Liv nodded. "She didn't know anything about it."

"I was researching it some more." Winnie motioned to her phone. "It opened in 1968 and closed in the 1990s. They collected over twenty-five years of predictions."

"Which is totally wild," Matty chimed in, opening the guava sticks next. Nothing on the bag was in English except the word GUAVA! in all caps.

"Totally," Winnie agreed emphatically. "I mean, this really could be a gold mine, Liv. We could document going through the letters. Start a YouTube channel or something. Catalog the ones that came true."

Matty tilted his head, considering the idea. Winnie had always been into psychic stuff. She read Tarot cards and swore she could see people's auras. He wanted to believe her about the auras—he really did—but Winnie had an overactive imagination. Almost as much as him. Which was why they were best friends.

His phone dinged. Nebony had tagged him in a post. "Hey, check it out. Nebony posted the Polaroids." He showed them the online picture of Nebony dancing, dramatically backlit by the attic window.

Winnie read the post. "Party in the attic. Hashtag summer fun."

The Polaroid photos looked like cool vintage photographs, and the post about the Premonitions Bureau was actually funny.

"I can't believe they came over." He was surprised how much he'd hit it off with Nebony. Matty had written so many articles on the football team and the cheerleading squad for the school paper, he'd practically been their paparazzi. Then when he had tutored Forester last year to keep him from failing English, he discovered what a genuinely good guy their star quarterback was. And Forester lived right across the street from Liv. He'd had no idea.

He went to Liv's window and looked out at Forester's house.

Winnie cast a side-eye to Liv. "So what's the deal with Jaxon? You're into him?"

Matty snorted, his mouth now full of weird-tasting guava cookies. "Her and every girl at school. Dream on." He cringed as the words came out of his mouth, remembering she had written about him in her dream journal.

Liv's cheeks turned pink, but she ignored his faux pas. She was sitting at her jewelry table, fiddling with the pendant around her neck, her face giving nothing away. "What was Jaxon's deal with the letters? Why did he think we were pulling some kind of elaborate prank on him?"

Matty jumped to answer first, still trying to make up for the journal. "Because freshman year he saved some girl at school from a car crash and the car exploded." He used jazz hands for effect.

"What?" Liv stopped fiddling with her necklace.

Winnie nodded. "Kaitlyn Neilson was sitting at a bus stop when Jaxon dragged her away from the bench. A minute later a car swerved out of control and ploughed right into where she'd been sitting and caught fire."

Matty dropped his voice, now in full gossip mode. "Kaitlyn told me that Jaxon told her he saw the car careening out of control from across the street and happened to be there. But Kaitlyn didn't believe it. She'd gotten notes in her locker earlier that week, warning her not to take the bus that day and to stay home. She became convinced it was Jaxon who tried to warn her."

Winnie added, "Jaxon never confirmed or denied it."

"It only added to his mystique." Matty rolled his eyes. "Like he needs any help in that department."

Liv frowned. "So that's why he was upset?"

"Maybe all the rumors about it bothered him more than he let on." Matty took a wild guess. "And finding boxes of predictions from the Premonitions Bureau is pretty cuckoo. How did they end up at your house?"

"I really don't know." Liv shrugged helplessly.

Winnie started bouncing on the bed to rev them up. "Let's go upstairs and read some more!" She held out her phone to record herself and pitched her voice low and dramatic like the movie trailer guy. "On this psychic Sunday, we have found *the* actual Premonitions Bureau letters in an attic. Thousands of predictions. Let's go find out what they say."

Liv covered her face in her hands.

Matty, playing along, leaned into the camera frame and lowered his voice too. "Warning folks, predictions are usually bad, so finding boxes full of them is like walking into a haunted house—you know it's going to scare the hell out of you, but you're still going in." He zoomed the camera back and forth on his mouth, making a reverb effect. "In . . . in . . . in . . ." He stopped the video.

Winnie was laughing. "Did you say *folks?*"

"Yeah, I'm thinking cheesy 1950s narrator. We could do a noir feel with black-and-white video." He was beginning to see the possibilities. An attic full of psychic predictions was out there. They could totally have fun with this.

Liv stood up. "You guys are too much. Please don't post that."

Matty and Winnie both laughed maniacally as they all went back upstairs. Liv grabbed the box cutters and started opening up boxes. Every box was stuffed with premonitions, grouped by years, and Liv's grandfather had all the years spanning from 1968 through the seventies, eighties, and a few years in the nineties.

Matty chose a box. Before he dived in, for a split moment he looked at the writing scrawled across the outside.

DO NOT OPEN

He angled the box away so he wouldn't have to stare at it. The box was already opened—so there was no point turning back now.

Soon he forgot his unease as he got sucked into reading a whole variety of predictions, from natural disasters, to plane crashes and election results, to the collapse of civilization and UFOs landing on the White House lawn. There were also sports game predictions for the Super Bowl and World Series and races at the Kentucky Derby and NASCAR he didn't know or care about.

He debated. "Should we organize them by premonition genre?"

Winnie laughed, busy sorting the earliest box dated 1968–1969. "This isn't a bookstore, M. I think we should organize them by whether they came true. That's what people will want to know."

The investigators had been unable to verify most of the predictions in his box. Some premonitions were downright preposterous.

In 2001 a solar flare will wipe out the Earth.

In twenty years the automobile will be replaced by a car that runs on water.

Next February an earthquake will plunge the California coast into the ocean.

He reached the bottom where he found a thick file folder full of letters, all without envelopes, labeled *Verified Predictions*.

Stacks of letters were clipped together, each labeled with an event.

World Trade Center Bombing.

Hurricane Andrew.

Presidential Election.

LA Riots.

"Hey guys," he said. "I think I found the ones that came true."

"Me too." Winnie held up a file from her box. "There's a ton of letters here for Robert Kennedy getting shot." She looked at them wide-eyed. "A mass prediction."

Liv was rooting around in her box and confirmed, "I have a file."

Matty pulled the paper clip off of the World Trade Center bombing letters and started reading. Over thirty people had sensed what was going to happen: a bomb set off by terrorists in the parking garage in 1993, killing six people and injuring a thousand. Letter after letter, people saw the same catastrophe. The more he read, the more his imagination ran wild. What were real premonitions like these doing hidden in an attic?

The next thick stack of verified predictions stunned him even more—because they had all been written by the same person. A real psychic.

When he saw the psychic's name, at first he thought it was a joke. Then he read one of the letters and the analysis stapled to it and realized it wasn't.

"Uh, guys? You need to take a look at this."

5

JAXON

precognition:
foreknowledge of an event

LIV HALL. JAXON HAD FINALLY MET her—finally knew her name and where she lived. Two pieces of information he had hoped to avoid for as long as possible. He'd known her face for months, well before her arrival to town. That first day when she got out of her friend's car at school and he saw her across the parking lot, his world had tilted off its axis for a split second.

He couldn't believe she was really there—that he was finally seeing her. Ever since, he'd been avoiding her, basically playing dodgeball with fate. His life was way too complicated to get involved with anyone, and Liv Hall wasn't just anyone.

Today when she opened the door, he couldn't believe her house was *the* house Forester had asked him to come to.

Then he had followed her blindly upstairs—only to discover her attic was filled with boxes of predictions. It was like a sick joke from the universe, and all he could think was—*what the actual hell?* He didn't know what to do.

His phone rang, interrupting his thoughts, and he looked to see who was calling. He let it go to voicemail, not wanting to deal with Nebony anymore today. Her plan to win back Forester didn't seem to be working, and he had no advice left to give. Forester was being beyond a jerk to her, and Jaxon was friends with them both.

Whenever he tried to talk to Forester about it, the guy shut him out. Life had been so much easier when Nebony and Forester were together. Instead, now Jaxon was stuck in the middle of their broken relationship. Forester had announced he needed "space" and ghosted Nebony in the worst way. Nebony still had no idea what she'd done. Jaxon personally didn't want to tell them their relationship had been doomed from the start. Neither of them had any idea what he could see when he wanted to.

Though he rarely wanted to. Usually he tried to block out visions of the future, not wanting the tidal wave of information they brought. But seeing Liv today had unleashed a wild storm of feelings. Just the thought of her now brought an image to the forefront of his mind of a vivid memory yet to happen . . .

Liv is sitting beside him, their bodies so close their knees are touching. They are in her attic reading the letters, open boxes surrounding them. He has a letter in his hands. What it says shocks him to his core.

The moment played like a movie in his mind. He slowed it down to focus on the letter. When he read the words on the page, goosebumps rose on his arms.

In disbelief, his mind raced. Suddenly the boxes in Liv's attic were taking on a whole new light. He would read every single letter if he had to until he found the one he'd just seen in his mind.

"Jaxon! Dinner," his mom called, yanking him from the vision.

"Coming! Be down in a sec!" He stood up, his body now flush with adrenaline.

Hurrying to the bathroom, he splashed water on his face and tried to shake off the shock from the letter. He wasn't even certain. He had to see it first, really hold it in his hands to know.

"Jax?" His dad called up, his voice laced with impatience.

"Coming!" Jaxon hurried downstairs to find his family waiting at the dinner table, their dog already at their feet on the lookout for crumbs. He flashed them a smile, trying to act normal.

His dad announced, "We've got a mean-looking enchilada casserole tonight, courtesy of our celebrity chef." His parents were both in their scrubs, having just gotten off work from the hospital.

"They're French crepes, Dad." Jaxon's little sister, Tia, corrected him with the gravitas of a twelve-year-old deadly serious about her cooking. "I've been recipe testing all weekend and just uploaded the demo." She had her iPad at the table and was keeping an eye on all the action on her YouTube Kids channel, *Chef Tia*.

Jaxon helped himself to a big portion of the enchilada-looking crepes.

"You both ready for school to end?" his dad asked, then added to Jaxon, "How are the summer job applications going?"

Jaxon nodded and said, "It's going," with his mouth full. He didn't know how (or want) to tell his dad he didn't see himself in Hyde Park this summer. The problem was, he didn't know where he'd be. He just knew in his gut he wouldn't be working a summer job at home.

He asked his parents, "Did you guys know there used to be something called the Premonitions Bureau?"

His father's fork slipped from his hand with a clatter, and he picked it back up.

Jaxon went on. "They got letters from—" He didn't have a chance to finish because his dad accidentally spilled his wine all over the table and broke the glass.

Tia wailed, grabbing her iPad. "Dad! The salad! The salad!"

His dad grabbed the salad bowl and started mopping the mess. "Oh shoot. Mr. Butterfingers. I'm so sorry." His dad stood up and picked up the glass. "Why don't you ladies go relax in the living room, and Jax and I will clean this up. Then we can start over."

Their mother led a sniffling Tia away. Jax turned to find his father staring at him with a stricken look. "Let's go get a trash bag." He abruptly turned and headed into the kitchen.

Jaxon followed him. His father was standing at the kitchen sink. He turned the faucet on full blast. Then he turned on the stove vent and ran the fan. There was so much noise, Jaxon barely heard his whisper.

"Don't *ever* mention that again."

"What?" Jaxon stood there in shock.

"Remember what I said that day at the ballpark? It applies to this." His dad searched his eyes, as if trying to impart a deeper message through osmosis.

They never talked about that day at the ballpark. Jaxon tried hard not to think about that day. The revelations his father told him had changed his whole life. "I'm sorry. I didn't know—"

His father pulled him in for a fierce hug, his arms two steel bands around him. He whispered into his ear, "It's okay. I'm sorry too. But what I said before hasn't changed." His dad pulled away, his eyes full of sadness and regret. Then he turned off the sink and fan, grabbed the trash bag, and left to clean up the mess.

Jaxon stood alone, staring at the sink, utterly shaken. Two years ago, after he saved Kaitlyn Neilson from a fatal car crash he'd foreseen, his whole world had turned upside down. Only his father knew the reason why, and a second ago he had looked terrified.

If anything, his father's reaction tonight when he mentioned the Premonitions Bureau confirmed what Jaxon already knew. The letters in Liv's attic held the answers.

Dear Premonitions Bureau,

I've never shared a prediction with anyone before. For years, I kept them bottled up, not sure if they were real or my imagination. They started out as simple knowings of what would happen that day. Then the visions began to expand out into the world and further into the future.

I've decided to write to you, for they are a burden. I don't know if the future can change simply because I tell someone about it, but I can try.

Early next month, there is going to be a horrible train accident in Philadelphia. On the morning train with hundreds of people. The back three cars will derail, causing the fourth car to shear in half. I don't know what causes the accident, but I've seen it happen. So maybe this is more of a confession than a premonition because I cannot live with the guilt of having seen it first.

The Oracle of Delphi

6

WINNIE

cartomancy:
to see the future through cards

THE LETTER GAVE WINNIE CHILLS. SHE got out her phone and hit record, videoing for the camera. "In ancient history, the Oracle of Delphi was the most powerful seer in Greece, delivering messages from the heavens and telling the future to all who traveled to the Temple of Apollo at Delphi. Now thousands of years later, someone has used her name and predicted an event with stunning accuracy."

She zoomed in on the words and whispered for dramatic effect. "There was a train accident in Philadelphia on March 7, 1990. The bureau investigator said he forwarded the letter to authorities in Philadelphia, warning them. On March 7, 1990, Train Number 61 left Thirtieth Street station. The accident happened just as the Oracle described, one hundred sixty-two injured, four dead. Premonition Verified."

Matty seamlessly took the phone from her and aimed it at himself. "What else did the Oracle of Delphi predict? A lot." He waved the letters in front of the camera. "Stay tuned to find out more from a modern-day oracle who tried to warn us." Matty cut the video and handed it back to Winnie.

She nodded to him. "That was perfect."

"I know. We're cooking."

Liv nibbled her bottom lip. "You guys aren't really going to do a YouTube channel, are you?"

Winnie assured her. "If we do, we won't say we're at your house or give out your address or anything. But these letters are incredible. Don't you feel like we kind of have to?"

"Yeah, Liv. Read all these." Matty nodded, splitting the Oracle letters up. "We've got Clinton's election. Nelson Mandela becoming president of South Africa. The Gulf War . . ."

The next letter stopped Winnie in her tracks. "Oh my God. Look at this one!"

Matty grabbed Winnie's phone and started recording her. He made an excited "rolling" action with his fingers.

Winnie held up a letter. "The Oracle of Delphi even predicted the bombing of the Oklahoma Federal Building in 1995—three years before the date." She showed the analysis. "The investigator forwarded a copy of the letter to the FBI to warn them. In the Bureau's notes it says the letter was sent to both the FBI and the NSA."

Matty aimed the camera at himself. "They obviously didn't take it seriously. It still happened."

Winnie countered, "Would you? Getting something like this years in advance? Signed by the Oracle of Delphi? It reads like fiction."

"They all read like fiction, except they're not," Matty deadpanned into the camera. He stopped filming and handed the phone back to Winnie. "Am I like totally delulu or are we naturals?"

"I know. This is awesome. And we still have more verified predictions to read from other people." Winnie checked the time, surprised. They'd been up in the attic for hours.

Matty checked the time too. "Maybe we should stop for the night."

Liv didn't answer or look up. She was preoccupied with her box. It was like she was searching for something and couldn't read the letters fast enough. Winnie studied her aura, seeing new shadows that hadn't been there before. Shadows brought on by heavy emotions. Winnie frowned. Finding the boxes had hurt Liv somehow. For a moment, Winnie wondered if maybe they shouldn't have opened them.

Matty stood in front of all the boxes recording himself and said in his cheesy narrator's voice, "There is a lost library of premonitions in these boxes. How psychic were these people? How psychic are we? Well, we're going to find out, folks. One letter at a time."

He pulled a stack of letters from the boxes, held them up in the air, and let them fall like rain.

After they called it a night, Winnie drove home in her little Toyota coupe. ABBA's "I Have a Dream" was playing on the radio, and the lyrics grabbed her attention. The song was about angels and crossing the stream. She could feel the prick of sentimental tears coming on, and she turned the music off before her mascara started running.

When she got home she took out her Tarot cards and gave them a good shuffle.

Usually she got her deck out at night and pulled a few cards. She'd learned how to read Tarot on a whim and discovered the things she saw in a reading generally came true. Maybe she had a gift. She really didn't know. But the symbols on the cards helped her to make sense of things.

She drew a card, the *Wheel of Fortune*, and her mind started culling through all the meanings. The Wheel of Fortune signified many things: Change. Destiny. Fate. Luck.

She felt like she'd experienced all those things today. From the discovery of the letters to hanging out with Nebony, Jaxon, and Forester—

which had been completely surreal. At school they were in entirely different circles, different orbits really. Winnie had been an outcast for years, labeled weird and eccentric by her classmates. Before meeting Matty, school had been a toxic place for her. She was hyperaware, self-conscious, and often sensed things about people. Seeing auras didn't help either.

She pulled a card for tomorrow and stared at *The Tower* card with utter dread. The image was a burning building with lightning bolts and people falling from the windows. She tried to figure out what the card meant and all she could think was, *This week is going to be bad, a disaster of some kind.*

She drew another card to get a better sense.

Death.

She stared at the skeleton in the knight's armor sitting on top of his horse and an ominous feeling took root inside her. She had to remind herself the Death card didn't literally mean death.

But it was the second time she'd drawn it today.

"Awesome sauce," she muttered.

To top it off, the light beside her bed began to flicker, as if on cue in a scary movie right before the jump scare.

She gave the bulb an impatient tap with her fingers and the flickering stopped. She'd been meaning to change it forever. No longer in the mood to do a reading, she put away her cards and turned out the light.

The next morning when she and Liv pulled into the school parking lot, Winnie saw Nebony standing by the main doors, busy on her phone and surrounded by friends.

Today she was wearing an outfit few people could pull off. If a Tarot card symbolized a person, Nebony was definitely the *Queen of Wands.* Passionate. Powerful. Ambitious.

Then Winnie saw Ian nearby talking with a friend and she slowed down, trying to calm the heart palpitations now happening in her chest. Ian was her secret mad crush. He was the bass player for the Nomads, the coolest band in school, and he wrote all their lyrics. He was quiet and intense, and his aura was pure purple. (She should know. She'd stared at him enough the past year.) Purples were mysterious, intuitive, philosophical, and private people. She did Tarot spreads on him every Saturday night and stalked him online after the band started their own YouTube channel. In her Tarot deck, he was *The Lovers* card.

As she and Liv headed to the doors, she tried to think of what to say to Nebony. Something cool to get Ian's attention. She ran over options and instead panicked and went with a super cheesy car salesman finger point. "Hey Nebony, party in the attic!" Mentally cringing at her delivery, she sounded fake and giggly. Then her face turned beet red to boot. It was an epic fail of a hello. She shouldn't have said anything.

Nebony glanced up at Winnie and cocked an eyebrow. That was her only response before going back to her phone. Some guy on the football team asked Nebony if she was friends with "the Blue Man chick." Nebony rolled her eyes like she couldn't be bothered, busy texting. The guy took that as a no and mimicked Winnie's "P-p-party in the attic!" His friends all laughed. Ian looked in their general direction but returned to the conversation with his friend.

The Tower. There it was. Crashing and burning in front of the love of her life who didn't know she existed. Nebony was beyond lame. The Queen of Lame. Winnie stewed all morning, drowning in mortification. Why had she tried to be nice to her? Or said hello this morning? She didn't even like cheerleaders. They had nothing in common. She had a slow metabolism and hated PE.

At lunch, Winnie was still mad when she joined Liv and Matty at their table.

"Why did Nebony post the stupid photos in the first place if she won't even say hi the next day? It's so lame!" Winnie got out her phone and unfollowed her—not that Nebony would notice. She hadn't followed her back yesterday.

"Someone's grumpy today," Matty said primly. "She said hi to me." Today he was wearing a bow tie, round black glasses, and a 1940s bowler hat. Matty's style changed daily, and it was always theatrical. They were sitting together at their usual lunch table in the back corner where they could have their eye on the whole cafeteria. Sometimes a fellow Drama Club friend would join them or someone from the LGBTQ Alliance Matty helped lead.

Their table was open to anyone, like the United Nations, although on days when no one stopped by, to Winnie it felt like they were the Island of Misfit Toys.

Winnie had a clear view of Nebony's table in the center of the room where invisible barbed wire had been put up. To score a seat at the table, you had to run with their crowd or been invited to their last party. If only Nebony had been cooler, Winnie could have been over there right now three seats away from Ian. Forester would have totally made room for her. He had been surprisingly sweet yesterday. Winnie's eyes landed on Jaxon to find him watching Liv.

Less than a minute later, Matty said under his breath, "Oh my God, don't look don't look don't look don't look."

"What?" Winnie fought the urge to look.

Suddenly a voice behind her asked, "This seat taken?"

Winnie looked up to find Jaxon staring down at them.

"No," Liv said, suddenly fascinated by her pizza sticks. Winnie stared at her and saw the rush of pink blooming in the space around her. It was emanating from Jaxon's aura too, in multiple shades. All of a sudden, their table had the aura colors of a Valentine's Day card.

Well this was a surprise. Jaxon liked Liv back?

He took the seat across from Liv. "Did you go through the letters last night?"

Liv's face flushed and she admitted, "A few boxes."

"Yo yo yo," came Forester's greeting as he crossed the wilds of the cafeteria to move to their table too. He plopped down beside Matty. "It's the Premonitions Bureau. You guys talking letters?" he asked, taking a monster bite of his burger.

Winnie caught Nebony watching them and looked away.

"You read some more after we left? Anything good?" Forester sounded sincere, which was surprising.

"Yeah," Matty teased him, "You totally missed out, big guy."

"Totally." Winnie leaned forward and dropped her voice dramatically to make it look like they were having an intimate conversation. "We found mass predictions and some amazing letters from someone who signed them the Oracle of Delphi. Most of her predictions were verified."

"The Oracle of Delphi?" Jaxon leaned forward too, completely invested in the conversation. "Who do you think verified them?" he asked, his question more for Liv.

Liv tucked her hair behind her ears, looking uncomfortable. "I have no idea."

Matty snorted. "She has no idea how the letters even ended up in her house!"

Liv shot Matty an irritated look.

Matty then surprised Winnie by suggesting to the boys, "We're meeting up again today after school to read some more . . ." He trailed off, clearly inviting them.

Liv's eyes widened with a silent *what-is-he-doing* look. But Winnie chimed in, "Yeah, you two should come over." If Jaxon and Forester came over, Nebony would want to come too, and they could tell her no and see how she liked being treated like dirt. Winnie could. Not. Wait.

"Cool. You don't mind?" Jaxon asked Liv.

"Uh, no." Liv's eyebrows shot up. "But I thought you didn't want to read the letters."

"I changed my mind. If you're going to read them, I'd like to read some too." He gave her a lingering look. Even Matty caught the vibe and flashed Winnie raised eyebrows. Winnie nodded in agreement. Jaxon was acting all about Liv.

"I'm down," Forester added.

"Okay, come over then." Liv shrugged like it was no big deal, but Winnie could tell she was flustered and trying to hide it. The lunch bell rang, and Liv jumped up.

"Cool." Jaxon looked up at her. "I'll see you later."

"Cool." Liv nodded nonchalantly, even though her aura was exploding like a kaleidoscope.

Winnie walked away with her, feeling vindicated. She gave the boys a breezy "Ciao" and a little wave just like Nebony did. Winnie could feel the eyes of the cafeteria still on them, including Ian's. If she couldn't sit at the cool table, then she'd make the cool table want to sit at hers.

For the first time ever, things at school were beginning to look up, and she thought maybe, just maybe, the cards might be wrong.

7

LIV

ESP:

to perceive remote information or imagery

AFTER SCHOOL, MATTY CAUGHT A RIDE with Winnie and Liv. Of course he insisted on being in the front seat. Liv rolled her eyes to herself and got in the back. When they arrived at her house, Liv was relieved to find her mom wasn't in her bathrobe. Winnie's mom's art gallery opening was today, and she was about to head out. At least they would have the house to themselves. Liv didn't know when—or if—Jaxon and Forester were planning on making an appearance.

Winnie and Matty headed upstairs to the attic, and Liv ducked into the kitchen to say hi. Her mom was having coffee and eating pistachio brittle straight out of the box while watching the news about the upcoming New York primary for the presidential election.

The anchorman said, "If I were a betting man, I'd say Charles Becker and Tom Miller are going to be the ones facing off with each other at the end of this race to the White House."

The screen displayed two side-by-side pictures of smiling old white men.

"Please no," her mom complained to the TV as if it could hear her. "Come on! This is the best we can do?"

"I take it you don't like the candidates?" Liv teased her.

"Could you consider running for president when you're older please?" her mom asked, only half joking.

Liv laughed with an offhanded, "I'll think about it," and opened the pantry to eye the meager offerings. It was all bizarre food samples. She shut the cabinet, refusing to eat more guava cookies.

Her mom gave her a sheepish look. "Sorry, I need to go the store."

"So you keep saying." Liv shook her head. Her mom was a wreck, but she was a lovable wreck.

Her mom closed the brittle box and handed it to her. "Please keep this away from me." She downed the rest of her coffee and washed out the cup. "Oh listen, we're set for Wednesday, and someone from the attorney's office is coming to the house on Thursday."

"What?" Liv turned to her in a panic. "But—but I need more time to sort stuff before they come." She wasn't even halfway through the letters or closer to finding out why her father had left them there.

"I'm sorry. They insisted."

Liv's mind raced to find a solution. She needed more time. "Then do I have to go to the city on Wednesday?"

Today was Monday. That gave her only a few days. Maybe Wednesday she could stay home and spend all day in the attic while her mom was gone.

"Yes." Her mom shot down that idea. "The attorney is reading the will and asked for you to come. We'll need to get up early to make the drive."

Liv grimaced at the idea of a two-hour early morning drive to Manhattan. She'd have to read faster if she was going to get through all the letters by Thursday. If she had to go Wednesday, then maybe she'd ask the attorney about the boxes at their meeting. It was possible he knew about the Premonitions Bureau.

With a sigh, Liv took the pistachio brittle with her upstairs and quickly changed into shorts and a tank top that showed off her armband. Then she twisted her hair up, trying hard not to think about Jaxon and how he'd held the hair clip yesterday. Like a caress. Or maybe she was absolutely, completely delusional. She debated putting makeup on and settled for lip gloss. Then she joined Winnie and Matty, who were already busy reading.

Winnie had her cell phone out and was recording again.

Liv decided to lay down some rules. "Absolutely no recording when Jaxon and Forester are here. I don't want to weird them out."

Winnie reluctantly agreed and Matty grabbed the box of brittle from her with an over-the-top, "Oh my God, thank you! I'm literally starving and about to become a size zero!"

Liv held back a sigh. Matty was such a drama queen, and she still hadn't forgiven him for reading her journal. She had yet to write in it again either. Her dreams were private. She never talked about them to anyone, not even Winnie.

Last night, she had dreamed about Jaxon. *Again.* The dream had felt so vivid, when she woke up this morning she could have sworn it was real. Her journal was riddled with such entries. How when she slipped off to sleep, she floated and hovered over her body and then flew in the air like Peter Pan. In her dreams, she could move through walls like a ghost and go anywhere she wanted.

Lately, she always found herself at Jaxon's house, the same two-story brown brick on a cul-de-sac. She'd slipped in with moonlight while Jaxon was asleep in bed. He looked so angelic, his face peaceful. She would curl up beside him, burrowing into the crook of his chest. Her favorite place to be. Every time, she was tempted to kiss him.

Last night, she almost had. She leaned forward, their lips a breath apart, when suddenly his dog, a big golden retriever, sat up, cocked its head as if he could see her, and gave a gruff bark. The sound jolted her, and the next thing she knew, she was back in her bedroom, waking up to her alarm.

So today, when Jaxon had come over to their lunch table, she was sure the guilt was all over her face. Technically, she was a dream stalker, a girl who liked to spoon with him while he slept. Her face burned at the thought. She wanted to ask him if he had a dog, but she didn't know how to without sounding weird. Plus, if she did, she was sure her face would turn bright red.

The doorbell rang, yanking her from her thoughts.

Matty said, with his mouth full of brittle, "Juliet! Romeo's here."

This time Liv did roll her eyes at him and got up, feeling a fluttering in her stomach that hadn't been there a second ago. "Jaxon's just here because of the letters." She reminded Matty what he said yesterday. "Me and all the girls, right?"

Matty shook his head. "I changed my mind. He's definitely into you. He couldn't take his eyes off you at lunch."

Liv was surprised. "Really?"

Winnie glanced up from reading and nodded in agreement. "Pink's all over his aura too. Trust me. It's the Pink Parade."

"Trust me too," Matty said flippantly and waved the premonition letter he was reading in the air. "And I don't have to be psychic to know that!"

8

JAXON

oneiromancy:
seeing the future through dreams

JAXON WAITED ON LIV'S DOORSTEP WITH Forester. "I was surprised you wanted to come back today."

Forester gave a lazy shrug. "Got nothing better to do than watch you crush on my neighbor."

Jaxon gave him a side-look. "How about you handle your love life and I'll handle mine? Nebony still deserves an explanation. She's not over it."

"She'll get over it," Forester insisted, a stubborn set to his chin.

Jaxon shook his head in disgust, ignoring Forester while they waited, and he tried to look relaxed. A second later, Liv opened the door. Seeing her always made Jaxon feel like he couldn't get enough air. She had changed into shorts that showed off her long legs, and her hair was falling out of that clip again. It distracted him to no end. They stood staring at each other for a suspended moment.

Forester cleared his throat on purpose. "Thanks for having us over."

Liv gave them a hesitant smile. Jaxon could tell she absolutely had no idea what to make of his interest in coming over again to read the letters.

She opened the door wider. "Come on in. We're already upstairs."

She led the way, and Jaxon looked down at her bare feet, noticing her two silver toe rings. His eyes made their way slowly back up to her hair clip, remembering. When he held it in his hand yesterday, he saw their first kiss. The premonition had hit him square in the chest out of nowhere.

Distracted by the memory, he almost missed a step and heard Forester comment from behind. "Easy there, cowboy."

Jaxon turned back and shot him a *shut-up* look. Did Forester really have nothing better to do than tag along and make fun of him? When they reached the attic, he found Liv's friends surrounded by piles of letters and open boxes.

"Hey guys." Jaxon nodded, trying to play it cool. He really needed to learn these people's names. Minnie and Matt? He waited to see where Liv sat before he chose his spot.

"Whoa, check it out," Forester said. "It's the premonition factory." He ducked under the doorway, his big frame shrinking the room.

"The cavalry's arrived," the little guy joked. Jaxon remembered meeting him once last year. The guy was a total brainiac and had kept Forester from flunking English and getting kicked off the team.

"Yo, Matty." Forester fist-bumped him and then wandered toward the mountain of boxes to assess their progress. "Find anything good?"

Matty held up a stack. "These are pretty wild. Hey Winnie, check it out. This guy calls himself Nostradamus."

Winnie laughed. "No way, I love it," she said, taking the letters from him.

Liv sat back down on the blanket, and Jaxon parked next to her. Their knees touched and déjà vu rained on him like a shower of electricity. His prediction was happening exactly as he imagined it.

Liv scooted a box toward him without looking, her lashes hiding her eyes. She seemed embarrassed by something. He'd felt it at lunch too. Was it because he wanted to come back?

"Who's Nostradamus?" Jaxon asked to fill the silence.

"Jax, Jax, Jax," Matty teased him, explaining, "he's only one of the most famous psychics of all time."

Matty's friend added, "His prophecies were used as propaganda in World War II."

"Sorry. I don't know any World War II psychics."

She shook her head. "That's what's so wild. Nostradamus lived in the 1500s with his BFF, Catherine de Medici." She showed the letters to Liv. "These are like that kidnapping letter we read."

Forester asked, "So he's trying to stop crimes before they happen?"

Matty nodded. "And they're all legit." He motioned to the organized piles he'd been making. "Basically, we've got fake predictions and real ones. For the real ones, like a mass prediction or when the Bureau realized a psychic was legit, they forwarded copies of the letters. Although I'm sure the authorities didn't put a lot of stock in the letters when they got them."

"Maybe they would now." Forester turned to Liv and pressed, "You don't know why your grandfather has all these? Does your mom know?"

Jaxon was surprised by his best friend's intensity.

Liv shook her head. "I asked her yesterday. I'm supposed to meet with my grandfather's lawyer Wednesday. I was planning to ask him about it."

Matty nodded approvingly. "Good plan."

"Thank you," Liv said dryly, and Jaxon caught a flash of irritation in her eyes.

The doorbell rang and Liv jumped up to get it.

Liv's friend followed her out, announcing she was grabbing drinks.

"Bring more snacks!" Matty ordered. "Nothing that says guava!"

The attic grew quiet after the girls left and the guys got to reading. The shuffling of papers between them was the only sound.

Jaxon put down the Nostradamus letters in frustration. This wasn't what he wanted. "Hey, Matty," he tried to fish, "where are those letters you were talking about? Written by the Oracle of something?" Even though he knew the name.

"Delphi." Matty reached behind him and pulled out a thick file. "Enjoy. She's good."

Jaxon took the letters, unable to control the slight quiver in his hand. But no one noticed. Matty and Forester were both preoccupied.

Afraid to look, he opened the file. The handwriting immediately jumped out at him. The unusual way the cursive capital *E* looked like a backward three, the way the *T* crossed in a long line, the strong right slant to the *I*, as if the letter were stretching to the future.

As he read each of the Oracle's premonitions, his eyes watered and his nose began to run. He furiously blinked and took a deep breath.

"You okay?" Matty looked up from his organizing.

"Dust. Got to me for a second." Jaxon made a big show of rubbing his eyes. He took a few breaths, trying to get his feelings under control.

He knew who had written these letters.

9

WINNIE

auramancy:
divination through auras

WINNIE DETOURED TO THE KITCHEN AS Liv opened the front door to find Nebony holding two Starbucks trays and six coffees. "Hi . . . Nebony." Liv sounded speechless.

Nebony gave Liv a full-wattage smile, the head cheerleader kind that made your face hurt from being on the receiving end of it. "Hey you!" Nebony gushed. "I heard we were back up in the attic, so I brought caramel macchiatos." She held up the trays.

Winnie listened from the kitchen, in disbelief Nebony had the nerve to show up uninvited—or maybe Jaxon had invited her, which was more than presumptuous of him.

"Oh my gosh, that's so sweet." Liv tried to downplay her surprise. "Come in. We're all upstairs."

Winnie rolled her eyes and grabbed some sodas before joining Liv on the stairs. Nebony went ahead of them, sashaying up to the attic with the coffee like a flight attendant. Winnie gave Liv an irritated *What is she doing here?* look. Liv shook her head, just as clueless. Winnie stared at Nebony's back, seeing all the red in her aura. Reds were temperamental, stubborn, and tended to want to be number one at everything. Forester was the exact same. They were both Reds. The question was, was Nebony trying to get Forester back or was she here to stake her claim on Jaxon? Not that Winnie cared. She just didn't want Liv to get hurt.

When they got to the attic, Nebony announced, "Coffee delivery, gang!"

Jaxon looked up, surprised to see her too, and Winnie reconsidered. Maybe he hadn't invited her.

Matty was the only one sincerely happy she was there with coffee. "Oh my gosh, you're a lifesaver. I love you I love you I love you."

Nebony laughed and handed him one. "Hey, MacB." She turned to Forester. "Cappuccino for you, heavy on the foam like you like." He grudgingly said thanks and took it. She handed one to Jaxon. "Americano for you, Jax." She offered one to Liv and Winnie. "I got you both macchiatos. They're my favorite," she said with a grin, as if that made her impromptu arrival okay.

Liv took hers. "Thanks so much," and she motioned to the extra one. "Winnie?"

Winnie cracked open a soda loudly instead. Free Starbucks did not equal forgiveness.

Nebony ignored the snub and eyed Forester. He was acting preoccupied, looking through an open box. She curled up next to Jaxon. "Anything interesting so far?"

"Yeah, some amazing letters from the Oracle of Delphi," he murmured, still reading.

"Ooooh, the Oracle of Delphi. I love it." Nebony held her Polaroid camera up high and leaned back toward Matty. She took a photo of them surrounded by stacks of letters and envelopes. Matty flashed a silly grin to the camera and Nebony gave a sexy model-pout.

Winnie tried to ignore them and read the Nostradamus letter in her hand about a volcanic eruption in the Philippines.

"That's a great picture of us," Matty said as he and Nebony watched the Polaroid picture develop, their heads close together. "I love it."

"I know. Super cool hat, MacB."

Winnie gritted her teeth. It was the second "MacB" out of Nebony's mouth in less than two minutes. Was Nebony seriously trying to go with *we're-good-friends* nicknames already? The whole idea of Matty and Nebony becoming friends didn't sit well with her. It wasn't just that Winnie didn't like Nebony. It was more than that—she got a bad feeling. She sighed, trying to focus on the letter, and Googled the volcano prediction.

June 15, 1991. Mount Pinatubo exploded in a cataclysmic eruption.

She skimmed. *Fortunately, scientists forecasted the eruption and were able to save thousands of lives.*

Winnie flipped back to Nostradamus's letter and read the back analysis.

It said, *Given the track record of this psychic's premonitions, the Bureau forwarded this warning to the Philippine Institute of Volcanology and Seismology and the US Geological Institute. We stressed its validity.*

Had this letter, in fact, helped save countless lives?

Matty interrupted her thoughts, announcing, "Hey, listen to this one, guys. It's from that same psychic with the kidnapping letter and the little girl." He read it out loud. "Thank you for inviting me to the conference. It was wonderful meeting other psychics and taking part in the panel discussion. Best regards, Jerald Peterson." He held it out to her and Liv. "He went to some psychic conference hosted by the Bureau."

Jaxon looked up from the Oracle letters, suddenly interested. "They had a conference for psychics?"

Forester was rifling through a stack. "There's more letters from him here. He's like a psychic police detective." He handed them over to Matty. "I bet my dad would have loved to work with him."

Winnie glanced at Forester in question. Nebony caught her look and was the one who answered. "His dad is a cop."

"*Was* a cop." Forester corrected her sharply. "Before he was shot in the back. Now he's in a wheelchair for life."

"Oh my gosh," Winnie said, unprepared. "Forester, I'm so sorry." She hadn't known. She looked at Liv, who hadn't known either, and then at Matty. Matty had a subdued expression, like he had known. Why hadn't Matty ever told her? Winnie vaguely remembered Forester's dad was a police officer, but that was all she knew.

"They're still doing rehab." Nebony assured them. "He may walk again."

"No, he won't!" Forester suddenly exploded with anger. "Why are you talking about stuff you know nothing about?"

Nebony was taken aback. "Because you said—"

"Well I was wrong! He had his last surgery, and the doctors are giving up. Got that, Miss Pom-Pom? Not everybody wins." Forester stood up. "You know what? I'm done here." He stormed down the stairs.

Nebony jumped up. "Forest! Wait, I'm sorry!" She hurried after him, her voice trailing off. "I didn't know. Why didn't you tell me?"

Winnie glanced to Matty, who looked back at her, wide-eyed. They were both silently thinking the same thing: *Drama*.

Jaxon let out a sigh. "Sorry guys. They have some unresolved issues," he said, as if he should apologize for his friends.

"That's so horrible about his dad," Liv said.

The mood had totally turned weird. Winnie felt the urge to clarify the Forester-Nebony-Jaxon triangle for Liv. "Jaxon . . . so you and Nebony aren't together?"

Jaxon's eyebrows shot up. "No, just friends. And call me Jax." He said to Liv, "I didn't invite her over here today either. Just so you know." His eyes lingered on Liv and the pink was back. Winnie swore she was going to have to wear sunglasses around them in order not to throw up.

He asked Liv, "Do you want to take a break and go grab a quick bite?"

Matty answered before Liv could, "Sure, Jax. Sounds like a *date*."

Winnie and Matty grinned at each other. Liv shot Matty a pained look.

"I can drive," Winnie offered. "Let's go to Eveready."

Liv went to her room to grab her purse and Jaxon headed outside while Winnie and Matty waited by the front door. Winnie was touching up her lipstick in the hallway mirror when from the corner of her eye she caught Matty going through the stack of mail on the entry hall table.

"What are you doing?" She turned to him, incredulous, and lowered her voice. "Are you going through their mail?"

Matty dropped the letters. Guilty. "I just wanted to know what her grandfather's name is."

"Clement Spencer. Why?"

"Shouldn't we investigate his connection to the Bureau before we start posting anything?"

"*Investigate?* Are you serious?"

"A house of premonitions is a house of secrets, Win."

Winnie cracked up. "You did not just say that."

Matty dropped his voice to a whisper. "Come on, admit it's creepy. He's got twenty-five years of premonitions like a hoarder. A psychic hoarder."

Now they were both laughing. She said, "I'm sure there's a logical explanation. He was the sweetest granddad."

"The sweetest granddad who collected predictions instead of stamps."

"Would you stop?" Winnie was trying hard not to laugh.

They dropped the conversation when Liv joined them, though they still shot each other looks and giggled.

The group piled into Winnie's car. Matty took the front with a teasing look to Liv, letting her get into the back with Jaxon. "Have you guys read the book called *The Pink Parade?*"

"No, but I hear it's good." Winnie grinned, and Liv pretended like she wasn't listening. They were pulling out of the driveway when Nebony crossed the street from Forester's house. Winnie stopped with a sigh and rolled down the window.

"Hey, where are you guys going?" Nebony asked. Her eyes were bright, as if she'd been crying.

"To eat," Winnie said. Nebony stood there, looking lost and alone, her aura dulled with defeat. Winnie took a long look at her, feeling a knot in her heart unravel. Pity for the Queen. She unlocked the doors. "Get in."

<ENCRYPTED TRANSMISSION>

<DEFENSE INTELLIGENCE AGENCY SERVER>

<From: MIRIAM>

<Priority: HIGH>

Premonitions Bureau letters have been
identified and authenticated in recent post
from @nebonycheergoddess

Subject: Nebony Price
Driver's License: 015 361 978
Social Security: 921 98 9876
Address: 3157 Dew Point Drive,
Hyde Park, New York
Phone: (845) 555-3209

*Subject's phone records and contact
list attached.
*Subject's email records and contact
list attached.

Have a team watch her house and search it
tomorrow when no one's home.

10

NEBONY

instinct:
an intuitive reaction not based on rational thought

NEBONY IGNORED EVERYONE IN THE CAR and looked at the post she'd just shared online. It was one of her more artistic photos. Using her phone's camera, she took a snapshot of the Polaroid of her and Matty in the attic and caught a cool rainbow flare from the late afternoon sun hitting the car window.

Party in the attic! Found a bunch of old predictions
from the Premonitions Bureau.
We know the future and you don't. Ha!

#atticfind #PremonitionsBureau #psychic #oldletters
#NostradamusIsAlive #premonitions #prophecy #psychicreading
#paranormal #oracle #psychicpowers #crystalball #OracleOfDelphi
#goddess #WomenRule #cheer #TeenVogue

The post was different from her usual content and already getting a ton of likes. She dropped her phone back in her purse and looked out the window, furiously blinking back tears. She refused to cry in this car. Her hope she and Forester could patch things up was dead. Today he'd been cruel and made it clear they were done.

Liv was sitting beside her, crammed between her and Jaxon. She asked softly, "You okay?"

"Never better." Nebony gave a fake laugh. "Forester was just being a jerk. Nothing new."

"He's going through a really hard time," Jaxon said quietly.

"Whatever, Jax." Nebony gave a bitter smile. "Let's not bore the car with my problems." She'd been an emotional wreck for weeks and was still trying hard to act like she didn't care. One minute she and Forester were making serious plans for the future and the next he wouldn't even answer a text. Now she was done trying to give him another chance. He didn't deserve another chance. Not after what he'd said to her.

Winnie turned on the radio to cover the awkward silence, and Liv crossed her arms in front of her. Belinda Carlisle's "Heaven is a Place on Earth" was playing for Throwback 80s Night. Matty started full-on singing it. By the end, he had them all laughing and riffing on the song. Even she was singing, pretending like her heart wasn't shattered.

They pulled into Eveready. The diner was one of her favorite places. A 1950s retro cafe with padded leather booths and great coffee. She and Forester used to go all the time.

They got a booth. Winnie and Matty shared one side, leaving Nebony to sit on the other side with Liv in the middle again. Matty was going on about how Eveready's disco fries were the best.

"Let's share, MacB," Nebony suggested while the others opted for omelets. She got her phone out and glanced at her feed again and laughed in surprise. At least one thing was going well today. "Check it out—my post with us has two hundred likes already." She showed Matty their picture.

"You posted about the letters?" Jaxon looked aghast.

"Yeah. Why not? It's just a bunch of old letters."

"Because some of them are real predictions and Liv's granddad didn't want the boxes opened." Jaxon ran his hand through his hair. "Delete it," he said, tight-lipped.

"No," she fired back. "It's a fun post and it's my feed. What's your problem?"

"Right now, *that's* my problem." He pointed to the phone.

Nebony looked at the post, not getting it. "I never said whose attic it was. It's not like I gave out Liv's address. I could be anywhere."

Liv shrugged it off. "Jaxon, it's fine. It's pretty vague. I don't care."

"*Thank you,*" Nebony said pointedly while glowering at Jaxon.

Jaxon let the argument drop, although he still seemed agitated, and their food arrived. The disco fries were amazing, a mountain of gooey cheesy deliciousness. She and Matty dug in, chatting over anything and everything. Music, fashion, books, school. She'd had no idea he was the editor of the school paper.

Winnie glared as they cracked each other up, while Liv and Jaxon pretty much stayed quiet. Nebony was sure Winnie hated her and had no clue why, except for the fact they had nothing in common. Winnie was just too weird. From her clothes to her hair to doing Tarot cards in the cafeteria like she was some kind of teen fortune teller. Not to mention she stared at people with a silent, judgy look. Winnie probably thought she was a self-absorbed, empty-headed cheerleader who lived for her Instagram feed.

Whatever.

She'd worked hard for her posts to start earning money to help pay for college. She was constantly training and filming her progress. High-Vs, pikes, thigh stands, flips.

She was the pinnacle of the pyramid, the fearless flyer. She'd suffered more injuries than she could count. Sprained wrists, ankles, a dislocated shoulder, and three concussions. She shared those too. Now she had over two hundred thousand followers. The irony was, some days she felt more alone than ever. No one cared about her, not even Forester.

On the drive back to Liv's, Nebony scrolled through the deluge of comments and emojis that kept coming for her attic posts. The latest had five hundred likes and a hundred comments. So when they got back to Liv's, Nebony tagged along up to the attic to get another photo. She leaned back, using a pile of letters as a pillow and held her Polaroid up in the air to take another selfie.

"Jesus, don't post one again," Jaxon said, sounding irritated.

She sat up and shot him a perplexed look. Jaxon had been acting strange ever since they'd come over yesterday. It was like he was totally obsessed with the letters—and Liv, which was bizarre because he'd never given her the time of day before.

She shoved her camera in her purse, ready to go. Everyone else was reading letters like they were starring in a *Paranormal Hunters* episode. She leaned back on her elbows with a sigh and caught the annoyed look Winnie shot her. It was obvious Winnie didn't want her here. *No one invited you* was written all over her face from the moment Nebony walked in the door. Now that Forester had left, there was no reason to stay—except she had nowhere else to go. She didn't want anyone to know she was afraid to go home.

Luckily, Matty stretched and announced, "I think I'm done for tonight. You ready?" he asked Winnie.

"I can give you a ride, MacB," Nebony jumped to offer and flashed Matty a hopeful smile. Maybe she could hang at his house for a while.

Matty agreed, and Winnie gave them a sharp frown. Jaxon asked Liv if he could come help tomorrow. (Of course she said yes.) Winnie chimed in she'd come over too. Matty said he'd try. Nebony kept a blank face and didn't say anything, knowing she wasn't invited. Plus, the last place she wanted to be was stuck in this attic again. Tomorrow after the homecoming pep rally, she'd find somewhere else to go.

She and Matty got into her car, a green Mini Cooper her dad had gotten her for her birthday. A "guilt gift" because he lived across the country with his new wife and perfect twins. Sometimes she thought about driving to his house on the West Coast, knocking on the door, and announcing she'd like to live with them. She might have to if the situation got any worse.

Trying not to think about home, she drove, blaring music with the windows down. She had been listening to breakup songs all month. She and Matty belted out the lyrics to Fleetwood Mac's "Go Your Own Way" at the top of their lungs, laughing, and Nebony felt happy for the first time in weeks.

Matty's mom lived in a townhome near the historic Vanderbilt Mansion with a view of the Hudson. His parents were divorced like hers. Matty said his dad lived in town, but Matty stayed more with his mom because she'd been the most supportive after he'd officially come out. His dad not so much.

His mom was out of town for two days at a school conference, and he had the house to himself. He invited her in and Nebony checked the time, still needing to kill some more until her mom came home. That was generally the safe zone. She almost confided in Matty tonight, but it wasn't like they knew each other well enough. He was still Team Winnie and not a hundred percent sold on her yet.

They ate ice cream and watched TV. She kept sneaking looks at the clock, willing time to move faster. When Matty started yawning, she took the hint and said she had to go—but she purposefully left her purse behind in case she needed to call or come back over tonight with an excuse.

She took the longest route home and drove slow, killing another half hour while singing Kelly Clarkson's "Since U Been Gone" on repeat. She finally pulled up at home, a small two-bedroom cottage house that kept getting smaller every week since Travis moved in. She killed the engine and put on Forester's hoodie. Her face in the shadows, she took a mysterious selfie and typed: *Nighttime hoodie. My security blanket. Missing my ex for the very last time. It's time to move on. #goodnight #kisses #love.*

Not that Forester was ever online and would see it.

She hit share and sat in the darkened driveway a few minutes longer. Her mom must be running late again. She recently got promoted to manager and had to close up the restaurant. Nebony compensated by staying out.

She stared at the house, debating what to do.

Her problems with her mom's latest boyfriend had gotten worse to the point last week she went to Home Depot and bought a wedge for her bedroom door so it couldn't be opened from the outside. She had tried to tell her mom about his innuendoes and lingering touches, and it'd ended in a fight with her mom accusing her of trying "to ruin her chances at happiness." Now they were barely speaking.

Nebony waited five more minutes in the car, staring wistfully at her bedroom window. She wanted to go to sleep.

Unable to wait any longer, she came up with a plan and hurried inside, pretending to be on the phone. "Forester! I told you it's too late to come over," she said, exasperated, and shot Travis a distracted wave as she passed by. He was sitting on the couch watching TV and drinking beer, empty cans all around him. She made a beeline to her room at the end of the hall, pretending to argue. "No really, my mom's going to be home any minute." She shut her door and kicked the wedge under it to keep it in place.

A minute later, she heard footsteps.

Travis knocked. "Nebony? Come out here and say a proper hello," he demanded, sounding drunk. "Don't be rude."

"I'm on the phone!" she called out. The door handle began to turn slowly, straight out of a horror film.

Travis tried to open the door but was unable to because of the wedge. "What do you have blocking the door?"

Nebony didn't answer, frozen with fear.

"Open this door right now!" he yelled, shoving it harder.

Suddenly her phone rang. She saw who was calling and answered, putting him on speaker. "Hey MacB! What's going on?" She sounded breathless as if she'd been working out and tried to calm down.

"Hey you!" Matty's voice came booming into the room. "You left your purse, ding-a-ling. Do you need it tonight or can it wait until tomorrow? You could come get it or I could bring it over. Although I am in my pajamas and my mom doesn't like me driving at night when she's out of town." Matty was rambling on in that sweet way of his and she watched the door handle turn back. Travis retreated down the hall. Matty asked, "Nebony? You there?"

"Yeah, sorry, bad connection. No, it's okay. I can get it from you tomorrow at lunch." She tried to keep him on the phone a little longer, but he said he had to go.

Seconds after she hung up, Travis rammed the door like a bull. Nebony screamed as the rubber wedge went sliding across the carpet and he came barreling into her room.

"Don't ignore me with your stupid friends!" Travis stood in the center of her room, primed for a fight.

"I'm not! I wasn't." Nebony fought not to take a step back and show weakness.

"You think you're so high and mighty, Little Miss Prom Queen."

"I don't. I swear. I'm sorry if I offended you." She tried to talk him down.

"You're always giving me looks. On that stupid phone!" He yanked her phone from her hand, his face bottled red with rage.

"Give that back," Nebony demanded, watching him put her phone in his pants.

"Ask nicely." Travis grabbed her arms, holding her in a vise.

"Stop, you're hurting me." She couldn't keep the break from her voice or the tears welling in her eyes.

"I think you need to learn some manners."

Headlights flashed through the window blinds as her mother's car pulled into the driveway.

Nebony started sobbing, "My mom's home. My mom's home." She kept saying it over and over until Travis finally let her go.

He pointed his finger at her. "Don't you dare say a word to your mother or I'll make you regret it. Ask me nice for your phone tomorrow and maybe you'll get it back," he jeered, patting her phone in his front pocket. Then he left, slamming the door behind him.

Nebony raced to put the wedge back under the door and put her desk chair under the doorknob too for good measure. Her whole body was shaking hard from the shock. She looked around wildly at her room, her mind racing. Now that her mom was home she was sure Travis wouldn't try anything else tonight. But tomorrow he would.

Not knowing what else to do, she pulled the suitcase out from under her bed and started to pack. She would load up her stuff in the morning and figure out where to go while she was at school. Because one thing was certain—she couldn't stay here anymore.

<ENCRYPTED TRANSMISSION>
<DEFENSE INTELLIGENCE AGENCY SERVER>

<From: MIRIAM>
<Priority: HIGH>

Letters not found at Nebony Price's residence.

Second subject in photograph identified:
@flymattytothemoon
Matthew Jacobs
Driver's License: 016 373 979
Social Security: 921 48 9126
Address: 2495 Hudson View Terrace,
Hyde Park, New York
Phone: (845) 555-3008

Search subject's house tomorrow.
Extraction and interrogation needed if letters not found.

11

JAXON

paraphysics:
coined by the CIA, the study of paranormal applications

TWO YEARS AGO, JAXON HAD SAVED Kaitlyn Neilson, a fellow student, from dying.

All because of a premonition.

In his vision, he saw her waiting at the bus stop when a car slammed into her. He saw her bones break. He saw her body fly through the air and land twenty feet away. He saw her die.

And once he saw it, he couldn't unsee it. Her tragic death was branded in the cortex of his brain.

He didn't know Kaitlyn well, but suddenly he was in charge of keeping her alive. He'd never felt responsible for anyone's life before. It definitely had been a turning point. To have that kind of responsibility was terrifying.

After agonizing over what to do, he left anonymous notes in her locker, warning her not to take the bus on Thursday. Of course, she thought it was a prank and still showed up. He had stood behind a tree and waited, his adrenaline racing, sweat on his face, as he deliberated other options—until he had no other option but to come out of hiding and join her. As the car swerved out of control toward them, he picked Kaitlyn up and ran, clearing the crash.

There'd been a big stir about the almost fatal accident. The local paper even reported on his saving a fellow student. The details were embarrassing. How he had swooped in "like a knight and whisked her to safety." The reporter romanticized it to no end until every girl at school was staring *at him* with hearts in their eyes. His sister proudly put the article on the refrigerator. Jaxon tried to downplay the whole thing, saying he had been at the right place, the right time. Only his parents knew he had a gift, though they had tried hard his whole life to downplay it.

Two days after the incident, his father took him to a baseball game in New York City. The Yankees were playing the Red Sox. At the time, Jaxon thought it was strange. They'd never gone to a game together before and his father didn't even like baseball.

Midway through the game, as the crowd was cheering, his dad leaned over and talked softly to him.

"Listen carefully, because we can only talk about this once. Your birth mother had the same gift—the gift of seeing the future. It's what enabled you to see that car crash."

Jaxon sat there frozen in shock. His father never talked about his birth mother, his first wife. She died when Jaxon was a baby, and his dad married his stepmom when he was two. Sarah was the only mom he'd ever known, and Tia was his half-sister.

In the din of the crowd, his father went on. "I believe your mother died because of her gift. Her death was ruled a suicide, but I know she didn't kill herself. I know." His eyes burned into his. "Forester's dad tried to help me find out the truth. Drew investigated for years, coming up with dead ends. But *I know*." His dad stressed. "I know the truth. So whatever visions you have, son, whatever premonitions come to you, don't ever act on them, and never, *ever*, tell anyone what you can do. The people who came for your mom don't suspect her ability transferred to you. If they did, it would put you at risk."

Jaxon had a million questions, but his dad said they couldn't talk about it anymore.

He said, "All we can do is honor her memory and live our lives by staying safe. Do you understand?"

Jaxon nodded solemnly, trying hard to comprehend what his dad was telling him, but it was a bombshell.

His mother's death hadn't been a suicide.

She had been *killed*.

Because she was psychic.

Jaxon stared at the baseball field, his eyes unfocused on the game.

His father took his hand. "We can never speak of this again. For your own safety. You have to trust me on this, Jax. We both have to let your mother go."

Jaxon and his father never talked about that day again, and Jaxon never shared another premonition with anyone. He even tried—and failed—to stop getting them altogether. But sometimes the knowledge came unbidden, delivered by the universe or his brain's faulty synapses or whatever it was. Sometimes the premonitions came as a thought or an image or like the clip of a movie playing inside his mind. Now he'd been at Liv's all afternoon wading through an ocean of them. Every single letter, whether it was a real prediction or just a dream, whether it'd come true or not, had meant enough for someone to write it down, lick the stamp, and mail it off to a stranger. The majority of the letters had never come true—and never would—but some of them had. They were real, and it was the real ones he was there for, because he felt a kindred spirit to those people. If the Premonitions Bureau still existed, he would have written to them too. Now that he'd found the letters, they were filling his head and calling to him.

Because his mother had written some of these letters.

He couldn't ignore the feeling deep in his bones or the voice inside his heart whispering she was the Oracle of Delphi.

From the way his father had acted at dinner, he knew it too.

His father said his mother had been killed because of her gift.

Had she been killed *because* she was the Oracle?

Part of him wanted to tell Liv what he was discovering, but he couldn't. His father had warned him it wasn't safe. But for the first time, he felt connected to his mother, like a seed buried deep inside him was finally getting water, and he didn't want to lose that feeling. No matter what the cost. He was meant to find her letters.

Suddenly New York City's skyline loomed in his mind, and a whole slew of thoughts and images slammed into his brain at once. Like a series of film clips that hadn't been edited properly.

He is driving with Winnie in his car. Downtown buildings tower around them. What are they doing there?

The image jumps. *Liv stands outside One World Trade Center in a black dress. She's with a woman. Her mother. It looks like she's been crying.*

Then the image jumps again—*He's looking out a window at Central Park. He's high up in a building . . . someone's apartment. No one's home. A feeling of emptiness surrounds him. Jaxon looks over at Liv. She is absorbed in reading a letter addressed to her. It's from her grandfather—or no, that's not right. Confusion clouds his mind. Winnie sits beside her. A Picasso painting hangs over their heads.*

The image holds his mind's eye captive—until his vision jumps to nighttime. To a premonition he's already had before. *He and Liv are outside on the apartment balcony kissing in the rain. Her hair is down, his fingers twined in it. They're both soaking wet, in each other's arms.*

He blinked, pulling away from the whirlwind in his mind, now left with only questions. What was he doing with Liv and Winnie in New York? What letter was Liv reading? Whose balcony were they on?

The only thing he did know was the letter Liv would read was going to change everything.

12

LIV

inevitable:
an event certain to happen

LIV WAS HAVING LUNCH WITH WINNIE and Matty at their table when Jaxon sat down across from her, as if they'd been eating together all year. He gave her a rare smile that made her stomach flutter.

She could have sworn she heard him say, "How am I going to ask her?"

But his lips didn't move.

Or had they? She frowned. Then he did say something. But she couldn't tell if it was "How am I going to ask her?" or "How are you doing?"

What in the world? Liv tried popping her ears, opening and closing her mouth.

"Liv is practicing her miming techniques." Matty stepped in to rescue her—although was it a rescue? He put his arm around her. "That's what mime school does to you. She could never be called Chatty Kathy."

Winnie laughed hard at that. Even Jaxon looked amused.

Liv was going to kill Matty. Before she could think of a comeback, Nebony slid in next to her with a peppy, "Hey guys!" Today she was dressed in full head cheerleader regalia for the afternoon pep rally. Her hair was done up in two Princess Leia buns and her makeup looked heavier than usual. She asked Matty, "Got it?"

"But of course," Matty said in a bad French accent. "One Kate Spade handbag *pour toi* is in my lockeeeeeur." Nebony laughed and started going on how fun last night was at his place and asked if he wanted to hang out again tonight. "I was going to be at Liv's." Matty joked, "Partying in the attic."

"Oh." Her face fell then brightened again. "Maybe we can meet up after?"

Winnie dropped the french fry that had been on its way to her mouth, looking annoyed as they made plans. Liv listened to Matty and Nebony's easy rapport and wished she could be like that with Jaxon. Whenever he was around, she couldn't think straight.

Nebony and Matty left together to go get her purse from his locker. Winnie made a big production of checking the time. "Oh gosh, I totally forgot I want to check out that book *The Pink Parade* in the library. See ya." She shot Liv a look and dashed off, leaving her alone with Jaxon.

He asked her, "Have you read the book she's talking about?"

"Uh, no." Liv fought to keep from laughing. Lunch was an official disaster. Feeling nervous, she took off her armband and fiddled with it.

Jaxon surprised her by reaching over and gently taking it from her. She watched as he turned it round and round. "This is seriously cool."

"Thanks." She cleared her throat. "I made it."

"You made this? Wow." He looked up, pinning her with his eyes. "You're really talented. What's the design?"

Liv could not look away, becoming lost in his eyes. What were they even talking about? She forced herself to think. *Right. Her armband.* "It's a triple spiral called a triskelion." Now a bundle of nerves, she looked down at his hands and fiddled with her pendant, running it up and down the chain.

Jaxon's eyes went to her neck, as if he wanted to touch her necklace too. "Are you going through more of the letters today after school?"

Liv nodded. She didn't mention Winnie's YouTube idea. She was still on the fence about it. Until she found out why the boxes were addressed to her father, she didn't feel comfortable broadcasting anything on the Internet. He clearly hadn't wanted them opened.

But she had opened them. Maybe she'd subconsciously done it to spite him.

On second thought, maybe she would greenlight Winnie's idea. Then he might see it online wherever he was up in Alaska and be pissed.

"Can I come hang out again?" Jaxon surprised her by asking.

"Sure." Liv tucked her hair behind her ear and tried to play it cool. She pretended to check the time on her phone, already well aware the bell was about to ring. "Um, can I?" she motioned to her armband and he gave it back. This would be the third day in a row Jaxon Coleson was at her house, and she didn't know why. Either he was really into old psychic letters—or he was really into her.

<ENCRYPTED TRANSMISSION>

<DEFENSE INTELLIGENCE AGENCY SERVER>

<From: MIRIAM>

<Priority: HIGH>

Letters not at the Jacobs' residence.

Storlie wants to interrogate both subjects in the morning.

Schedule their extraction tonight.

13

MATTY

omen:

an event with prophetic significance

AFTER LUNCH, MATTY USED HIS ENTIRE study hall in the computer lab researching the Premonitions Bureau. He was determined to find out why all those letters were in Liv's attic. But even he, editor and star reporter of the school paper who had a nose for a story, was ready to give up. He couldn't find anything about the Bureau except what they already knew. It shut down in the early nineties.

He couldn't find names of anyone attached to it either. A lot of the Internet links were broken, probably because the information was so old. He read a few archived newspaper articles. The Bureau's offices had been in New York City and closed after a building fire. He found a small article about how a longtime paranormal study had gone up in flames. Literally.

Matty shook his head to himself. *Well that was a lie.* The letters hadn't gone up in flames. They'd been hidden in Liv's attic.

He tried researching the psychic Jerald Peterson who'd helped that kidnapped little girl and found several mentions. How the Bureau sent his letter to the police. How the psychic from New York went on to help the NYPD on several more cases. Matty tried googling Premonitions Bureau + CIA + FBI + NSA and only got websites riddled with conspiracy theories. If the Bureau had sent predictions to the government, there wasn't any mention online. But then, all of this had happened before the Internet.

He was about to give up when an article caught his eye:

Psychic who helps police killed. He clicked on it in shock and covered his mouth with his hand as he read *Jerald Peterson found murdered.*

The details were grisly. Jerald had been stuffed in a sack and thrown into the East River. Matty checked the date and found the Premonitions Bureau closed the same year.

This could be lead he'd been searching for. A psychic who had written the Bureau and helped the police was murdered, and then the Bureau closed for good.

Was it a murder and then a cover-up?

And how did Liv's family factor into it?

He focused next on her grandfather, Clement Spencer, and came up empty. Matty needed Liv's parents' names, but he didn't want to wait to ask Winnie. He glanced over his shoulder and quickly logged into the school's database with his mother's password. He rarely did it and if he ever got caught, his mom would expel him herself.

L-I-V-_-H-A-L-L

He typed her name into the fields and hit enter.

Her record came up with the transfer date from this spring. He clicked on the file.

Record Not Found

He clicked back and tried again. Maybe it was a glitch. He checked his own record and Winnie's. They were both there.

Only Liv's school record was missing.

Then a thought occurred to him, and he couldn't believe it hadn't occurred to him sooner. Who the hell was Grayson Spencer? The name on all the boxes wasn't Clement. He was about to jump back on the Internet when the bell rang and he had to log off. He headed to his next class, now in a grumpy mood. His research expedition had only led to more questions.

"Hey MacB!" Nebony called from down the hall. Every head turned to watch her catch up and give him a hug. "I need to ask a big favor. Since your mom's still out of town, can I crash at your place tonight? My mom texted she's having friends over and I know I won't be able to sleep."

"Of course." He waved his hand in the air and gave a snap. "Slumber party!"

She laughed and gave him another hug. "Thanks, you're the best."

The bell rang and they hurried to class. As he walked down the hallway, he noticed people saying "hey" to him who never had before—girls and guys. Even the bullies from the football team looked like they were reevaluating their stance on the principal's kid. Ever since Nebony posted that cool picture of them, things were definitely improving.

After school he headed to his car. Winnie was parked beside him, waiting for Liv.

"You okay?" she asked. She was staring at him with that funny look she got whenever she was "seeing auras." Then she said, "Your aura's a little all over the place."

Yep. He knew it.

"It's got a lot of red. You've never had red before."

According to Winnie, his aura was normally orange and blue. Orange people had loads of creativity and energy and blue signaled he was an excellent communicator and writer. He could have told her that.

"So?" He unlocked his door and threw his stuff on the seat. "Isn't red like fire and passion?"

"Among other things. Nebony's a Red."

He whipped back around to her. "OMG. Would you stop with the Nebony bashing?"

"I'm not bashing! Chill. I just said she was a Red."

"Like it's a bad thing. Come on," he pointed out, becoming irritated. "You're just mad because she didn't follow you back and she followed me."

"No. People rub off on each other. That's all I'm saying." She hesitated. "And I get a *really* bad feeling when it comes to you two hanging out together."

He rolled his eyes. "Well don't. Because we're becoming *really* good friends." He stressed the really like she had. "I accepted Liv for you. You can be more open-minded about Nebony."

"Whatever." She sighed. "But don't say I didn't warn you."

"About what?"

"I don't know. Just be careful," Winnie said cryptically. God, she could be so annoying sometimes.

They waited for Liv, both leaning against their cars, the silence now like a lead weight between them.

He studied his nails before remembering he wanted to ask her. "What's Liv's parents' names?"

"Why?" Winnie glanced over at him.

"Because I'm trying to find the connection to the Bureau."

She rolled her eyes at him. "Hazel and Bodhi Hall."

"Who's Grayson Spencer?"

"No clue."

"What about her grandmother?"

"Why don't you ask Liv instead of being so secretive? Here she comes." They watched Liv head toward their cars. "It's like you're trying to think the worst of her."

"Like you think the worst of Nebony?"

Liv reached them and they dropped it, not happy with each other. Matty followed them to Liv's. When they arrived, he was surprised to see Jaxon pull up. Matty looked across the street to see if Forester was joining them too, but it was only Jaxon. Why Jaxon was so clearly into Liv, Matty had no idea.

The four of them headed up to the attic and returned to their same spots. The vibe was definitely more rushed than yesterday. Liv said they only had two more days with the letters before the estate attorney came. She seemed determined to go through every single box, Winnie too.

Only the rustling sound of paper filled the silence. Liv kept shifting in that nervous way of hers. He caught Winnie discreetly recording video footage of the letters she was reading without drawing Jaxon's attention. Jaxon was glued to the Oracle letters again. It was weird—he wasn't even trying to talk to Liv. Not that Liv was interesting to talk to. Matty was beginning to feel the need to take a big break from the attic after today. There were only so many premonitions someone could read.

With a sigh, he picked up a stack of verified predictions they hadn't gotten to yet. They were all written by the same person. The letter on top was dated 1993, the year the Bureau closed.

Dear Reader,

Omens are real. They are a warning of an event yet to happen.

I've seen your omen: when the raven hits the round window. The glass splinters but does not break. The fear you feel in that moment is not imagined but real, because you have found the letters. You have found my letters. Tell no one or you will not survive the summer's end.

For those who can see the future and how its threads are woven together have been hunted by people in power for thousands of years. Knowledge is power, and knowing what tomorrow will bring is the ultimate power.

The future can be changed. The trick is you have to see it first.

Mad Merlin

Matty's breath hitched in his throat as he read the letter again.

"What is it? What's wrong?" Winnie was the first to notice he was freaking out.

"There's a bizarre letter here from someone named Mad Merlin."

Winnie startled. "Mad *what?*"

"Mad Merlin." He handed it to her and looked at the attic window, at the crack running down the center. This letter being for them was not possible or feasible or remotely realistic. He must have been up in this attic too long to even be considering it. But the raven *had* crashed into the window the first day they were here.

Right when they found the letters.

Was that an omen? Seriously, for real? They were dealing with bird omens now? What century was he living in?

"Uh, guys?" Winnie sounded unnerved and handed the letter to Jaxon and Liv.

Matty went over to the window. "It can't be for us. There's just no way."

Winnie joined him. Her finger traced the crack in the glass. "What if it is? A raven flew into the window. And it's round." Her hand circled the window frame as if he couldn't see the shape. "And we're the ones who found the letters."

"That letter was written in 1993. He couldn't have been talking about us. It's like twenty years ago."

"Thirty," Jaxon corrected.

"See?" Matty turned back to Winnie. "There's no way."

"But what if he was?" Winnie crossed her arms defensively. "The real Nostradamus predicted stuff hundreds of years in advance."

"Please don't bring Nostradamus into this," Matty snapped. "None of his writing even makes sense. It's all quatrain gibberish!"

"I'm making a point!" she snapped back. "Predictions don't have expiration dates on them like a carton of milk. And that letter is more than a premonition. It's *an omen*, a curse."

"So you're saying we've all been cursed? Like Cassandra in the *Iliad*?" Matty ran his hands through his hair. Great. He was trapped in a book.

He looked at all the boxes full of premonitions. DO NOT OPEN was written a gazillion times. Why hadn't they listened? What were they thinking? Screw the YouTube idea. They never should have opened these boxes. It was like opening Pandora's box, which technically had been a jar in the myth. Pandora was stupid and they were stupid too.

Liv was still reading the letter, looking shocked.

Jaxon joined in the argument. "I agree the letter is freaky. Why don't we try to find this guy and ask him?"

"Because this was written decades ago and there's no address on any of the verifieds," Winnie pointed out. "All the envelopes are missing."

"Okay, then why don't we find out who ran the Bureau and go try to talk to them?" Liv suggested.

Matty looked up to the ceiling, praying for patience. "All I've been doing is researching the Bureau, and I can't find anything."

Winnie added, "Plus, the letter says we can't tell anyone we found the letters."

Jaxon suggested, "We have an address for Jerald Peterson. His letters were written on letterhead and he's in New York. Plus he's a verified psychic. We could ask him if he knows Mad Merlin. Maybe they were both at that conference together?"

Matty rubbed his forehead, feeling a headache set in. How had Mr. Popular suddenly become such a part of this?

"That's a good idea," Liv said.

Matty finally erupted. "No, that's *not* a good idea because Jerald Peterson is dead!" Everyone turned to him in shock. "I researched him today. He helped NYPD with his predictions and ended up murdered. The Premonitions Bureau shut down the same year and all the letters were put here!"

Liv crossed her arms defensively. "What are you saying?"

Winnie chimed in. "Yeah Matty. That kinda sounded like an accusation."

"I'm not saying her grandfather killed Jerald Peterson or anything. I'm saying there is a cover-up going on. A big, massive Watergate cover-up for psychics! Her school record is even missing."

"You looked up her school record?" Winnie sounded dismayed, like he had infringed on her privacy or something.

"My school record is missing?" Liv sounded confused.

Matty was already regretting his outburst. "Yes, it's missing," he told Liv with a sigh and turned to Winnie. "And no, I'm not saying she's a suspect. I'm just saying someone was murdered and the letters were hidden *here*. Which sounds like a mystery to me." Sarcasm dripped from his voice. "But what do I know? I'm just a reporter who runs the school paper." He had been planning to ask Liv who Grayson Spencer was, but now he didn't care.

Right now he wanted to go home and forget this whole fiasco. He didn't want to know about the Premonitions Bureau anymore. He just wanted to leave. Nebony was waiting for him at his place.

Jaxon tried to steer the conversation. "Look, I say let's go to Manhattan tomorrow and talk to Jerald Peterson's family. Maybe they know what happened with the Bureau."

Liv said to Jaxon, "I'm supposed to take off school and go to the city with my mom to meet my grandfather's attorney."

"So we'll meet up afterward and get you," Jaxon offered. "I can drive. We'll all skip school." Suddenly he seemed dead set they were going to Manhattan tomorrow.

"Well I can't go," Matty announced, throwing a wrench into the plan. "I have a physics lab."

"Are you kidding me?" Winnie exploded. "We have a cursed-omen-death letter written to us and you're worried about your GPA?"

"What if the cursed-omen-death letter wasn't written for us, and we're all just being paranoid?" he countered. "Reading premonitions for three days straight can do that to you. Make you go cuckoo in the head! I'm sure in the last twenty years a lot of birds flew into windows!"

"Thirty," Jaxon corrected him again.

"Do you really want to take that chance?" Winnie asked. "Pretend we didn't get the memo? Because I can't! Ignore an omen at your own peril."

"No, it's the opposite," he countered. "Think about Oedipus. He had an omen and he acted on it. That's the irony. I'm saying let's not act."

"Whether he acted or not, he was still screwed! That's the real irony!"

"No, he was screwed because he tried to change what he couldn't!"

"It's the same thing!" Winnie shot back.

Matty couldn't believe he was arguing a twenty-five-hundred-year-old play right now. *Damn it if Sophocles wasn't good.*

He turned away and stared at the window. Were they unwittingly fulfilling a prophecy that would kill someone? What if they were doomed either way?

The attic suddenly felt like a dangerous place—a real haunted house that had cursed them.

"Just forget everything I said. I'm out." He grabbed his bag to make a swift exit.

"Matty?" It was Jaxon who called him back. He held out the letter. "Do you want to take a picture of Mad Merlin's letter to show Nebony? She was here too when the bird hit. The omen is for all of us." Jaxon looked so serious, like he really believed the omen was for them.

Matty swallowed the lump in his throat and shook his head. He wanted nothing to do with the letters anymore. "You can show her. Count me out on the letters from now on." He looked at Winnie. "I'm done. Good luck tomorrow," he said flippantly and left.

He jumped into his car and sped away like it was a getaway car. When he arrived at his house, he noticed a plumbing van in front of the complex. Nebony was parked across the street and waiting in her car. As he pulled into the driveway, his phone rang. He fished it from his bag and answered, but there was no one on the line.

"Hey you!" Nebony got out of her car, still in her cheerleading uniform. She walked toward him with that cute strut of hers like she owned the world. "Perfect timing!"

"Cool! I texted you earlier. I wasn't sure if you were waiting or not." He grabbed his bag, his phone still in his hand.

"Oh, I lost my phone." She held up a Taco Bell bag. "I brought us 7-Layer burritos and Cokes." They both cracked up, and Matty felt all the stress leave his body. Getting to know Nebony was one of the only good things to come out of the past few days.

"You read my mind, Missy. I'm starving!" He started down the driveway to meet her halfway when he heard the doors of the plumbing van swish open behind him.

It all happened so fast. Two men in black ski masks jumped out— someone grabbed him. His phone slipped from his hand. He heard Nebony's scream as his body was wrenched off the ground, his gravity gone.

A gloved hand covered his mouth with a wet cloth, the reeking fumes making the world around him go dark.

Greetings to the Bureau of Premonitions,

Did you know the Earth hurtles through space at 67,000 miles an hour and the galaxy at 490,000? Well our futures are hurtling toward us at an even greater speed. Like a race to the finish line, whichever future reaches us first is called "inevitable." So let me share with you some of the inevitables I see ahead on the horizon.

I'll start with what is being called the WorldWideWeb. (Yes, it is all one word.) Created last year by Tim Berners-Lee at CERN to share computer files. Soon the WorldWideWeb will change life on Earth as we know it, and Mr. Berners-Lee will be knighted. (Don't tell him yet and spoil the surprise.) In April of 1993, CERN will release the code into the public domain, donating it to humanity like the world's digital ocean for anyone to freely access. Next year, the first web camera will go online with a live shot of a coffee pot. (Riveting, I know.) But this is only the start. From computer files to letters to pictures and videos, all of these can be shared within moments.

A person's life will become a TV show and be watched around the world. We will all have tiny telephones in our pockets with this ocean accessible anytime. This feat of magic will happen in just ten years. All the while, Artificial Intelligence will be growing smarter, running the race alongside us. In 1997, a computer will defeat the world's chess champion for the first time, proving its thought capacity equals ours. The only question remaining will be whether there are aspects of the human mind which cannot be copied by Artificial Intelligence. But that is for another letter.

Yours truly,
Mad Merlin

LIV

arithmancy:
divination by assigning letters or phrases numerical value

AFTER MATTY'S ABRUPT DEPARTURE, LIV READ more Mad Merlin letters with Jaxon and Winnie. They passed them back and forth. Mad Merlin's predictions were all over the place. Some were broad. Others detailed. For the ones that could be verified, Mad Merlin had gotten everything right. From historic hurricanes to plane crashes to earthquakes. Winnie held up the letters. "He predicted two gas explosions, one in Turkey and one in Mexico, that killed hundreds of people."

Liv shook her head at what she was reading. "He mailed in a list of everyone who would win a gold medal in the 1992 Summer Olympics in Barcelona."

"Now that's just showing off." Winnie laughed and took the letter from her to read it.

There was a flair to his writing, a wild recklessness that made Liv agree there was something definitely *mad* about him.

She went through more letters and read the analysis on the back. The majority were verified. On the premonition about the Internet, just as Mad Merlin predicted, CERN released the code for it in April of 1993. He even got the month right.

"Listen to this. Mad Merlin predicted it years before it happened in 1997," Jaxon said, reading from his phone. "'On this day in history, World Chess Champion Garry Kasparov was defeated by Deep Blue, an AI computer designed by IBM. Garry Kasparov was a twelve-time chess champion and considered the best chess player of all time. Deep Blue could calculate one hundred to two hundred billion chess moves in three minutes. Kasparov resigned midgame.'"

Liv picked up the Mad Merlin letter Jaxon was referring to.

He kept reading, "The chess community was shocked, thinking Kasparov could have won. He had defeated Deep Blue the year before by being spontaneous. But this time, he resigned because he said he knew he'd lose."

"I guess Mad Merlin knew it too." Liv handed the letter back to Jaxon and caught him staring at her again in that peculiar way of his—as if he was looking at her but thinking of something else.

Winnie read from her stack. "He predicted the fall of the USSR. The Bosnian War. Czechoslovakia separating into the Czech Republic and Slovakia. The Great Blizzard of 1993. The flooding of the Mississippi River. The Internet. He predicted basically www dot everything."

"Yeah and gave us a bird omen too." Jaxon rubbed his face.

Liv felt the need to ask them, "Are you sure you want to go to New York tomorrow? Maybe we should see what the attorney says first?"

"No, we should go." Jaxon sounded certain.

Winnie agreed. "If the omen is for us, we need to track down every lead."

Liv tried to joke, "You're starting to sound like Matty."

"Well, maybe Matty has a point," Winnie countered. "These predictions are incredible, and they've been hidden up here in boxes. It doesn't make sense. Why are they even up here? And why do *we* have a letter written to us?"

No one said anything because they all had same the questions. Liv swallowed and nodded. "I know. It seems unreal."

"So we're going tomorrow," Jaxon confirmed, looking set on the plan.

"Yeah, we're going." Winnie checked the time and started gathering her things. "It's getting late, and I think I want to read more of *The Pink Parade*. It might help take my mind off everything. See you guys tomorrow."

She flashed Liv a look and left. Liv pinched the bridge of her nose, trying hard not to react.

Jaxon commented, "She must really like that book. Do you know what it's about?"

"Uh . . . no." She couldn't help the heat rising to her face. She was going to give Winnie such a hard time tomorrow.

Jaxon stood up and stretched. He held his hand out to Liv and helped her stand. They kept hold of each other's hands a lingering moment as they stood facing each other, the air between them becoming charged.

Liv held his gaze. He had to know how she felt—he *had to* see it on her face, in her eyes. Never had she liked someone this much or wanted to kiss someone so, so much. It was ridiculous.

She parted her lips and leaned forward, certain it was about to happen. Not in her dreams but right now in real life.

Jaxon studied her face. Then something flickered in his eyes like regret, and he stepped away from her, clearing his throat. "I should be going too," he said, looking embarrassed, and basically rushed out with a quick, "I'll see you tomorrow."

Liv tried to play it cool when really she was dying inside. Had she actually puckered her lips? God. Talk about absolute mortification. That had been a serious bad call on her part.

"Bye, see you," she forced out, trying to sound normal. "Have a good one!" She cringed as she said it. *Have a good one?*

Then he was gone, leaving her drowning in embarrassment. She could have sworn they were going to kiss. It'd been the perfect moment. Any guy who even semi-liked her would have read the signs. She'd practically closed her eyes and swayed.

Maybe he wasn't into her—actually there was no *maybe* about it. He definitely wasn't. He'd just expertly extricated himself from the awkward moment of a girl who wanted to kiss him and he didn't. She had seriously gotten his signals wrong. Winnie, too. Jaxon was a pretty reserved guy, some would even say arrogant, and he didn't let many people get close to him. Forester was his best friend, and look at Forester. He'd dumped his girlfriend out of the blue, given her the cold shoulder, and made her cry yesterday. And that was Nebony Price. The most popular, confident, beautiful girl at school. What if Jaxon was a player too? And he was only here because of a weird fascination with psychic stuff?

Now she regretted ever opening the boxes. The attic looked like a tornado of paper had hit it. Hundreds of premonitions were scattered over the floor, and it was going to take her forever to box them all up before the attorney's office came on Thursday. Part of her couldn't wait for them to come. Maybe she'd even ask them to take the boxes away. She just wanted the letters gone and her life back to normal.

15

WINNIE

bibliomancy:
foretelling the future by interpreting a randomly chosen page in a book

MAD MERLIN. MAD MERLIN. MAD MERLIN . . . the name was circling around in Winnie's head like a buzzing fly that wouldn't go away. She could not remember where she'd heard it before, but she knew she had. It sounded so familiar. The answer was right on the cusp of her memory. When she got home from Liv's, she fanned out her Tarot deck, closed her eyes, and drew a card, hoping for clarity.

The King of Swords.

She stared at the card with a frown. In her mind, the King of Swords was her father's card. The card symbolized intellectual power, wisdom, and truth.

She gasped, suddenly realizing where she'd seen the name Mad Merlin before.

For a moment, she sat there in stunned disbelief.

It couldn't be possible, but it was.

She hurried downstairs to the living room where her mom lovingly displayed all of her dad's novels next to framed family photos. Winnie ran her fingers over the weathered spines, having read them so many times. It was one of the ways she kept her father's memory alive, through his stories. Sometimes she could imagine his voice reading them to her. She studied the titles: *Split Horizon*, *The Zodiac Race*, *Time Wars*, *The Omega Maze*, and her favorite, the last one he wrote before he died, *Quantum Silence*. That one had been his breakout success, landing him on the *New York Times* bestseller list. Then he died in a plane crash. His tragic death had seemed straight out of one of his books.

She flipped through them all, not quite sure what she was looking for. She was speed-reading *Split Horizon* when *Quantum Silence* fell to the floor. Right on her foot.

"Ow." She startled, wondering how that had happened.

She bent down to pick it up. Then she remembered exactly where she'd seen Mad Merlin.

In the back of this book.

Adrenaline hitting hard, she flipped to the back page of *Quantum Silence*, to the teaser for his next novel—the one he never published.

THE GNOSIS TRAP
Sawyer Scott's exciting new novel
Coming next summer!

A secret government organization is hunting psychics in order
to map their minds and transfer their ability to a powerful
supercomputer named Miriam. The future has become a
chessboard and only one man can play the game and possibly win.
A psychic who calls himself Mad Merlin.

Winnie stood there frozen in the living room, trying to make sense of the words on the page.

Her dad had written a book about Mad Merlin?

Her brain was overloading with questions. She flipped through *Quantum Silence* several times to see if she could find any other mention of *The Gnosis Trap*, but that was it.

She found her mom in the back den having tea and watching TV. One of the presidential candidates, some powerful billionaire white-haired dude, was making his spiel in a commercial. "If I have the honor to become the President, I will cement the United States as *the* super-power of the future. And that future is technology. AI. Quantum computing. Space exploration and mining. I know what it will take to keep America on top as we race up the mountain of scientific breakthroughs. These are exciting times." He smiled at the camera, full of charm and charisma. "No matter what party you belong to, what religion you hold dear, your race, your tax bracket, I'm the only candidate who can lead this great nation into a bright future." He ended with a wink, as if the American public was in on the joke. "I'm Charles Becker, and I approve this message."

Winnie shook her head. Charles Becker ads had been blanketing the airwaves with the upcoming primary along with the other leading candidate, Senator Tom what's-his-name, who looked like even more of a snake. "There's something so fake about him."

"His message is a strong one though. He'll probably win." Her mom noticed her dad's book in her hand and raised her eyebrows in surprise.

"I thought I'd reread it," Winnie explained and tried to sound normal. "You know, I was wondering whatever happened to Dad's last book? *The Gnosis Trap*. There's a summary about it in the back of this. It sounds good." *It sounds real*, was what she was thinking. "I'd love to read it."

Her mom got that sad look on her face whenever Winnie brought up her dad. "He never finished it. I think it's on his old computer."

Winnie pressed, "Where is it?"

"In my closet. I don't know if it works anymore."

"Do you mind if I get it out and see? I really want to read it."

Her mother swallowed and nodded, visibly fighting back tears. "Your father would have loved how much you enjoy his stories."

"Oh Mom." Winnie gave her a tight hug.

Her mom pulled away with a soft laugh and wiped her eyes. "Go on, you can have the computer. I hope you find it. Maybe I'll even read it someday." She gave her a forced, bright smile, trying to lighten the mood.

Winnie hurried upstairs. Her mom's bedroom had a big walk-in closet. She had cleared out her dad's clothes years ago. Winnie found his computer on the floor in the back corner, along with a keyboard, a printer, and a box of discs. She picked up the monitor. It weighed a ton and reminded her of an old TV. She brought it to her room and went back for the hard drive, keyboard, and mouse. There were countless cords. She untangled them and connected everything—at least she hoped she did it right. The computer made gurgling noises as it booted up.

Winnie sat at her desk, anxiously waiting. "Come on come on come on." The booting-up took a good five minutes and felt like an eternity. While the computer was running through all its system checks, she flipped through the disks. There were both CDs and floppy disks, small and square. Her dad had been organized, and he had a ton of files. Each novel had two floppy disks, one labeled "drafts" and one "research."

There were no disks for *The Gnosis Trap*.

The computer quit making noises, and she turned back to it. Her shoulders fell when she saw the prompt.

ENTER PASSWORD

_ _ _

She tried some random ones without luck. She ran downstairs to ask her mom if she knew it, but she didn't. "Try his birthday," her mom suggested.

Winnie tried it. Then she tried her birthday, her mom's birthday, all their names, first and last. She tried every combination she could think of, but nothing worked. Before she knew it, the clock said midnight. They had a big day tomorrow with their last-minute road trip. She'd have to think more how to crack the password, because no matter what, she needed into this computer. She needed to know why her dad had created a character named Mad Merlin and whether he was fictional or not.

<ENCRYPTED TRANSMISSION>
<DEFENSE INTELLIGENCE AGENCY SERVER>

<From: MIRIAM>
<Priority: HIGH>

Subjects are in holding and sedated.

Their cell phones weren't with them.
Cannot yet determine target location.

Have a team standing by and await orders
pending interrogation.

16

FORESTER

sixth sense:
power of perception beyond the five senses

THE DAY FORESTER'S DAD WAS SHOT, Forester had no idea when he said goodbye to him that morning at breakfast the next time he would see him would be in the ICU. Forester had been at football practice while his dad was fighting for life from a gunshot wound. Forester hadn't known after that day they'd never go camping again, go rowing again, or hiking again. The two of them were off in the woods every weekend and had a trip planned for the following one. But on that day, life unexpectedly rearranged all the pieces.

In the beginning and for a long time after, Forester tried to be strong. He kept hold of the belief his dad would walk again and their lives would go back to normal. Although at night, he would lie awake staring up at the ceiling in the dark, looking for answers.

Why did this happen? How could it have happened? Why did this happen to us?

Until he finally came to the conclusion sometimes there were no answers, and the idea "everything happens for a reason" was a crock. Sometimes life just dealt you a bad hand.

The reality was, his dad was never going to walk again. There was only one possible surgery left, and their insurance wouldn't cover it because it was an "experimental procedure." A doctor in Los Angeles was the only surgeon who could do it. They didn't have the money to pay for it, and even if they did, there were no guarantees it would work. His dad's salary, now he was part-time working admin at the precinct, barely paid the bills together with his mom's florist job. Forester took care of his own expenses with his weekend job, but his parents had sat him down a month ago to break the news there would be no more surgeries. This summer they were putting the house on the market to pay the outstanding medical bills. They'd be moving into a small apartment on the outskirts of town. As far as college went, maybe Forester could get student loans or a football scholarship. They didn't have the money to pay for tuition. Forester said not to worry. He'd be fine.

He broke up with Nebony the next day and told his coach in private he'd be quitting the football team at the end of the year to put in more hours at work. He wouldn't have time to play senior year. He doubted he would have been able to get a football scholarship anyway. His grades were lousy. But still, all he could feel was rage at the unfairness of it all. It was like life was caving in on him. The past year had been all about fighting to get his dad to walk again, of not giving up hope, and now they were giving up.

So when he saw the Premonitions Bureau letters had been shipped from the same town upstate where his father was shot, for the first time Forester thought maybe he could make sense out of what happened. Now the idea seemed ridiculous. The Bureau closed decades ago, and a stack of predictions about the future didn't change his.

It was time to give up. He honestly thought Nebony had given up on him too. She should have by now. So her showing up with Jaxon at Liv's house both days had completely thrown him. Her initial shock and anger at their abrupt breakup and his vanishing act on her had subsided. Now she wanted answers and was ready to forgive him. She'd said as much in Liv's yard.

She said she loved him, and in response he told her they were done and she needed to get on with her life. He said to stop following him around like a lost puppy. It was pathetic.

He'd been half tempted to call and apologize, but that would only bring them back to square one. He'd done the best thing for her by ending it with a clean break. If he told her the truth, she wouldn't want to break up. She didn't need him holding her back. Nebony had huge dreams, and they couldn't include him anymore. There could be no college together, no future plans. He didn't want to have to tell her how bad it was at home. He didn't want her pity. In twenty years, he'd be a faint memory, the lame high school boyfriend who'd thrown away something good. They'd meet at their twenty-year reunion. She'd have become super successful and famous, and he'd be the loser in the corner because this was his life, and his life sucked.

So he kept his phone off, not wanting to see if Nebony had called or texted after last night. He doubted she would. She was the proudest person he knew, and she would never forgive him for what he said yesterday. She said she loved him, and he'd thrown it back in her face. He'd made her cry and Nebony never cried. Now he was still agonizing about it. Tonight he was watching a game on TV with his dad, eating burgers he'd gotten them. His mom was working late. The florist shop had a ton of orders for prom next week. Not that he was going.

"You been friends with Liv Hall long?" his dad asked out of the blue.

"No," Forester said, surprised by the question. He left it at that. They ate in silence a while longer.

"What were you doing over there the other day?"

"Helping move some furniture." Forester didn't mention the letters.

"I think it'd be best if you stay away from the Halls, son."

"Why?" Forester gave him a sharp look. His father was a man of few words and seemed to have something on his mind.

"Nothing but problems with that family."

That family? What about our family? Forester wanted to say. He waited for his dad to explain, but he didn't. "Dad, you can't say 'stay away' all cryptic-like and not tell me why." Forester's antenna was up. What beef did he have with the Halls?

"Yes I can, and I just did." His dad pursed his lips sternly, giving him what Forester called his *resting cop face.*

Forester was about to demand an explanation when a knock at the back door interrupted them. Jaxon peered through the window.

Forester got up. "Want me to stay away from Jax too?" he asked flippantly. His dad pursed his lips tighter and went back to watching TV. Forester took his burger and fries and left, meeting Jaxon outside. "Hey." He headed up the stairs to the garage apartment his parents had finally let him move into this year as a birthday present.

"What's up?" he asked Jaxon, sounding more curt than he meant to as they headed inside. He sat down to finish his burger. The garage apartment was basically an oversized bedroom with a kitchenette. An old family couch and his dad's broken La-Z-Boy took up the center of the room.

Jaxon looked like he didn't know where to start. He seemed flustered, which wasn't like him. "Something happened. We found a letter today . . . a premonition that's pretty out there." He opened up his phone and handed it to him to show him a picture.

Forester held up his hands. "Dude, I'm so done with the letters."

"Just read it."

Forester took the phone and zoomed in on the picture of a letter. He usually didn't like reading with people because he was dyslexic and slow at unjumbling the words. But Jaxon knew. He was the one who'd helped him learn to read when they were kids. It took him a few minutes for the words to sink in.

Then he read it again. "Mad Merlin? This some kind of joke?"

"No. He wrote a lot of predictions that happened. Big ones. This is his only letter like this."

"And you think it's meant for us?" Forester shook his head and laughed. "Bro, you are so far gone. I'm sorry man, but no. There's no way."

"You tell me." Jaxon ran his hand through his hair with a shaky laugh. "A bird hit the window right when we found the letters."

"That letter was written in the *nineties*, dude. It's coincidence," Forester pointed out, sure Jax had officially lost it.

"What if it isn't?" Jaxon looked so earnest, and Forester was pretty sure why. Jaxon had been the one who'd saved Kaitlyn Neilson based on a dream—no, a premonition. At the time, Jaxon confided in him about it but then clammed up and never wanted to talk about it again. Forester always wondered if Jaxon had had other predictions, saw bad things before they happened.

Deep down, he wished Jaxon would have had one about his dad. Maybe he could have saved him.

"Liv, Winnie, and I are driving to New York City tomorrow to try and talk to one of the psychics' families. See if we can get answers. Want to come?"

"No." He handed the phone back. "I'm done with wacked-out letters from psychics, and I refuse to believe in bird omens. I've got a shitload I'm dealing with. So you go have fun with Liv Hall and leave me out of it."

Jaxon looked disappointed, but right now Forester really didn't care. He didn't believe in psychic ability or sixth sense. He didn't believe in anything.

Jaxon stared off into space with a troubled look. Then he said, "Listen. I'm afraid it's more complicated than that. I've never told anyone this." He sounded grave and leaned forward.

Forester leaned forward too and waited as Jaxon struggled to say whatever it was.

Jaxon dropped his voice to barely a whisper. "My mom . . . my real mom . . . was psychic. My dad told me after I saved Kaitlyn. And I think your dad knew about her ability too."

"What do you mean?"

"I think she was the Oracle of Delphi."

It took a minute for Forester to grasp what he was telling him. "The letters in the attic? You're saying she wrote those letters?"

Jaxon nodded. "I think it's why I was drawn to Liv and ended up at her house. It's like I was meant to find them." He expelled a breath. "After I saved Kaitlyn, my dad told me my mom was killed because of her gift and I could never use mine again. What if it's because of the letters? He said your dad investigated her death for years and came up empty-handed."

Forester sat there stunned. His mind went into overdrive.

Suddenly his dad's weirdness about his hanging out with Liv was starting to make sense. His dad had investigated Jaxon's mom's death for years. What if the address on the boxes being linked to his father's shooting wasn't a coincidence? What if Forester's initial gut reaction had been right?

"That must be why my dad's so uptight about me going over there. He knows about the letters." Forester deliberated. "There's something I need to tell you too." He found he was whispering as well. "The return address on the boxes is the same town where my dad was shot."

"What?" Jaxon covered his mouth with his hand. "Why didn't you say something?"

"Why didn't you?"

The two stared at each other. They'd both been keeping secrets from each other.

Jaxon rubbed his face with his hands, looking overwhelmed. "Jesus. Should we go talk to him?"

Forester shook his head. "He wouldn't even answer my questions tonight."

"So what do we do? We need to find out."

Forester saw the raw pain in his friend's eyes and realized there was a lot Jaxon hadn't told him. Maybe they hadn't been the best of friends to each other. "Come over tomorrow afternoon after you're back in town. I know where he keeps his old case files, and he'll be at work. We'll see what we can find."

17

NEBONY

psychic:
phenomena that are inexplicable by natural law

NEBONY OPENED HER EYES AND BLINKED several times until the room slowly came into focus. She was lying on a concrete floor with Matty beside her. Pain lanced through her skull like metal spikes. Her head was pounding.

All the memories came flooding back, and a sob rose up in her throat. They'd been attacked by somebody outside Matty's house. Kidnapped. Shock hit her next, and she started shivering so violently her teeth chattered.

"Matty?" she whispered, frantic. "Matty!" She reached for him, wild with fear, as she took in their surroundings. They were in a box cell. One entire wall was made of mirrors. An open toilet sat in the corner near an oversized cot. Two overhead cameras in the top corners of the room pointed down at them. A red light glowed, as if they were recording.

"Matty, wake up! Wake up now!" She shook him again and again, hysteria overcoming her. Matty finally came to with a moan and sat up with a dazed expression. It took him a minute to catch up to Nebony's state of terror.

"What happened?" He looked around in panic.

"I don't know!"

"Where are we?"

"I don't know! Prison?"

"*Hello.*"

A deep warped voice came from a speaker somewhere. Nebony and Matty screamed and grabbed onto each other. A man's voice, heavily manipulated, said, "Answer my questions and you will not be harmed. Tell me where the letters are."

Nebony's brain felt scrambled. She couldn't make sense of his words. "What letters? What's happening?" Uncontrollable sobs rose up and racked her body.

"The Premonitions Bureau letters you photographed." The voice went on to quote her post. "Found old letters from the Premonitions Bureau. We know the future and you don't. Ha."

Matty started saying "Oh my God. Oh my God. Oh my God," over and over while Nebony was speechless.

They were here because of Liv's letters?

Matty threw his arms around her and put his mouth to her ear. He whispered in a frantic voice, "We found a letter last night. A warning for us not to tell anyone about the letters or we'll die. This must be the omen!"

"What are you talking about?" Her voice was rising. "What omen?"

"Shhhhh!" he hissed hysterically, covering her mouth with his hand. "There was a bird omen! When the raven hits the glass! Someone named Mad Merlin predicted this. Remember the raven?"

Nebony could only stare at him blankly.

Matty had lost his mind.

He jumped up and ran to the mirror, only able to see his own reflection. "I want my lawyer. I want to make a phone call. I know my rights! This is highly illegal!"

The voice said through the speaker, "You have no rights here. I suggest you cooperate. Where are the letters? Where did you take those Polaroid pictures?"

Nebony came to the mirror too, ready to take charge. The man had to be on the other side of it watching them. "A girl's house. Her name is Liv Hall."

"Nebony!" Matty yanked her arm to get her to stop. "What are you doing?"

"Getting us out of here!" She turned to the glass. "She's a new girl at school, from New York City. She lives on Garden Street. I don't know the address. I was just there because—" She stopped, not about to mention Forester to this wacko. "The letters are in her attic. I swear." The voice didn't say anything. Nebony knocked on the mirror. "See? We're cooperating. Sir? Hello?" Her reflection stared back, her black mascara streaked down her face. "Please let us go. Please!"

Matty broke down into a weepy mess. "Psycho killers don't let their victims go, Nebony! Don't you watch TV?" He started crying hard, his nose running.

"How many letters are there?" the man asked.

"Thousands!"

"Nebony, shut up! He's just going to kill us." Matty put his head in his hands, hyperventilating. "We're gonna die. We're gonna die."

"Withhold information, little boy, and you *will* die," the voice threatened.

Matty staggered back and pressed himself against the far wall.

"Tell me about the letters. How did you find them?" A moment passed. "*Speak!*"

Matty whimpered. "I came over to help Liv go through the attic. They're all in boxes addressed to Grayson Spencer. I don't know who he is. I swear. The labels were old, and the boxes had been there forever. It said 'do not open' all over them."

The voice taunted, "But you did open them. I've seen the pictures. Who is Mad Merlin?"

"One of the psychics who wrote a bunch of letters that all came true."

"What did his letter say? The omen?"

Matty shook his head frantically, looking even more terrified. "I can't talk about it."

"Are you willing to die today?"

Matty broke down sobbing. "Please."

Nebony wrapped her arms around Matty and screamed to the voice, "Why are you doing this? We're telling you everything we know! He's just scared!"

"Who else saw the letters?" the voice demanded next.

Matty stared at Nebony, stark fear blazing in their eyes. "Only Liv!" Matty sat up straighter. "We were at her house, and it was just the three of us," he lied. "I swear. No one else."

Nebony nodded emphatically. "All the boxes are in her attic. We were just helping her organize."

"Like Marie Kondo or *Dream Home Makeover* or *Hot Mess House*," Matty babbled through his tears, trying to sound helpful. "We're an organizing team."

A long moment passed. A red laser from one of the cameras scanned the room—and them. Matty and Nebony held on to each other for dear life. Then the voice spoke. "Your elevated blinking, speech pattern, and increased heart rate all indicate you're lying. I'm going to give you time to think on how much you value your lives and then I will ask you again. Because I'm one push of a button away from killing you with lethal gas. We'll talk when you wake up—if you wake up—and are ready to cooperate."

The speaker clicked off. They both jumped up and ran to bang on the mirror, begging him to come back.

But there was no answer. He was gone.

Nebony was holding Matty's hand in a death grip, waiting for the gas. "Do you smell it?"

Matty shook his head. Tears streaked down his face. "Why does he think we know anything?"

"Because I posted about it." Pure terror was choking her, thick and viscous, rising up from her chest and blocking her ability to breathe. They were trapped here by a madman because of her Instagram post. She'd unintentionally attracted a psycho from the Internet, and now they were going to die. "I didn't know." She sank to her knees, full-on wailing with her hands on the ground. "I'm sorry. I'm so sorry, Matty. I didn't know." Her shoulders shook as she sobbed.

Matty knelt too and gathered her in her arms, trying to comfort her as they cried together. "It's not your fault. We didn't know. No one knew." Then he hesitated with a hiccup, wiping the snot from his face. "Except Winnie. She tried to warn me something bad would happen, but I wouldn't listen."

"I don't want to die," Nebony said it again like a mantra.

They hugged each other fiercely. Suddenly she heard a hissing sound coming from above.

Nebony looked at Matty in a panic. "Do you hear that?"

They both jumped up and searched the ceiling, seeing two glass valves spewing something into the cell and turning the air noxious.

"It's the gas!" Matty sniffed.

"Don't breathe it!" she screamed, but Matty was already losing consciousness. He slid down to the floor like a rag doll. Nebony held her breath, desperately fighting the urge to breathe, until her lungs burned for air and she had to.

Immediately, her body felt weightless, and she slid down to the floor beside him. Her plea, "Help me," was only a faint whisper no one else could hear.

18

LIV

fate:
the development of events beyond a person's control

THE LAW FIRM HANDLING HER GRANDFATHER'S will was fancy, much fancier than Liv would have imagined. Their offices were on the hundredth floor of the One World Trade Center. The elevator whisked Liv and her mother up like a spaceship, and the doors opened to the lobby. An enormous reception desk spanned the entire back wall, looking more like the lobby of a five-star hotel.

The receptionist escorted Liv and her mother to the conference room, where they sat quietly and waited, staring at lower Manhattan through a wall of windows. They were high up in the sky, an arm's reach from the clouds. The view of the skyscrapers below was magnificent, and it made Liv think back to her dream last night.

This time she could have sworn she was awake, flying in the sky. She'd dreamed of her father again—her real father. In the dream he was in Alaska, out on a boat on a river. Only this time she was with him.

For the first time, he could see her. Even stranger, they were laughing together. Salmon swam in the water, some jumping in the air. The landscape was alive with colorful flowers blooming by the thousands.

She could even hear bird songs.

The sound was so vivid it woke her up.

She went to write the dream down in her journal but then decided not to bother. What was the point? If dreams were messages, she had no idea what that one was.

She absently ran her stone pendant back and forth on its chain, comforted by its familiar weight.

Her mom interrupted her thoughts by saying quietly, "Your dad emailed me again to see how you're doing. He really wants to talk to you."

"You mean Bodhi—he's not my dad." Liv corrected her more sharply than she intended, knowing her anger wasn't fair since she'd called Bodhi "Dad" for years. She puffed out a sigh. "I don't want to talk to him right now." Maybe she never would, though she didn't say it out loud. Her mom was enough of an emotional wreck without needing to worry about her.

"I know. I said you weren't ready." Her mom shrugged helplessly, looking lost, and it broke Liv's heart. Bodhi was not her mom's first failed marriage and history was repeating itself for her in the worst possible way.

Liv's real father had left her mom too, right after Liv was born. Her mom had told her the story, how she'd met her dad when she was in college. He'd been a computer programming major, and she had come to the computer lab, looking for someone to help her design a web page. Her mom was a journalism major, but her real passion was astrology. She did a compatibility "couples chart" with Liv's dad and found all their signs, houses, and planets were perfectly aligned. Astrologically speaking, they were meant to be. After graduation they got married, got pregnant, and then when Liv was born the dream shattered. Her father bailed on them, saying he wasn't cut out to be a husband or a father. He announced he was going to move to Alaska to go "find himself," whatever that meant.

After the abandonment, Liv's mom's belief in astrology crashed and burned too, like a comet falling to Earth. How could she have been so wrong? About him. About them. Astrology charts were supposed to be like cosmic fingerprints of someone's life, and she had completely misread theirs. Instead of being a dreamy-eyed astrologer married to her soulmate, she became a single mom, firmly grounded in reality, and tried to put her degree in journalism to good use. She never looked back on that time of her life. It was Liv who often wondered about the past and her real father with dreams of him up in Alaska, lost in the vast wilderness, with the aurora borealis twisting in the sky above him. Wherever he was, he'd missed out on her whole life. Father's Day was when she thought about him the most.

The man hadn't even shown up to his father's funeral. Grayson was Clement's only child, and he couldn't even rejoin civilization to pay his respects. At the time, Liv wondered if he might come. She hadn't wanted to ask her mom and risk her having a bigger breakdown. Her mom had been like a daughter to Clement, and Clement had never forgiven his son for abandoning them.

Liv stewed in silence, trying to control the churning emotions inside of her.

"Stop kicking your foot under the table, sweetie," her mother said, and Liv realized she was tapping her foot in a nervous staccato rhythm.

"Sorry." She offered her mom a small smile. Her mother took her hand and gave it a reassuring squeeze. This morning, her mom had curled her hair and put on makeup. It was the best she'd looked since the divorce. "You look really pretty today, Mom," Liv told her right before the door opened and the estate attorney, Mr. Steiner, joined them. He was an older gentleman, polished in a three-piece suit, and looked to be about Liv's grandfather's age.

"Thank you for making the drive down," he said, sitting across from them at the conference table with a file in his hands. He had a slight accent, German if Liv had to guess. His assistant, a young man, asked if they would like a coffee, and they both said yes. Liv noticed her mom seemed nervous and kept glancing at the door, like she was waiting for someone to join them.

Mr. Steiner said, "Mrs. Hall—"

"Please, call me Hazel," she insisted.

"Hazel, I've received copies of your divorce papers with Bodhi Hall. They were signed before Clement's death, so fortunately there will be no conflict of interest in how the estate is to be distributed if Mr. Hall were to make a claim."

Her mom looked confused. "I doubt my ex-husband would try to get anything of Clement's."

The attorney gave her a kind smile. "Mr. Hall might have if he knew how much your previous father-in-law's estate is worth." He kept saying the word *estate* like it meant something. Liv shot a look to her mom, but the attorney didn't give them time to ask any questions. "I've been Clement's attorney for many years. His wishes were straightforward. He left the house, his accounts, investment funds, and the other property to you."

"What other property?" her mom asked, confused.

"Clement owned a second house in Alaska on the Kenai Peninsula," the attorney said, and Liv watched her mother shrink before her eyes.

Alaska?

Liv was suddenly swimming in confusion. Her grandfather had a house in Alaska? That didn't seem possible. Alaska was where her father ran off to after she was born. Liv's mind whirled with questions, beginning with the most obvious one: Had her grandfather been seeing her father all these years and not told them?

Liv refused to believe it. She hadn't heard from her father her whole life, and she was sure it'd been the same for her grandfather.

Her mom looked shaken and asked, her voice barely a whisper, "What about Grayson? He isn't going to be here today to read the will?" A twinge of hope crept into her voice.

"Clement's son is not in the will. He is not a beneficiary and will not be coming today," was all the attorney said.

"I see." Her mother nodded, trying to keep her composure, but her expression fell, and her eyes welled with tears. And then it hit Liv. Her mom had been expecting to see her father today. Sixteen years later and she was still carrying a torch for the guy. That's why she'd gotten so dressed up. The designer black dress, the makeup, the hair. It had all been for *him*.

The well of anger inside Liv began to simmer into a hot rage. She was so angry with her father she could barely think straight. She wished he *had* come so she could tell him exactly what she thought of him. Angry tears welled in her eyes, and she blinked them back.

The assistant came with their coffees at the perfect time and her mom gratefully took hers, the quiver in her hands noticeable. The attorney seemed to understand she needed a minute to compose herself. Liv poured a sugar pack into her own, wondering when she'd get the chance to ask the attorney about the Bureau letters. She didn't want to make a big deal of it in front of her mom. But ever since they'd found the warning from Mad Merlin last night, it was all she could think about.

Liv checked her phone. Jaxon and Winnie were supposed to meet her downstairs in a half hour.

Her mother asked, "How long has he had the house in Alaska?"

The attorney referenced his file. "The property was bought sixteen years ago."

The year her father left. The year she was born. Liv closed her eyes with a silent groan, knowing her mom was going to take this hard.

The lawyer continued, "I have all the details in the paperwork I'll send home with you. It's right on the Kenai River outside the town of Soldotna." He sounded like a vacation home salesman. Her mom was nodding but Liv could tell she had completely checked out, in too much shock. "The property, though, is the least of his holdings. His investment accounts have a worth of twenty million."

"Twenty million dollars?" Her mom gaped at him.

"I just need your signatures." He slid the paperwork toward her.

Her mom looked like she was going to fall out of the chair. Liv was barely holding on to her coffee cup at this point. How had her grandfather accrued twenty million dollars and two houses? All without telling them. He was a retired psychiatrist who bought produce on sale and drove a Hyundai.

Her mom stood up, looking shaky. "I'm sorry. This is . . . I need to use the restroom." Liv could tell her mom was going to go cry. The whole meeting felt like a betrayal. Why hadn't her grandfather shared any of this himself? Why had he waited to die to have some stranger tell them his secrets?

"Of course." Mr. Steiner nodded and watched her walk out of the conference room.

The moment the doors closed, the lawyer's whole demeanor changed. He leaned forward, an urgency now in his voice.

"Liv, I'm afraid there's not much time. I need to know—and please answer truthfully because it will determine how we move forward—your mother mentioned on the phone you were going through your grandfather's things. I asked her to wait for us. Were you up in the attic?" He suddenly looked grave.

Liv was taken aback and stammered, "Yes, sir. I wanted to ask you about it. I found boxes of letters . . ." She trailed off because he was silently shaking his head.

"Are you telling me," he lowered his voice, "you found the Bureau letters?"

"Yes," she admitted, her throat constricting.

"Please tell me you did not read them."

"I'm sorry," she said, suddenly feeling like she was in the middle of an interrogation.

Mr. Steiner said something in another language. Liv thought it was probably a swear word. "We were contracted to take those boxes away immediately after Clement's passing. Why do you think we were coming to the house?"

"I'm sorry. I didn't know." Liv fought to keep from crying.

"You do not understand the danger this puts you in. Or the efforts that have been made to protect you. Your grandparents went to great lengths to keep your family's life private. Why do you think you can't keep a cell phone since moving into that house?"

Liv startled at that. Was he saying her grandfather stole her phone?

Before she could ask, he quickly got on the phone with someone and said, "We need to push up our schedule with Clement Spencer's estate. Immediately. Yes, I need someone there today." He hung up and opened his desk drawer and pulled out a manila envelope. "There's no time to explain. This key is to an apartment near Central Park. Here's the address. There is a letter waiting for you." He handed her the key and a slip of paper. "He hoped you would never have to go there. He instructed me that if you did, you were not to tell your mother about any of this for her own safety." His eyes darted to the door. Her mother would be back any second. He rushed on. "Go there today. Convince your mother to stay in town overnight. We'll need today to clear out the attic. Put the key in your purse. Now."

Liv's whole body was shaking in shock. She slipped the key and paper into her purse right as her mother came back.

Her mom's eyes were red, half of her eye makeup gone. She murmured, "So sorry."

"Not at all," Mr. Steiner said with a gentle smile, as if the last few minutes with Liv never happened.

Liv sat immobile, not knowing what to do. Her mother signed the paperwork with a shaking hand and gave the pen to Liv. Liv signed too, her vision a blur, and she gave the pen back. Mr. Steiner, with his eyes on Liv, said to call him if they had any questions. Liv and her mom left, both in a daze.

When they got into the elevator, her mom turned to look at her. Shock was all over her face. "I can't believe this."

Liv's heart was racing. Why had the attorney stressed that her mother couldn't know about the letters? And what did the letter her grandfather left for her have to say? What secrets had he been keeping from them? People did *not* inherit twenty million dollars and a house in Alaska without some kind of warning.

Liv asked her mom, "Are you going to be okay to drive?"

"No." Her mom tried to smile but failed.

The attorney had said she needed to convince her mom to stay in town. "Why don't you go check into a hotel and order room service? Spend the night." She tried to joke, "We can afford it now."

Her mom gave her a weak smile but seemed to be seriously considering the suggestion. She tucked a stray piece of hair behind Liv's ear. "We could turn it into a long weekend, and you could play hooky from school."

For a moment Liv wanted to tell her mother about the letters, the warning from Mad Merlin, and the key in her purse to an apartment she'd never been to before. But she couldn't. Not yet. First she had to read her grandfather's letter and find out what he'd been hiding from them. There had to be a reason he hadn't wanted her mother to know. Liv shook her head. "My friends are picking me up, remember? We're going to hang out and drive back. But why don't you stay?" They made it outside. "I'll sleep over at Winnie's."

Liv promised to call her from Winnie's when they made it back tonight, and her mom agreed to the plan, giving her a fierce hug. "We'll figure this out," her mom promised, as if inherently knowing there was a big mystery to solve. She just didn't realize how big.

<ENCRYPTED TRANSMISSION>
<DEFENSE INTELLIGENCE AGENCY SERVER>

<From: MIRIAM>
<Priority: HIGH>

No Halls or Spencers registered in Hyde Park or Halls living on Garden Street.

Liv Hall enrolled at Roosevelt High School in March.

Transferred from Brooklyn Technical High School.

All her school records have been erased. Someone is going to a lot of trouble to hide.

Scan databases for any reference to Mad Merlin that can be connected to Hyde Park.

Scan databases for any reference to the name Winnie.

19

chance:
the probability of something happening

WINNIE WAS GOING TO KILL MATTY the next time she saw him. Now he wasn't even answering her texts. He and Nebony had probably stayed up all night watching TV at his place and overslept. She sent him several more messages.

Where r u?

Call me

R U ignoring me now?

What's up?

Finally, she gave up and sent him one last snarky text.

Give me an L. Give me an A. Give me an M. Give me an E.

What's that spell?

She shoved her phone away, highly annoyed. She'd hoped Matty might change his mind after he cooled off and decide to come with them today. Jaxon didn't seem surprised it was just the two of them.

They were both quiet while he drove, each lost in thought. She'd never hung out with Jaxon before. Over the years they'd been in a few of the same classes but never said two words to each other. The past three days together had been a surprise in a good way. Jaxon had a comforting vibe about him. A quiet solitude. She didn't feel self-conscious around him either.

She studied him while he drove. Jaxon's aura was pretty amazing actually, a fascinating indigo, more purple but with blue threaded throughout and a hint of pink. Purple guys were *the best* in her opinion. And from the swirls of blue she could sense he was intuitive. A deep thinker. And the pink . . . well he was a softy. Jaxon Coleson. Who knew?

"You stare at people a lot." Jaxon glanced over at her. "You know that, right?" He shot her a little smile. "It can be disconcerting. Your eyes go all out of focus and kind of cross-eyed."

Winnie laughed before she could catch herself. Jaxon ended up laughing with her, and she found herself admitting, "I see people's auras. That's when I go kind of cross-eyed." She grimaced.

Jaxon looked over to her in surprise. "For real?"

"Yeah, for real." She tried to explain. "People can unconsciously sense auras—like getting someone's vibe—but I can see them if I try hard enough. It's like bird watching but with people," she tried to joke.

"So you've been able to your whole life?"

Winnie hesitated. The confession bubbled out of her on its own free will. "The first time I really saw one was in third grade. My best friend Stephanie was surrounded by this beautiful orange and yellow glow. Like sunlight. Once I saw it, I couldn't stop. I told her and she told her mom and her mom told my mom. She took me to the eye doctor, the pediatrician, a neurologist. They couldn't find anything wrong with me. Everyone was so concerned with *what was wrong* with me. My mom was flipping out, so I stopped talking about it. Stephanie didn't want to play together after that. She thought it was contagious." Winnie gave a rueful smile, still remembering the hurt.

"Do all auras glow like sunlight?" he asked.

"No." Winnie shook her head. "Everyone's is different."

"How so?" Jaxon seemed genuinely interested. It made her feel more comfortable sharing.

"Generally a person is one or two colors. Swirls and hues can change depending on their mood. It can grow brighter or duller. You can tell when someone's sick too. There's a shade . . ." She trailed off, then said, "Remember Mrs. Jenson?"

"The librarian?"

"She started having dark spots and holes in her aura the year she passed away." Mrs. Jenson had been a sweet lady. Winnie had started noticing the change about six months before she died of cancer.

"That's incredible."

Winnie tried to gauge his reaction. "You don't think I'm making it up?" Matty barely believed her, and he was her best friend.

"Why would I?"

"Because most people can't see what I see."

"Some people can do things that can't be explained yet. Doesn't mean it's not real." Jaxon shrugged, staring straight ahead. "Maybe one day it won't be considered so out there. Look at science. Amazing break-throughs happen every day. It makes you realize how much we don't know."

Jaxon was deep, way deeper than she'd thought, and Winnie found herself wanting to confide about her dad. No one knew who her dad was—or had been. Only Matty and Liv. She never wanted to see any-one's pity or fascination. A famous father who died in a plane crash was like a double whammy.

She'd been planning to tell Liv first what she discovered about Mad Merlin, but Jaxon was surprisingly easy to talk to and they had time to kill.

"My dad was a writer, a novelist. He died in a plane crash a long time ago when I was a baby." She could feel Jaxon's confusion, won-dering why she was telling him this out of the blue. "His last published book has a teaser in the back. Like a trailer for his next novel." She took a deep breath and dropped the bombshell. "It was going to be about a psychic named Mad Merlin."

"You're kidding."

"No. Dead serious."

Jaxon looked over to her in shock for a moment too long, forgetting he was driving.

Winnie gripped the dash. "Watch the road!"

Jaxon swerved back into his lane as a car passed them with a blaring honk. "Sorry. You're telling me he wrote a book about Mad Merlin?"

"It looks that way, but he died before it could be published. I only found this out last night." She rushed on. "I know it's unbelievable. I think the manuscript's on his computer. I just need to figure out his password so I can read it."

"How could your dad have known about Mad Merlin?"

"I have no idea." Winnie stared out the window. She'd ended up pulling Tarot cards late into the night asking the same question. The King of Swords, her dad's card, had been next to the King of Wands in several spreads.

Repeatedly.

It was as if her father's spirit was trying to tell her something.

All her life, she'd felt like her dad was watching over her. She'd even read a book about receiving signs from loved ones on the other side. They could come through a song on the radio, or a presence in the room, or by smelling the person's scent. There were also *Ghostbusters*-like appearances, ranging from flickering lights to apparitions. Or seeing symbols that had meaning.

Last night, the more she stared at the two kings, the more her intuition kept telling her Mad Merlin knew her dad and her dad had written about him, turning nonfiction into fiction—but didn't writers do that all the time?

The Gnosis Trap.

The word *gnosis* meant knowledge about spiritual mysteries. And *trap* didn't sound good. What happened in the story? Tonight when she got home, she'd work some more on cracking the password. Her mom swore she didn't know it, but maybe she just needed help remembering.

She and Jaxon didn't say much the rest of the drive. Finally, they made it to Manhattan, lining up in traffic on the FDR and inching their way to the Financial District.

"There she is," Winnie said, spotting Liv outside One Word Trade Center with her mom. They were both wearing black today, Liv in a simple shift dress, and Hazel more dressed up. Liv's mom looked really beautiful, like she used to. Winnie rolled down her window and waved, but as they got closer, she could tell Liv's mom had been crying. Winnie gave a bright smile, pretending she didn't notice. "Hi, Mrs. Hall!"

"Hi, Winnie!" Liv's mom called out. Liv gave her mom a hug good-bye and jumped into the backseat, rolling the window down.

Her mom reminded her, "Call me tonight and drive safe." Hazel wiped her eyes and called out, "Nice meeting you!" to Jaxon. Cars were honking, waiting for them to move on. Jaxon cast a worried look to Liv in the rearview mirror and pulled out into traffic.

"Thanks for getting me," Liv said, her voice thick with emotion.

Winnie twisted around to look at her. "How was the meeting? You okay?"

"No." Liv's eyes started watering up. "Guys, I think we're in trouble."

"What do you mean?" Jaxon looked ready to pull the car over as he glanced back at her in the rearview mirror. "What happened?"

Liv started talking in a rush. "When my mom left the room, the lawyer got all serious and started asking me about the letters. He said we weren't supposed to find them. Someone's going to the house today to take them away."

Winnie and Jaxon both erupted in alarm, talking over each other. "They're taking the letters?" "Why?"

"I don't know. He gave me a key to some apartment and then my mom came back in the room and he pretended like we never talked." She put her face in her hands and started to cry.

"Liv, we're going to get through this." Jaxon tried to calm her down. "What's the address to the apartment? We'll go there and read the letter and see what it says."

Liv looked up at him in confusion. "What?" she asked, her voice barely a whisper.

"We'll go to the apartment and read the letter."

Winnie looked back and forth between them in confusion. Liv now seemed afraid.

"How do you know that?" Liv demanded. "I never mentioned the letter to you."

Winnie was just as confused too.

Jaxon hesitated and then said, "I saw it happen."

"Saw what happen?"

"The three of us. At the apartment. There's a letter there you're going to read."

Liv was shaking her head at him. "How do you know that?"

Winnie added, "Yeah, and what do you mean *you saw it happen?*"

Jaxon expelled a deep breath and confessed to them, "It's called a premonition, and I get them all the time."

20

JAXON

clairvoyant:
clear sight

JAXON KNEW AT SOME POINT HE would share his secret with Liv, but he hadn't foreseen he'd be telling Winnie at the same time. He tried to explain to them as best he could. "I have visions of the future. They're like future memories in a way, because whatever I see in my mind happens. So it's like a double memory—or watching a movie twice" was the simplest way to explain.

"So you really did save Kaitlyn," Winnie said, sounding floored.

"That's why you were so weirded out about the Premonitions Bureau." Liv met his gaze in the rearview window.

He nodded, averting his eyes. He wanted to tell Liv he'd inherited his gift. He wanted to tell her his mother had written some of the letters but wasn't sure how. *Oh by the way, my mom's the Oracle of Delphi* wasn't something he could just drop on them. They might even think he was delusional and needed help. Plus, what if it was dangerous if they knew? He needed to find out what he could about Forester's dad's investigation.

"You're like a closet psychic." Winnie shook her head in disbelief. "I'm the one who's labeled the freak at school, and you're the one who can really see the future."

"Well I don't stare at people for five minutes at a time," he shot back, and Winnie rolled her eyes at him.

He glanced back again at Liv in the rearview mirror. She seemed stunned, her mouth parted in shock. Whether it was from what he'd said or what the lawyer had told her in his office he couldn't tell.

They headed to the apartment, deciding it was more important to read the letter than try to find Jerald Peterson's family. As they drove, Winnie filled Liv in on her father's never-published book and the connection to Mad Merlin.

"Your dad knew Mad Merlin?" Liv asked her, wide-eyed.

"I don't know. I need to figure out how to access his computer when we get back." After that, Winnie started peppering him with questions.

How long had he had his ability? Did his parents know? What else had he predicted?

He tried to answer as best he could. He knew he sounded vague but couldn't help it. He'd never tried to explain his gift to anyone. The premonitions had started when he was a child. Instead of the fuzzy dream fragments people usually had, his dreams were fully formed memories. Then those memories would actually happen. As he got older, they grew stronger, like extreme déjà vu.

Liv stayed quiet while they talked. He was relieved when they arrived at their destination so Winnie's interrogation could end. The apartment Liv was supposed to go to was right by Central Park, where the buildings were worth a fortune. They parked and walked past the Guggenheim Museum and a row of stately buildings until they finally found the address of an elegant condominium.

A doorman in uniform stood like a sentry at the door. Jaxon could feel Liv's stress skyrocket. She stopped walking and turned to them, dropping her voice. "Guys, what if they won't let us in?"

"Liv, relax. You have a key," Winnie insisted. "Tell them to call your creepy lawyer if they give you a hard time. He said to come here."

Liv still looked nervous, and Jaxon tried to reassure her. "It'll be okay. I already saw us inside."

She frowned at that but nodded and led the way. The doorman opened the door without question.

Inside, an indoor fountain ran down the back wall like a waterfall. Koi fish swam in the pond beneath it, and a dramatic metal sculpture of orchids sat on a raised platform in the center of the lobby.

An elderly man in a posh suit was behind the reception desk and looked up when they approached. "Welcome, Ms. Hall. I was notified you'd be arriving today. The kitchen is fully stocked, and the house-keeper has prepared the bedrooms. Please let me know if you and your guests need anything else."

Jaxon could feel Liv silently flipping out. Winnie too. He fought the urge to look over at them. The man came out from behind the desk, walked over to the elevator, and inserted a key. The elevator doors whisked open. As they got in, the man instructed Liv, "When you arrive at the twelfth floor, only your key will open the elevator doors. It's the only way to access that floor." Liv nodded and then the doors closed, leaving them alone in the elevator. Liv crossed her arms nervously over her stomach.

They were all aware of the security camera above their heads. Cheesy elevator music began to play over the speakers. The moment had become beyond surreal.

As the music played on, Winnie's shoulders shook with silent laughter. "Is that Guns N' Roses?" she whispered. Her laughter was contagious. Muzak had made an elevator version of "Knockin' on Heaven's Door."

"This is so beyond," Liv said under her breath. Then they were all three laughing the entire way up to the twelfth floor.

The elevator arrived with a ding and their laughter died. Liv inserted her key to open the doors, and they stepped out into the hallway to find only one door.

There was only one apartment for the entire twelfth floor, suite 1200. Liv looked afraid to unlock it.

"I think it's safe to go in," Jaxon said, trying to sound confident. He'd seen them already inside reading the letter. In his vision there hadn't been anyone jumping out at them.

She gave him a searching look. Winnie elbowed her. "Just do it."

"Okay, okay," she whispered and inserted the key. The door swung open to reveal a long, shadowed entry hall with a black marble floor.

Jaxon flipped on the light and tentatively moved forward. "Hello? Anybody home?"

The hallway opened up to an enormous living room with a grand view of Central Park. A kitchen and dining room were tucked behind the living room along with two bedrooms on each side. The place was huge.

Winnie came forward to the windows. "Liv, who lives here?"

She shook her head. "I don't know."

Jaxon walked around the living room. Every detail was impeccable but impersonal, like a hotel. "It doesn't look lived in at all."

Winnie headed to the kitchen. "Wow, when he said the kitchen was stocked he wasn't kidding. Can we eat this stuff?"

Jaxon and Liv joined Winnie in the kitchen. A carafe of fresh orange juice had been set out along with a warmed teapot and a catering tray with finger sandwiches, scones, mini quiches, and fresh fruit.

"Is this all for us?" Jaxon wondered.

"I guess." Liv looked dazed and headed back out to the living room.

Jaxon followed her and the déjà vu hit hard. A Picasso print hung on the wall over the couch. The image was exactly the same as his vision.

His eyes landed on the table where a large envelope sat.

Liv's name was written across it in a bold script.

Jaxon recognized the handwriting. The same person had written on all the boxes.

From the envelope, Liv took out a folded letter along with two rolls of cash. The money was bound into tight bundles, all hundred-dollar bills. Startled, she dropped it on the table as if it had burned her.

Jaxon stared at it with raised eyebrows. That was a lot of cash.

Winnie came from the kitchen holding a cup of tea and a blueberry scone. She stopped. "Why are there two rolls of cash on the table like it's a Scorsese movie?" Liv didn't answer and opened the letter. Winnie tentatively sat down beside her.

Jaxon stared at the Picasso print hanging over their heads. The painting was the image of two girls reading a letter.

Just like Liv and Winnie were doing now.

Was the painting a coincidence? Or a message? Had someone purposefully picked the print out, knowing one day reality would mimic art?

Jaxon tried hard to shake off the powerful déjà vu still gripping him. As Liv and Winnie read the letter, he watched the color drain from Liv's face. Then she looked up at him, handing him the letter so he could read it too, and said, "This isn't from my grandfather. It's from my father."

Dear Liv,

I've tried to keep you from all of this, but if you're reading this letter then I no longer can. Whatever you do, do not go home. Wait for me at the apartment. I am on my way. Your mother is safe as long as she doesn't know about the letters. Steiner's office will take care of everything. Right now, go walk into Central Park and throw away your phones. This is a necessary precaution. Cell phones can be used to trace your location. So can any debit or credit card. Use only cash and ask the concierge downstairs for a temporary cell phone. They loan them out to guests who are traveling. When you go outside, do not look up. Do not look at streetlights. Do not look at people you pass. Wear a hat and sunglasses to avoid facial recognition. There is an assortment in the hall closet to choose from.

Whatever you do, do not get back in the car you drove in today. Leave it where it's parked. In case of an emergency and you need a car, there is one in the parking garage in the designated space for this apartment. The key is under the floormat.

Contact Detective Drew Torres with the Hyde Park Police. Tell him he was not wrong about Shelly McNeil's death and Dr. Alberty's study never ended. If anything happens to me and I do not reach you, stay there until you hear from your grandmother. She will call you from Zurich when she can. She has been waiting to talk with you for a long time. Until the man hunting us is stopped, no one in our family is safe. I know this is a lot to take in and to put on your shoulders. If my plan goes as it should, there'll be no more secrets. I promise.

I'm sorry our lives could not have been different.

Your Father

21

LIV

sciomancy:
divination through shadows

LIV HAD TOO MANY QUESTIONS TO begin to sort them out. The letter was more than a riddle. It was a betrayal, from her father and her grandfather. And her grandmother, who was apparently alive and well in Switzerland.

What did her father mean, no one in her family was safe? What was Dr. Alberty's study? And who was Shelly McNeil?

Liv handed Jaxon the letter. Winnie had been reading it with her. "Liv, what's happening?" she whispered, and Liv shook her head, floundering as well.

After Jaxon finished reading, for the first time since she'd met him, he seemed emotionally distraught. He looked up from the letter, his expression bleak.

"Shelly McNeil was my mom. She died after I was born."

She and Winnie were both speechless.

He went on. "They ruled it a suicide, but Forester's dad tried to prove she was murdered."

Liv wanted to stand up and go to him. To hug him. But her body felt weighted down from the shock.

"I'm so sorry. That's so tragic, Jax," Winnie rushed to say and shook her head in confusion. "But what does her death have to do with the Premonitions Bureau letters?"

Jaxon hesitated. "Because she was the Oracle of Delphi."

For a moment Liv and Winnie could only stare at him.

"You're serious?" Winnie said.

"Yes," he whispered. His eyes were on Liv when he said softly, "I didn't know how to tell you."

Liv didn't know what to say. It was a lot to take in. First he'd dropped the bomb he was psychic and now his mother was the Oracle of Delphi? What other secrets was he hiding? Suddenly he felt like a total stranger she didn't know at all. She crossed her arms defensively. Finally, she understood why he kept showing up at her house to read the letters. Now she felt silly for assuming she was the reason he was there at all.

As if reading her mind, he shook his head. "I didn't know it was her at first. I just felt drawn to the letters. And to you."

Her eyes darted back up to his.

He went on. "I was as much in the dark as anyone. Then I started to suspect when I saw them."

"And Forester's dad investigated her death?" Winnie asked. "Who's Dr. Alberty?"

"I don't know. I swear." He searched Liv's eyes, as if willing her to believe him.

Liv only nodded and walked over to look out the window, needing a minute. She was still trying to process what she'd just read as well. The letter made no sense. When had her father written it? How could he afford this apartment? Who was he hiding from? And why did her grandfather have so much money hidden away? Then a horrible thought entered her mind. Had her family been involved in something illegal? And they were somehow responsible for Jaxon's mother's death? She gripped her stomach, suddenly feeling sick. At this point, anything seemed possible.

Jaxon said, "I'm supposed to meet up with Forester at his place later. Hopefully we can find some answers."

"So Forester knows? About your mom?" Liv asked, but then, of course he knew. He was Jaxon's best friend. She was just the girl he met this week. Jaxon didn't owe her his secrets. She didn't know why it made her feel so bereft.

"I told him last night, after I left your place," Jaxon said, looking uncomfortable, and Liv couldn't help but replay the failed kiss in her mind. The single most embarrassing moment of her life. She rubbed her forehead, trying to banish the memory.

Jaxon laid her father's letter back on the table. "I think we need to do what he says."

Liv crossed her arms. "Just sit here and wait for him to show up? No way."

"No. I meant about the phones. And the car." Jaxon held his phone out.

"What—throw away our phones?" Winnie asked, incredulous. "That letter is for Liv. She doesn't even have a phone. She keeps losing it."

"No, more like my grandfather kept stealing it." Liv shook her head, still in disbelief.

Jaxon sounded resigned. "Winnie, he said phones. Plural. And we're here with her."

Winnie stared at her new iPhone, her mouth opening and closing like a fish. "But into a garbage can in Central Park?"

"Exactly!" Liv began to pace. "He's deranged! My father abandoned me, then he gets to waltz in sixteen years later and give us ridiculous orders?" She picked the letter up and put it back down. "Don't look up? Wear a hat and sunglasses?"

"Liv, my mom *died*." Jaxon's words stopped her cold. "And your dad is saying it wasn't an accident. Which is what my dad told me after I saved Kaitlyn. He said I could never do what I did again or tell anyone about my gift, that it had killed my mom. He said *they* would come after me. I don't know who *they* are. But it sounds like your dad does and he's trying to protect us."

His eyes bored into hers and Liv expelled a breath. She had so many questions she wasn't ready to ask about his past and what he'd been hiding.

Winnie was already standing and gathering her things. "Fine. We ditch our phones and borrow the car, but we need to get back. I have to read my dad's manuscript."

"Agreed." Jaxon nodded. "We go to Winnie's, get the manuscript, and go to Forester's. We do this together." He looked pointedly to her.

Liv nodded, feeling flustered, and shoved the money in her purse, never having carried this much cash in her life.

They went to the hall closet by the door, and sure enough they found an assortment of Yankees baseball caps, beanies, bucket hats, sun visors, and a fedora. A bin sat next to them filled with sunglasses. Jaxon chose a Yankees cap and put on his aviators.

"It's a good look for you," Winnie said, picking out a beanie and John Lennon sunglasses. Liv stood there in mutiny with her arms crossed. Winnie put a white women's tennis hat on her and, with a pointed look, handed her a pair of heart-shaped pink sunglasses.

Liv threw them back in the bin and fished out a pair of Ray-Bans. "Okay, the makeover is done. Let's go."

She locked the front door and they left. Downstairs, Liv approached the front desk, feeling like she was doing something wrong as she asked the concierge if she could borrow a cell phone. The man handed her one from a drawer.

"It's fully charged and has an Internet connection. Here's a travel case and charger and the number is on the back."

"Thank you," she said, and hurried out before he could either change his mind or start asking questions. They all had their hats and sunglasses on as they walked across the street and entered Central Park. Liv kept her eyes trained on the road and down at her feet, the sounds of Manhattan competing with the hammering of her heart. She was terrified to look up. Who could be watching them? *Were they being watched?* Liv didn't want to turn paranoid, but having to put on disguises and lose their phones seemed excessive. Jaxon was being forced to leave his Jeep on the street. Who knew when he'd get it back? For some reason, her father had felt all of this was necessary.

They walked a good five minutes until they found a private spot with a trash can.

"I seriously can't believe I'm doing this," Winnie said as she fished her phone from her purse. She tried to joke, "Maybe those rolls of money are for new phones?"

Liv couldn't believe they were doing this either. "Yeah, my treat."

"We should clear the contents, do a factory reboot," Jaxon suggested, doing it to his.

Before Winnie could, her phone rang. She looked at who was calling. "It's Matty's mom," she said, answering it. "Hi, Mrs. Jacobs." She listened with a frown. "No, I haven't seen him, but I'm not at school today." Her eyes took on a worried look. "Sure, of course. I'll let him know." She hung up. "Matty's mom is freaking out. She can't reach him, and he isn't at school." Winnie checked her phone. "I left him a ton of texts this morning and he never replied."

Matty ignoring Winnie's texts wasn't like him. A sense of foreboding bloomed inside her. She, Jaxon, and Winnie hadn't been the only ones to find the letters. Matty, Forester, and Nebony had been there too.

Mad Merlin had warned them all.

Winnie went to try to call Matty again, but Jaxon stopped her. "I know you're worried about him, but right now we need to lose our phones. Let's get back and you can check on him. Okay?"

Winnie stared at Jaxon, clearly conflicted, but she nodded. "Let's go then," she said, her voice tight, and she tossed her phone in the trash. She headed toward the park exit at a brisk walk.

Jaxon tossed his phone away, too, and they quickened their pace to keep up with Winnie.

Liv crossed her arms protectively as she walked and wondered how Jaxon's mother had died, but she was afraid to ask.

"Liv, I did want to tell you the truth—"

She cut him off. "It's okay. You don't have to explain to me. We barely know each other."

His lips tightened in a frown, but he didn't say anything.

Still, she did feel the need to ask him, "Have you had a prediction about what's going to happen?"

Jaxon was busy scanning their surroundings with an intent look. He shook his head, sounding grim. "Not yet."

When they reached the apartment building, Jaxon approached the man behind the reception desk with a confidence Liv couldn't bring herself to muster.

He asked the man, "Excuse me, where is the parking garage?"

"Straight through those doors, sir."

Jaxon thanked him and led the way, as if they had every right to drive off in a car that wasn't theirs.

Her father said he was on his way to meet them at the apartment and to stay put. When he did arrive, they wouldn't be there. From his warning, they were taking a huge risk by leaving, but Liv didn't see any other choice. Plus, she didn't know if she wanted to see him, because she couldn't help but feel what was happening was all his fault.

22

MATTY

providence:
timely preparation for future eventualities

MATTY WOKE UP ON THE COLD, hard floor with a sharp chemical smell in his nose. All his memories returned in fragments. They'd been kidnapped. He'd been kidnapped. With Nebony. In front of his house. They'd been thrown in the back of a plumbing van. Never in his life had he thought he'd be thrown into a plumbing van and wake up in a prison cell with the school's head cheerleader.

Killed by an Instagram post.

If Nebony hadn't posted that picture of the letters with him in it, none of this would have happened. The cell, the gas, his looming death at the hands of the psycho with the microphone. His head was killing him. He was dying of thirst and hunger, ready to puke, and really needed to pee, but he didn't want to do it in an open toilet in front of cameras. He held his bladder and thought about how much he was not ready to die. He had so many plans and dreams, starting with college in New York City. The place where his life would start to get exciting. He was going to act and write and direct plays on his road to Broadway. He was going to fall in love, find an amazing boyfriend, and have an incredible life together.

Now, instead, he and Nebony were going to die in a prison cell like the thrown-off cast in a low-budget slasher movie no one ever saw. Mad Merlin had gotten it wrong. It was only the two of them who were going to die. The gay guy and the cheerleader. The two most clichéd characters in any horror film. Winnie had even sensed it. She hadn't been happy he was hanging out with Nebony. Maybe because deep down she knew it would literally lead to his demise. He'd scoffed at her warning because he was an idiot. His best friend was a freaking Tarot card master. Why hadn't he listened to her?

"I can't believe we're here." Nebony was sitting against the wall with her eyes closed.

He whispered, "I keep hoping I'll wake up and this is all a bad dream and we're having our sleepover."

Nebony took his hand, and they sat there for a while in silence. Matty leaned his head back too and closed his eyes.

After a while, Nebony asked him, "Do you want to know something?"

"Always," he half joked, on his way to being delirious.

"I lied when I asked to spend the night. My mom wasn't having friends over."

Matty opened his eyes and looked at her.

"Her boyfriend's been threatening me, acting psycho. I was running away."

Matty sat up, holding her hand in both of his. "Oh my God. I'm so sorry. Why didn't you tell me?"

Nebony's eyes were luminous. "Because we just became friends, and I didn't want to lay that on you."

"Nebony, you can lay *anything* on me." He gave her a firm hug.

She rested her head on his shoulder and closed her eyes. "I'm so glad we became friends. It's the only good thing that happened to me this week."

"Same." Matty laid his head on her shoulder too.

"Even though I got you kidnapped?"

"You didn't. This is not your fault."

"What if he doesn't let us go?"

Matty was trying hard not to think about it. They both pulled away at the same time and sat leaning against the wall, their shoulders still touching. Matty drew up his knees to his chest and wrapped his arms protectively around his legs. He debated whether to tell Nebony something he had never told anyone, not even Winnie. Right now, Matty felt closer to Nebony than he had to anyone ever in his life.

Minutes passed. He finally said, "Can I tell you a secret? Since we might . . ." he refused to say *die* out loud. "It's something I haven't told anyone."

Nebony took his hand again and squeezed it in silent support.

"I've had a secret crush on Forester, like, forever." He saw Nebony's eyes widen in surprise and rushed to assure her. "I always knew nothing could ever come of it. I'm not that delusional. And I love watching you two together. You guys are the most amazing couple."

"Were," she reminded him.

"Of course he's beautiful and like God's gift to men, but I got to know him when I was tutoring him and he's so much more than a superjock. You know? He's sweet and kind and caring and even a little humble. I couldn't help but like him. He's one of those all-around great guys." He grimaced. "Like the guys that make sports halls of fame because of who they are as a person." Matty stopped talking, embarrassed. It was obvious he had given this a lot of thought.

Nebony gave him a watery smile, nodding in understanding. "Forester is all of those things. He's one in a million. He was everything to me." She wiped the tears from her cheeks. "Trust me, I get it."

Matty felt a pressure release in his chest. His mom always said sometimes the weight in your heart was lighter after sharing your burden with a friend. Because his feelings had been a burden. He'd been carrying that secret around for so long he never even let himself think about it anymore.

Telling Nebony, the girl who loved Forester, felt right. She was the only one who could understand. Which was why it made such sense Matty loved Nebony too. She was Forester's perfect match.

"Why did you guys break up?"

"I don't know." Nebony shrugged. "Suddenly he wouldn't talk to me. He clammed up. Shut me out. Said he didn't want me anymore." Fresh tears rolled down her face. "It was brutal. I couldn't tell anyone. It hurt so much. I couldn't even cry when it happened."

Matty frowned. It just didn't sound like Forester. The guy was sensitive, not cruel. "Did you try talking to him? He has to regret it. I've watched you two together for years."

"Yeah. I told him I forgave him. Confessed I love him, and he told me to quit following him around like a puppy. Can you believe that? He said I was pathetic."

Matty gasped in horror, putting his hand to his chest. "He did not!" Nebony nodded. "He called you a pathetic puppy?" Matty shook his head. "That! Bastard! Okay. My crush is gone." He waved his hand in the air like a magician. "Poof! I'll hate him with you. When we die, we can haunt him together." He froze, realizing he just said *die*, feeling like he cursed himself.

Nebony wiped her tears. "Do you think we're going to die?"

Suddenly the voice came over the speaker, "I think your chances are good."

Matty and Nebony both screamed and grabbed onto each other.

"I hope your little nap refreshed you and made you reconsider your situation. Now tell me the house number on Garden Street, and I may let you live. The decision is yours." The booming voice spoke again.

Matty was too terrified to speak. Garden Street was a major street that cut through several neighborhoods. There were at least sixty houses to choose from, if not more. If they gave him the address, their captor might not keep them alive.

Nebony screeched, "I don't remember the number! I told you, it's on Garden Street."

"I will find the house eventually. Perhaps I should start with your boyfriend's house. Forester. That is his name? Or I could start with Winnie's. If you don't tell me, I will kill you now and then your friends. You can either stay alive—or die. You have ten seconds to comply. Ten . . . nine . . . eight . . . seven . . . six . . ."

Hysterical screaming filled Matty's ears.

Wow, he thought, *can Nebony scream like a pro.* It was a high-pitched, shrieking, blockbuster of a scream. Then he realized he was the one who was screaming and blubbering like a baby.

"Five . . . four . . . three . . ."

He also realized when it came down to life or death, he was willing to do anything to stay alive.

He ran up to the mirror, splaying his hands on the glass. "15287 Garden Street! It's 15287! 15287!"

The counting mercifully stopped.

"Very good." The voice asked, "Who does she live with?"

Nebony joined him at the mirror. "Her mother! She got divorced and moved from New York City."

"What is the mother's name?"

"I don't know." Nebony shook her head. "She's a food reporter or critic or something."

"She eats guava chips!" Matty screamed, no longer making sense.

"*Her name.*"

"Hazel!" Matty answered, remembering. "Hazel Hall. She got divorced. It's why they moved. Her husband owns a restaurant in New York City and fell in love with his waitress." Winnie had told him that in confidence and made him promise not to tell anyone. Now he'd blown that secret too.

"Who else lives with them?"

"No one." Matty sank to his knees, feeling lightheaded. "Her grandfather Clement Spencer passed away. That's why we were in the attic. To go through his stuff. I think his wife died a long time ago."

"Clement Spencer." The voice repeated back. "And what about Liv? Does she show any psychic ability?"

Psychic ability? That question totally threw Matty off. He and Nebony stared blankly at each other.

"*Answer!*"

Nebony elbowed him. "Tell him! I don't know her."

"She keeps a weird dream journal. That's all."

"Have you read what she wrote in it?"

Matty couldn't believe this psycho wanted to know about Liv's diary. "Just a page. A dream about her dad and flying around in the air."

"Interesting. Now tell me about the letter from Mad Merlin. You said he warned you. What did he warn you about? What *exactly* did the letter say?"

Matty hesitated. He didn't want to talk about the letter. "I-I-I . . ." he stammered.

"You were doing so well, Matthew. What. Did. The. Letter. Say." Menace oozed from the man's voice.

"It said I can't talk about the letters or I'll die!" Matty began to sweat, his whole body shaking. He eyed the gas spouts, praying they didn't turn on.

"Then you will die."

Matty froze in terror.

"Make no mistake, the real countdown has begun. Ten . . . nine . . . eight . . . seven . . ."

Nebony was sobbing, saying, "I don't want to die. I don't want to die. I don't want to die."

He didn't want to die either, and hostages were only as valuable as the information they had.

"Okay! Okay!" He banged on the mirror again and begged, "Stop! Please! Please! I'll tell you everything. Just please don't kill us."

"Everything?" the man taunted. "Are you sure? I grow weary of this game."

"Just call off the gas. Please." Matty slumped in defeat. He couldn't fight this madman anymore.

After a moment's hesitation, their captor said, "I want to know about every letter you read, who wrote them, who read them with you. I need to know their names and every detail about their lives."

23

JAXON

paranormal:
events beyond the scope of scientific understanding

JAXON'S JEEP JUST GOT A SERIOUS upgrade. He gaped at the sleek black Mercedes AMG G 63, suddenly not minding leaving his own car behind. The car looked like a state-of-the-art Jeep but was technically an SUV, a very expensive one. The inside felt more like a cockpit and had all the bells and whistles. He slid behind the driver's seat to find an interior of natural wood and leather.

"Are you serious? This is our car?" Winnie climbed into the back seat. Liv looked afraid to get in.

Jaxon found the key under the mat. He held it up in the air. "Looks that way." He turned the car on and started fiddling with the control panel. Liv got into the passenger seat and buckled up.

No one said a word as the enormity of what they were doing hit them. Jaxon put both visors down so their faces would be shielded, and he pulled out of the parking lot before he lost his nerve. At least no one would be looking for three teenagers in this. They were silent until they got out of Manhattan and hit Interstate 87. Then he and Winnie debated whether to go to Forester's first or to Winnie's and get her dad's computer. Liv sat next to him, remaining silent, but he could feel the emotional turmoil rolling off her.

Winnie leaned forward from the back seat. "Forester lives right across the street from Liv. And the letter said Liv can't go home. What if they see us?"

"We'll park on the street behind Forester's house." Jaxon tried to assure her. "There's a back entrance. No one will see us. Then we'll go get your dad's file. I promise."

He tried to focus on driving. The sky had become overcast and heavy with dark clouds. A serious storm was coming. Right now, his family thought he was at school.

At some point he needed to figure out how to get a message to his dad. But until he knew what they were dealing with and how the letters tied to his mother's death, he didn't want to contact them and put his family in danger. What he needed was to find time to sit down and see if he could get a sense what would be happening.

Following that thought, an image flashed in his head, delivered straight from his subconscious.

I'll be back at the apartment in the city tonight with Liv and Winnie.

Jaxon gripped the steering wheel in surprise. They were going back to the apartment tonight? That made no sense. Except the image had been crystal clear. Tonight Liv would step out onto the balcony in the rain.

Ever since he'd had the premonition of their kiss, he'd been waiting for it to happen. It was the only reason he hadn't kissed her last night in the attic. He didn't want to risk losing what he'd already experienced, because the memory of that kiss lived in his head. And he had no idea how to explain it to Liv without sounding ridiculous. Instead, he'd botched things badly with her last night and wasn't sure how to fix it.

He glanced over at her, surprised to find her looking at him intently. "Do you have a dog?" she asked abruptly.

He shot her another look, trying to keep his eyes on the road. "Yeah, Alfredo."

That got Winnie's attention from the backseat. She leaned forward. "Your dog's name is Alfredo?"

"My sister named him. She's into cooking."

"What kind of dog is he?" Liv asked. "A golden retriever?"

"A golden retriever," they said at the same time. Jaxon raised his eyebrows at the guess.

"Does he sleep in your room at night?" she asked, sounding serious.

"Yeah, why?" He glanced over again, wondering the reason for all the questions.

"Nothing. Just curious." She clammed up again, frustrating him. Ever since his confession and her reading her father's letter, Liv had grown distant, like she was wrapped up in a protective shell.

He wanted to press, but they were almost to Forester's. He drove down the street behind Forester's house, eyeing all the cars. Nothing seemed suspicious, not that he knew what to look for. Forester's Mustang was parked by the gate. Jaxon parked half a block away, thinking it would be better to walk. "Let's go." He pulled his baseball cap down and hopped out. The back gate was always unlocked. Jaxon led the way to the garage apartment. He gave a sharp knock on the door.

Forester stuck his head out. "Hey." He looked at Liv and Winnie with surprise.

"We just got back." Jaxon motioned. "They know."

Forester raised his eyebrows but didn't comment. "What's with the baseball cap? Trying out for little league?"

"Long story." Jaxon took off his sunglass and the girls did too. "Is your dad home yet?"

"No, but I'm not sure what time he'll be back. We'll need to make this quick." He took them to the main house, through the living room to a small side den that was a home office. The cluttered desk and old desktop computer took up most of the room, surrounded by file cabinets and two bookshelves against the walls.

"He keeps his case files here. The important ones."

Forester went to the file cabinet and started rooting around while Jaxon hovered behind him.

The girls stayed by the door.

"Either M for McNeil or C for Coleson," Jaxon said, trying to rein in his impatience. Forester was a slow reader. Jaxon was ready to push him aside and look himself.

Forester finally announced, "Got it," and pulled out a thick file, laying it on the desk. They all crowded around.

Jaxon braced himself, not knowing what he'd find. Forester opened it.

On top were handwritten notes and an old photo of a group of young women. They were sitting on the grass in front of a beautiful college building that looked more like an English manor.

"Wait a minute," Winnie said. "That's Vassar." She pointed at a woman in the photo. "And no way. That's my grandmother."

"I think that's mine." Jaxon squinted. His grandmother looked to be about twenty and had a sixties beehive hairdo.

Winnie frowned at him. "They knew each other?"

The note on top said *Vassar College + Dr. Alberty*

Jerald Peterson – murdered

Ryland and Rachel Davis – missing

Shelly – suicide

Sawyer – plane crash

"What is going on here?" Forester's dad called from across the living room. They'd been so caught up with the file they hadn't heard him come home. He wheeled himself to the doorway of his office. "You have three seconds to explain what the hell you're doing in here." His face was beet red, his jaw clenched. He looked beyond furious.

Forester was speechless. Jaxon stepped forward. "Sir, I'm the one to blame. I begged Forest to help me. I'm trying to find information about my mom's death." He motioned to the girls. "This is Liv and—"

"Liv Hall?" Forester's dad cut him off.

Liv nodded, her words coming out in a rush. "My father said to tell you Dr. Alberty's study didn't end, and you weren't wrong about Shelly McNeil's death."

Forester's dad shook his head, as if it couldn't be possible. "Grayson contacted you?"

Liv nodded again, her voice breaking. "After we found the Premonitions Bureau letters."

Forester's dad was speechless for a minute. "You found the letters?"

Jaxon answered. "They're at Liv's. And now a bunch of wild stuff is happening. Who is Dr. Alberty and what do the letters have to do with my mother's death?"

Forester's dad put a hand through his hair, looking overwhelmed, and said wearily, "Jax, believe me, I've been trying to find the answer to that for years." He shook his head. "When the building housing Dr. Alberty's old lab came up for sale last year, I went snooping around again and ended up with a bullet in my spine."

Jaxon felt his chest constrict. He glanced at Forester, seeing the devastation on his face.

His dad went on. "So forget you ever heard the name Alberty. I'm serious. Nothing good can come of it. Does anyone else know about the letters?"

"Only Matty and Nebony," Winnie said, then hesitated, "and Nebony posted pictures online."

Jaxon and Winnie locked eyes. *The pictures.* Nebony and Matty were in a picture with the letters. And now they were missing. He watched the same realization dawn on her face.

"She posted a picture of the letters?" Forester's dad looked deathly afraid. "Did she say what they were?"

"Dad, it's okay. See?" Forester opened his phone and scrolled to find the post. "Nebony posts a ton of stuff. She never said where she was." He went to show him the picture. But another post caught his attention. Jaxon read it over his shoulder. Nebony was wearing Forester's old football hoodie and had written a heartbreaking goodbye to him. Forester covered his mouth with his hand.

His dad took the phone and scrolled up to the smiling picture of Nebony and Matty together, surrounded by letters and envelopes to the Premonitions Bureau. He looked even more grim and asked Forester, "Have you talked to your girlfriend since she posted this?"

"She's not my girlfriend—"

"Have you talked to her?" his dad cut in, his voice sharp.

"I tried. She's not returning my texts," Forester looked embarrassed to admit. "She wasn't at school today."

"Wait. Matty wasn't at school either." Winnie frowned. "I can't get ahold of him. He was with Nebony last night. They were together."

"Are you saying she's in trouble?" Forester immediately grabbed his keys to leave, but his dad stopped him.

"Son, you're not going anywhere alone. We'll drive by her place together in the van."

"They were at Matty's," Winnie interrupted. "I'll give you the address. Do you really think something might have happened to them?"

"I hope I'm wrong." Forester's dad was a man of few words. It was what he wasn't saying that was more terrifying. His earlier anger at them forgotten, he wheeled to the back door. "You kids stay here while we check. What's a number where I can reach you?" Liv gave him the number to the borrowed phone.

"Sir," Jaxon said, "we have to go to Winnie's and get her dad's computer. We think there might be a file on it that can help us."

"Come again?" Forester's dad turned to him.

Winnie crossed her arms. "My dad wrote about a psychic named Mad Merlin before he died. We need to find out what he knew."

Forester's dad stared at Winnie, as if seeing her clearly for the first time. "Who's your father?"

"Sawyer Scott."

Forester's dad looked dazed. "My God."

Winnie hesitated. "You knew my dad?"

"Yeah. I knew Sawyer."

To Jaxon, the past felt like an egg that was about to be cracked open. The time for secrets was over. "Mr. Torres, we really need you to explain what's going on. How did Winnie's dad know about Mad Merlin? And how is my mother's death connected to any of this?"

Forester's dad deliberated, then wheeled over to a cabinet in the living room. He took an old photograph from a drawer and held it out. The photo was of Forester's parents when they were young. A girl and two guys posed next to them.

"That's Jaxon's mother, Shelly." Forester's dad pointed. Next he pointed to the two guys with their arms ringed around each other's necks. "That's Winnie's dad and Liv's father."

Then he pointed to them all again.

"The Oracle of Delphi, Nostradamus, and Mad Merlin."

The room became deathly silent.

No one could say a word as they stared at the young faces of three psychics whose letters they'd been reading all week. They were all three gazing into the camera as if they knew this picture was significant.

Jaxon was unable to swallow past the lump in his throat. "You're saying our parents were all psychic? And someone killed my mother for it?"

Forester's dad nodded. "Shelly never would have . . ." He didn't go on. Then he turned to Liv. "Grayson left to protect you and your mother. After Shelly died, it wasn't safe."

"So he left us," Liv said softly.

"Had to," Forester's dad said in a tone that brooked no argument.

Liv crossed her arms defensively. Jaxon wanted nothing more than to give her a hug right now.

"What about my dad?" Winnie asked, crossing her arms defensively too, standing next to Liv. "He died in a plane crash."

Forester's dad measured his words again. "On his way to meet Liv's dad."

"But it was a plane crash. A hundred and eighty-six people died," Winnie said again, her eyes bright. "That's just pure bad luck."

Forester's dad was adamantly shaking his head. "I knew Sawyer, and believe me, if that plane had been *meant* to crash—been destined to crash—your dad would have seen it coming and never would have gotten on board."

24

WINNIE

second sight:
the ability to see the future or distant events

NO ONE SPOKE IN THE CAR on the way to Winnie's. She was glad the windows were tinted. She felt eerily exposed driving through the streets of her hometown. The sooner they left Hyde Park and got back to the apartment, the better. A sense of urgency was pressing on her to get to her house, get her father's manuscript, and get out.

"Can you drive faster?" She was in the backseat, pulling Tarot cards, trying to focus. She stared at the card in her hand, *The Magician*, trying to make sense of what Forester's dad had told them. The Magician signified many things. Talent. Concentration. Power. The ability to harness energy.

Their parents had been Magicians.

All three. They had incredible abilities and had been hunted for it. Forester's dad really thought her father's airplane crashed because he was on board, which was impossible.

Winnie couldn't even think straight right now. Matty and Nebony were missing. Where was he? She took a deep breath and pulled another card.

The Hanged Man.

She stared at the image of a bound man hanging upside down. The message was unmistakable. Matty was trapped somewhere, in pain and afraid.

Why would someone take them?

Because there is a bigger secret within the letters the Bureau tried to hide. Her intuition was speaking clearly to her. Winnie gripped the cards, mixing them up again. She pulled two more: *Judgement* and *The Devil.* Her mind worked to cull answers from the symbols. More thoughts came, as sharp as the cards' edges.

The Judgement card marks the end of a long journey and carefully laid plans coming to a head.

The Devil is who has Matty and Nebony. He is the one behind her father's and Jaxon's mother's deaths.

A memory came to her, something she had forgotten. Only now could she recognize its importance. She shared it with Liv and Jaxon. "I asked my mom once if my dad had a bad feeling before the flight, like he shouldn't get on the plane. She said he never said anything to her." Winnie glanced at Liv. "But she told me your dad called her that morning, frantic, trying to reach my dad. Your dad was in a panic, saying he had to talk to him, but the plane had already taken off. The plane crashed minutes later. Your dad must have had a premonition right before it happened."

"Only too late," Liv whispered. "I'm so sorry."

Winnie's father had been a powerful psychic yet hadn't seen his own death.

They'd all been robbed of their parents. Winnie didn't remember her dad. She only remembered the space he'd left behind. The empty chair at the dinner table, the other half of her mother's king-sized bed, the second sink in her parents' bathroom that was never used. Her mother had never gotten over his death. She still celebrated his birthday and their wedding anniversary and took flowers to his grave on the date he died.

Sawyer Scott.

Her mom had set up a website dedicated to his books and had her assistant at the art gallery manage all the social media. Readers and fans still wrote to Sawyer. There was particular lore on how uncanny it was several of his plots had actually come true, from the rise of AI to nationalism around the world. Everyone assumed he was simply a futurist. Futurism was a thriving industry where people predicted trends and global changes, and her dad had been really good at it. Now Winnie wanted to reread his books all over again. The stories were fiction, but still, maybe there were clues to understanding him he'd left behind, like breadcrumbs tucked between the pages.

Winnie stared out the window, wistful. If only she had known he had written the Nostradamus letters. What she wouldn't give to go back to the attic and read them again—her father's words, written in his own hand. He must have been in high school right about the time he'd written those. His premonitions had been right in front of her, and she'd been blind.

Now his letters were being carted off by strangers. She would never see them again. But at least she had his books—and his unpublished story. It was crucial she read it. The certainty inside her was unquestionable. She felt like her whole life was leading up to finding it. She looked down at her deck and saw the *King of Swords* on top.

Winnie glanced out the window as they drove past the school. Police cars were parked out front. Several officers were heading inside with dogs.

Liv asked, "Do you think they're there because of Nebony and Matty?"

"Maybe." Jaxon checked his speed to not draw attention. "Maybe they're searching the grounds for them?"

Winnie sat forward. Way down the block she noticed two black SUVs. An alarm bell inside her started going off to not let those cars see them.

"Jaxon, turn right. Right now. Turn right!"

"But your house is straight."

"Turn right! Turn right!" She was frantic. He was about to miss the corner. "Turn now!" she yelled and Jaxon made a hard right.

Liv gripped the dash. "Jesus, Win! I thought the plan was not to draw attention to ourselves."

Winnie put a hand to her neck, trying to calm down. "I'm sorry. I'm sorry but I got a serious bad feeling from those two SUVs up there." Something wasn't right.

"I did too." Jaxon kept checking the rearview mirror. "I just wasn't going to turn. Good call. We need to stay alert. Technically we shouldn't be here."

Winnie directed Jaxon how to get to her house from the back way. "Drive around the corner. We'll park behind the backyard, just to be safe. It'll be in and out." She was planning to bring the whole computer with them and figure out how to access the file at Forester's since she had yet to figure out the password.

They hurried inside through the back patio. Winnie's mom was still at the gallery. Winnie left her a note on the kitchen table.

Sorry my phone is broken. Spending the night with Liv. Have a big assignment. Will call you tomorrow. Love, W

It should buy her some time. At some point, she would have to call her mom and tell her what was going on. But what could she say? *Mom, I threw away my phone and am on the run because it turns out Dad was a superpsychic who called himself Nostradamus.*

Then she stopped, her heart racing when she realized, "Oh my God, guys. I know what his password is."

She ran upstairs and booted up the computer. The machine gurgled and made clicking noises as it ran through its endless process of turning on. "Come on clunker."

The computer was sixteen years old, practically a dinosaur in tech years. After endless minutes, finally the cursor was ready for the password.

Winnie took a deep breath. "Here goes." Liv and Jaxon both leaned over her shoulder to watch. They were all three braced as she typed in the letters:

N·O·S·T·R·A·D·A·M·U·S

Hardly daring to breathe, she hit enter.

And the screen came to life.

Winnie jumped up with excitement as they all yelled over each other. "Oh my God!" "You're in!" "It worked!" They did a spontaneous group hug, like a team who'd scored a touchdown.

While the computer took another endless few minutes to load, she connected her father's old printer to it.

Suddenly she was staring at the desktop and her dad's screensaver.

A picture of her dad, her mom, and her as a baby illuminated the screen. Her parents were holding her up in the air. They were outside on the patio, bathed in sunlight.

"Win, it's beautiful." Liv laid a soft hand on her back.

Winnie hadn't been expecting to see this photo, and the surprise hit her with such force it brought tears to her eyes. She never realized how much she looked like her dad. Black hair, brown eyes, wide smile, same nose. She had so much of him in her. Her dad looked radiant and happy and so alive.

This photo must have been taken weeks before the crash. For a moment, she wanted to stop right there with the picture and not go any further down the rabbit hole.

But they already were down the rabbit hole. Deep down the rabbit hole. To think her father was Nostradamus and Mad Merlin was his best friend.

Had he actually written a novel about him?

"Winnie, we really can't stay here much longer." Jaxon stood watch at the window, peeking out from behind the curtain.

Liv was at the far window, watching the other way. "I agree. This doesn't feel safe."

Liv's words pulled Winnie out of her daze. Then she saw the file folder icon on the desktop clearly labeled.

[THE GNOSIS TRAP]

"I've got it! This will just take a minute." She opened it and clicked print, and her father's printer came to life.

As the pages spit out, she looked around her room. Was she ever coming back here? They were literally on the run and reality was going up in flames.

Suddenly the same feeling she had in the car descended over her. They needed to leave. Like *now*.

Liv gasped. "A police car is coming down the street. Guys!" Jaxon ran to her side and looked out.

"Shit. Winnie, we've got to go now!"

"I need a minute." Winnie willed the pages to print faster. She couldn't leave until the last page printed.

"We don't have a minute! Come on!" Jaxon hurried to the door.

Hands shaking, Winnie grabbed a duffle bag and shoved all the disks in it. "You go. I'll catch up. I need all the pages."

"Winnie!" Liv pleaded. "They're coming!"

"And we need these pages!" She waited on bated breath for the pages to print.

"They're pulling into your driveway," Jaxon reported.

"Get to the car and start it. I'll be thirty seconds behind you," she promised.

Jaxon gave her a stern look. "Thirty seconds." Then he took off, dragging Liv with him.

Liv called out, begging, "Hurry, Win!"

The neighbor's dog started barking outside. Winnie heard her neighbor apologizing to the officers on the driveway.

Four more pages.

"Come on come on come on come on," she pleaded to the printer.

Three more. Two more.

Finally, the last page appeared and she yanked the plug on the computer from the wall to shut it off. There was no time for anything else. She crammed the manuscript and all the disks into her bag and crept down the stairs, trying to be quiet.

She raced through the back den to the patio door just as the doorbell rang. Pulling the backdoor shut, her hands were shaking so hard she could barely turn the key in the lock. Then she hiked up her pencil skirt and took off at a dead run to the car. She clutched the duffle bag to her like priceless treasure. Her father's writing was all she had left of him, and she wasn't about to leave a word behind.

<ENCRYPTED TRANSMISSION>
<DEFENSE INTELLIGENCE AGENCY SERVER>

<From: MIRIAM>
<Priority: HIGH>

15287 Garden Street is owned by a foreign trust in Liechtenstein, a principality between Switzerland and Austria. Unable to access further information due to their privacy laws.

Liv Hall is the daughter of Hazel Hall and Grayson Spencer, son of Maxine Spencer. Maxine Spencer attended Vassar College.

Based on Nebony Price and Matthew Jacob's interrogation, of the group who found the letters, three are offspring of the Alberty prodigies:

Liv Hall (daughter of Grayson Spencer)
Jaxon Coleson (son of Shelly McNeil)
Winnifred Scott — goes by Winnie (daughter of Sawyer Scott)

From the facts provided we must consider
they have inherited Enhanced Human Biological
Function from their parents. The odds of this
are incalculable. If EHBF can be genetically
passed down, proliferation will become
unstoppable.

Recommendation:

Offspring be classified as Alberty prodigies
and included in the program objective:

Terminate all prodigies and destroy any trace
of the study.

Local law enforcement has been fed a false
narrative Jaxon and Winnie are involved in
selling drugs at their school. When the
police bring them in for questioning, we
will have an extraction point.

Send a team to Liv Hall's residence this
evening. Wait for the cover of night to
transport the letters and be discreet.

Lethal force is acceptable.
Leave no trace.

.

25

THEGNOSISTRAP.DOC
<OPEN FILE>

prophecy:
prediction of what is to come, an instruction

IF YOU'RE READING THIS, THEN I didn't survive, and you get to decide whether this is real or fiction. I know a thing or two about stories, and I have one to tell. Once upon a time, there was a widely accepted belief humans use only ten percent of the brain while the other ninety percent lies dormant. We have since proven that is a myth. Humans use all of the brain. The question is how. At its core, the brain is a quantum-based operating system, far more powerful than any AI program, and brain mapping is only beginning to explore the mind's capabilities.

For years, science has already proven psychic ability, telepathy, telekinesis, and remote viewing are all repressed human mental functions.

The question never has been *Is it real,* but *Who controls it?*

The US military has always been seeking to develop the mind's hidden talents, and their research is well guarded. To understand the full scope of the problem, first we need to go back to World War II, when the psychic arms race began with the Nazis. The Nazis attempted to weaponize psychic abilities but then lost the war. So America swooped in and took all the research before Russia could. The US military had suddenly acquired countless studies on psychic phenomena—groundbreaking, mind-blowing studies—and they wanted to know more. If a spoon could be bent, if a mind could be read, the government not only wanted to know how, but how they could do it better than the Russians.

If Russia had a psychic who could stop an animal's heart with her mind, then the US had a psychic who could travel with his mind's eye thousands of miles to spy on them. A global tug-of-war ensued over which superpower could unravel the secrets of the psyche fastest.

Then China stepped in, late to the game, in the 1970s.

"Mental phenomena" and "psychic function" entered the Chinese public eye with a loud bang when children were discovered to have rare abilities, such as *eyeless sight* (to see without the eyes) and *psychokinesis* (the ability to manipulate objects with their mind). China's Politburo went into overdrive. They publicly praised the children and called these rare feats *EHBF*.

EHBF = *Extraordinary Human Body Function.*

China took all mysticism out of the idea of being "psychic" and turned it into cutting-edge science. They stated EHBF abilities are based on *qi*, the Chinese word for the body's life force.

The irony was well noted on the other side of the world. China, one of the most censored countries on the planet, wanted its psychic studies in the news and in the public eye.

The US, on the other hand, *did not.* The Defense Department wants psychics who can plant thoughts in the minds of others, read minds, bend metal, move objects, and know the future. They need remote viewers who can locate targets, from missile locations, to drug cartels, to kidnapped victims, halfway across the world without leaving their chairs. The military needs psychics. However, they discovered soldiers can't be trained to be psychic. Psychics are born that way, and they are few and far between. A rarity in nature.

An anomaly.

But what if they weren't?

What would happen if being psychic wasn't rare anymore?

What would happen if *everyone* became psychic?

Those in power do not want this question answered. And they will do *anything* to stop it from potentially happening. Because third-dimensional reality is one scientific study away from being blown to bits.

I know because I am an anomaly.

I was born with a natural ability to tune in to the future. It wasn't until I was older that I understood why.

The turning point came when I saw the news on TV about a missing girl named Carrie Williams. Her kidnapping and the psychic who found her had riveted the entire country. A man named Jerald Peterson contacted NYPD weeks before the incident, warning them it would happen.

When no one took him seriously, he wrote to the Premonitions Bureau for help. A bureau I was stunned to learn existed. A bureau who read people's premonitions, determined their validity, and tried to help stop potentially harmful events from happening.

The year was 1989, and email had yet to replace old-fashioned mail. We had no Internet or cell phones. We were still in the virtual dark ages. Even the microphone the TV news reporter held on camera had no digital components, no Bluetooth, only a thick cable disappearing out of frame.

Jerald looked to be no more than eighteen, two years older than I was at the time.

"The Bureau stepped in," he explained to the reporter interviewing him. Jerald had a reserved manner. He came across as quiet and shy. "Because of them, the police kept my letter on file. I hadn't known her last name."

The reporter prompted, "So when Carrie Williams was reported missing by the school . . ."

"They searched the marina where I saw her being held and found her."

The reporter listened with wide eyes. "You're saying your premonition saved a little girl's life?"

"I was just glad to help." Jerald Peterson looked into the camera, and the image froze on him.

I'd had premonitions for years, inklings about people and their future, but I'd never thought to write to someone. The reporter said Jerald would be a guest speaker at a conference the following week in New York centering around psychic ability. The reporter made a joke to "bring your tinfoil hat" and come if you believed in "that sort of thing." I shook my head at the idiot who just interviewed the person who'd saved a girl's life with "that sort of thing" and jotted down the conference information. I had to go.

The morning of the conference, I took the early train to Manhattan and made my way to the hotel near Times Square where it was being held. I made it in time to grab a seat in the back for the first panel. That's when I saw Grayson Spencer. All I could think was, *What is he doing here?* Grayson went to my school. We weren't friends but knew each other. He was a loner—and the smartest kid in our class. He intimidated most of the other students. I found out later that when he was a child, he'd been the youngest member of Mensa, the society for people with the highest IQs in the world. After high school, he went on to triple major in physics, computer programming, and math at Columbia University. To say he was a genius was putting it mildly.

That day, Grayson came toward me with a grin and plopped down in the chair next to me. "Sawyer! You're here. Good to know I'm not off the mark." He crossed his legs like a sophisticated adult would and checked his watch. "Now let's see if this really happens as it should. Today's the big day."

I had no idea what he was talking about.

While Grayson waited for something to happen, I glanced around the crowd. The hotel ballroom held about two hundred people. A stranger went to sit beside us, and Grayson put his hand on the chair. "Sorry, this seat's taken," he said, and the person moved on to find another spot.

Grayson grinned at me and turned back to watch all the people filing in. Then we both saw the girl walk past.

Shelly McNeil.

Shelly went to our school too. She was really odd, always off in a corner furiously writing in a notebook. I always wondered what she was writing because her pen never stopped. Everyone thought she was strange. I thought she was interesting.

Grayson waved and called out to her, "Over here! We saved you a seat."

Shelly looked behind her, as if not sure Grayson was talking to her.

"Of course, you," Grayson teased her, like they were old friends.

Shelly seemed as confused as I was but came over and took the seat.

"You go to my school." She said it to us like an accusation.

"Grayson Spencer and Sawyer Scott at your service," Grayson said and then asked us, "Don't tell me you didn't see this coming? Am I the only one here who saw this coming?" He looked from me to Shelly and back again.

I hadn't seen anything coming, but then I hadn't been looking. Color rose to Shelly's cheeks, and she hugged her notebook to her chest without a word.

That day was the start of our friendship. Grayson, Shelly, and I spent the entire day together, opening up to each other about our abilities. After that weekend, we were inseparable. For the first time, I could talk about what I could do. It was like being silent my whole life and finally having permission to speak. We were three budding psychics from Hyde Park who had found each other in the most populated city in the country. The fact we were all from Hyde Park should have been the first clue, the first warning, but we didn't see it. Not yet.

We had been brought together by Jerald Peterson. Only later would we understand why.

* * *

Before I go any further, first it is important you understand there is no one way to be psychic. Abilities fall into four categories, which we call the *four Clairs*:

1. Clairvoyance (seeing)
2. Clairaudience (hearing)
3. Clairsentience (feeling)
4. Claircognizance (knowing)

A person can be dominant in any one or all four Clairs at the same time. Each person is unique because psychic ability is like a fingerprint.

For example, a psychic who relies on touch and holding objects to get information is called a *psychometrist*. While other psychics use tools to have visions. They stare at objects like candles, water, mirrors, or crystal balls. Or they simply close their eyes. A psychic who gazes at a reflective surface is called a *scryer*.

Nostradamus, the most famous scryer recorded in history, used a bowl of water to see the future, and I became intrigued by the idea. I had never tried to use a tool to get a premonition. After the conference, I went home and started experimenting by staring into bowls of water. I felt ridiculous at first but found it worked.

Shelly was clairaudient. She could hear facts about the future in her mind and then would write them down. Her journals looked like they'd been through a war, battered and scribbled on all over, with not an inch of white space left on the paper.

Grayson can see the future simply by knowing it. Claircognizance. Numbers are his passion. *Numerology* predicts the future with numbers. He even boasted once how he could predict lightning strikes in a storm through the number coordinates on a map.

Grayson explained how numbers can tell you about yourself. For example, take the numbers of your birthday, add them together, and that is your *Life Path* number.

"Your Life Path number is a three," Grayson told me when we first met. "*The Communicator.* You're a writer," he said, as if I didn't know. But somehow, he knew just by looking at my birthday. He predicted, "You're going to write books one day."

Another important number to know is your *Destiny Number.* Mine is a nine. *The Humanitarian,* someone with a yearning to help people, which is true. I wanted to use my ability like Jerald, and I thought about sending letters to the Premonitions Bureau like he did. I brought up the idea to Shelly and Grayson.

What if we tried to help change the future for the better?

"If we do, we can't use our real names," Grayson stipulated. He was personally connected to the Bureau. His mother, Maxine Spencer, was one of the directors. Grayson was concerned we might ruin the Bureau's study if they discovered a psychic was related to one of the researchers. "We don't want to get on the news like Jerald Peterson."

None of us wanted to get on the news. We were high schoolers in a small town. My dad was the local dentist, and my mom taught at the elementary school. Grayson's mom might understand her son's ability, even embrace it, but my parents wouldn't. I had kept what I could do a secret until I met Shelly and Grayson.

So we came up with pen names. I thought the name Nostradamus was perfect. Shelly chose the Oracle of Delphi. And Grayson wanted to be Merlin.

"You can't just be Merlin," I insisted.

"Why not? You're *just* Nostradamus."

"Yours needs something more. A qualifier. How about Mad Merlin?" I suggested.

"Says the writer. I like it." Grayson nodded and raised his Snapple for a toast. "To Mad Merlin, the Oracle of Delphi, and Nostradamus. Once we put our predictions on paper, there's no turning back."

Shelly nodded. "The world needs proof. Let's give it to them." And our letter writing began. We got together on weekends to write to the Bureau, never putting a return address. Although many of our predictions would take years to verify, we still wrote them down so they could be a part of the record, of history yet to come. We didn't know if these letters would make a difference or not, but we had to try.

Conviction and will are two of the most powerful forces of the mind. Our conviction to help made seeing horrible events possible, knowing we were trying to stop them from ever happening.

We discovered the more time we spent together, the stronger our abilities became. A bond formed between us. Grayson calls it a triskelion, the power of three. In the world of energy, three creates an unbreakable bond. It's why the pyramid is the strongest structure in nature.

Out of all of us, Shelly was determined to understand why we were the way we were. Three kids from Hyde Park with psychic abilities who had found each other. Nothing could explain *us*.

Until something happened that did.

Like a spool unraveling, in 1993 Shelly discovered our connection at the end of our senior year.

She called a meeting at her house, saying it was urgent. "My mom went to college with Jerald Peterson's mother at Vassar. They were friends."

Goosebumps raced up my arms like an electric current. "My mother went to Vassar."

"Mine did too," Grayson said.

Vassar was the nearby college. The fact they had all gone there together felt significant.

"How did you find this out?" I asked.

Shelly looked grim. "Because my mom went to Jerald Peterson's funeral today. His body was found in the East River. He was murdered because of his ability." At first I couldn't believe what she was saying. She showed us her journal. "I got very clear answers."

I'd seen Shelly's pen fly across the page countless times as she wrote down predictions like someone taking lunch orders at a restaurant during rush hour. Her premonitions were never wrong.

She looked scared. "Someone connected to Jerald's death is going to contact the Bureau and demand to see the letters. I keep getting the name Stan Storlie. I also keep getting the name Miriam. And the words Clair Dominus."

Those names meant nothing to us. I took her journal from her and stared at the page.

CLAIR DOMINUS CLAIR DOMINUS
CLAIR DOMINUS CLAIR DOMINUS
CLAIR DOMINUS CLAIR DOMINUS
CLAIR DOMINUS CLAIR DOMINUS
CLAIR DOMINUS CLAIR DOMINUS
CLAIR DOMINUS CLAIR DOMINUS
CLAIR DOMINUS CLAIR DOMINUS
CLAIR DOMINUS CLAIR DOMINUS
CLAIR DOMINUS CLAIR DOMINUS
CLAIR DOMINUS CLAIR DOMINUS
CLAIR DOMINUS CLAIR DOMINUS
CLAIR DOMINUS CLAIR DOMINUS
CLAIR DOMINUS CLAIR DOMINUS
CLAIR DOMINUS CLAIR DOMINUS
CLAIR DOMINUS CLAIR DOMINUS
CLAIR DOMINUS CLAIR DOMINUS
CLAIR DOMINUS CLAIR DOMINUS
CLAIR DOMINUS CLAIR DOMINUS

She had written the words over and over in all caps down the page as if she was crazy. Only I knew Shelly was perfectly sane. By writing it, she'd been trying and failing—over and over—to get more information from the name. The repetition alone evoked a sense of dread inside me.

Grayson teased her. "Serial killer much, Shel?"

She rolled her eyes at him and sighed. "I have no idea what it means. I asked my mom how she knew Jerald's mom and she said they took part in some kind of mental enhancement study. It wasn't at the college. A doctor from the Neuroscience Institute recruited them. She said your moms did it too."

Grayson was the one who voiced the question. "And you think the people who did the study went on to have kids with psychic abilities?"

Shelly had a troubled look on her face. It would explain us—and connect us to Jerald.

The young psychic had been in the public eye and been killed. If whoever was behind Jerald's death got ahold of the letters, they would lead to us. Right now the only thing keeping us safe was our anonymity.

That was the day the letter writing stopped. We hoped it would be enough to keep us safe, but we were wrong.

26

LIV

stichomancy:
divination through the lines of books

LIV CAME TO THE END OF the chapter and stopped reading. *The Gnosis Trap* wasn't a thriller about Mad Merlin. It was Winnie's father's diary, his last story to tell. Reading it now, she didn't know what to think. She still couldn't believe her father was Mad Merlin.

She had questions for her mom. Big ones. Had her mom known about her dad's ability when they got married? Or had he kept it a secret? Liv had to believe her mom hadn't known. What about Jaxon's dad? Or Winnie's mom? Jaxon's dad seemed to have known the truth, at least some of it, because he had warned Jaxon.

Her father's letter said her mom was safe as long as she didn't know about the letters, and the attorney warned her she couldn't go home while they cleared out the attic. Which meant strangers were entering the house right now and carting off all the boxes. Her mom was still in the city, hopefully at a hotel. Liv wanted to call and make sure she was okay, but she didn't want to alert her what was happening and risk her coming home. One thing in all of this nagged at her. The omen. Mad Merlin had warned them decades ago with an omen—so if the warning really was meant for them, then her father had foreseen some version of this scenario of the future playing out.

If he had seen this future and the danger, why hadn't he moved the letters out of the attic years ago? Why were the letters up there in the first place? It didn't make sense.

If only the attorney's office had taken the letters sooner. If only she hadn't opened the boxes or invited Forester over to help move the wood. Then Jaxon and Nebony never would have come over. Nebony never would have taken that picture. She and Matty wouldn't be missing. If only her mom hadn't run away to Hyde Park and dragged her with her. Or if only Bodhi hadn't cheated on her mom in the first place. A clear chain of *if onlys* led to this moment.

Had everything been inevitable? Was that all fate was?

The sun cast a glare through the car window, and Liv watched Winnie swipe at her cheeks and sniffle. They were parked behind Forester's house, reading in the car and waiting for Forester and his dad to return. After Winnie finished a page, she handed it off to Liv, who handed it to Jaxon. Round and round the pages went while no one said a word.

Liv's phone interrupted them. Only Forester's father had this number. She answered with an anxious "Hello?"

"Where are you right now?" Forester's dad asked. The worry in his voice was clear.

"Parked on your back street."

"There's a key hidden under the big potted plant in the garden. Use it and get inside right away. The police are looking for Jax and Winnie."

"What?" Liv sat up in shock.

"The DEA got a reliable tip today they are the head of a drug ring at the school. They're wanted for questioning."

"But that's ridiculous! That's a lie!"

"I know that and you know that, but right now some very powerful people are trying to find you. They're enlisting all the help they can get. My guess is the only reason you weren't included in those allegations is because they don't want the police at your house finding the letters."

Liv began to shake. Jaxon put a comforting hand on her leg in concern, and Winnie leaned forward, anxiously trying to hear.

Forester's dad was saying, "We're at Matty's now. Both cars are here but no one's home." The stress in his voice was clear. "We're going to ask the neighbors if they saw anything. Get in the house and wait for us."

"Yes, sir," Liv said, flustered, and hung up.

Jaxon and Winnie were staring at her expectantly, but she didn't know where to start.

Matty and Nebony were missing, and Jaxon and Winnie were wanted by the police. Unable to hold back the quiver in her voice, she relayed what Forester's father had said while Winnie and Jaxon listened in stunned silence.

"He wants us to get inside so we're not spotted. There's a key in the garden."

They locked the car and hurried through the back gate, bringing the manuscript with them. They still had more pages to read. So far, all they knew was how their parents met and how they were tied to the Premonitions Bureau. A big gulf of time still existed between then and now. What had happened to cause Shelly and Sawyer to die? And who were Stan Storlie and Miriam?

Liv hoped Winnie's father explained, because Liv's father was the only one alive who might know the answers. And even with their whole world falling apart, Liv didn't know if she'd ever be ready to hear his side of the story.

<ENCRYPTED TRANSMISSION>
<DEFENSE INTELLIGENCE AGENCY SERVER>

<From: MIRIAM>
<Priority: HIGH>

Jaxon Coleson's car was found in Manhattan
near Central Park. Surveillance order issued
to see if he will return.

Grayson Spencer's mother, Maxine Spencer,
is the current director of the Mage
Foundation, a private research institute
in Zurich studying EHBF.

Have a European team place her under
surveillance. She may know where Dr. Alberty
and Grayson Spencer are hiding.

Confirm when the team has extracted the
letters from the Hall residence.

27

JAXON

presentiment:
a feeling something is about to happen, especially something evil

THE GNOSIS TRAP. AS JAXON READ Sawyer Scott's manuscript, he couldn't help the jealousy welling inside him. He had nothing from his mother. No words. No letter. No goodbye. All Jaxon had were the letters she'd written to the Bureau, and he'd been planning to ask Liv if he could keep them. Now those were gone too.

Shelly, the Oracle of Delphi who'd seen terrorist events and the rise and fall of presidents, hadn't seen her own death.

Because she wasn't meant to die.

The thought was now branded in Jaxon's brain, and a new kind of rage coursed through him, along with the certainty her future had been altered. Maybe by the same people who had taken Nebony and Matty. He *knew* Nebony shouldn't have posted that photo with the letters. He'd felt it in his gut.

What had happened to her?

He, Liv, and Winnie were hiding out at Forester's, waiting for him and his dad to come home. No one was ready to read more of the manuscript yet.

Forester's dad had dropped several bombshells on them with that phone call. Jaxon couldn't begin to process the fact he and Winnie were wanted by the police. Those police officers and dogs had been at the school *for them*.

Forester kept texting them updates.

Her car is unlocked

Found a phone near the gutter

WTH happened!!!!????

Jaxon stared at Forester's texts, feeling his mounting distress. He put the phone on the table and rubbed his face.

He tried to stay focused, but it was hard. It felt like the walls of reality were closing in on him and he was about to be crushed. He had to hope Nebony and Matty would turn up and there was a logical explanation for why no one could reach them. And he held on to the prediction that he, Liv, and Winnie would be back at the apartment tonight safe and sound. It was the only thing keeping him from completely freaking out. His family must be beside themselves right now. The police had probably come to his house too. At some point, he and Winnie would have to come forward. He just couldn't think that far ahead right now.

Liv hovered at the front curtain and peeked out, but her house seemed quiet across the street. If someone from the estate attorney's office had come, they were gone now.

Winnie was sitting across the room in the rocking chair, having retreated into her own world. Her rhythmic rocking, controlled by one foot, felt like a ticking clock. Liv came back and joined him on the sofa. She looked lost in thought as she held the stone pendant around her neck and moved it back and forth along the silver chain. Jaxon noticed that, like the armband, she always wore it.

Trying to distract himself from his thoughts, he asked, "Is it obsidian?" resisting the urge to touch it. He didn't need anything else filling his head right now.

He'd started to notice sometimes when he touched things he got a premonition.

Sawyer had called it being a psychometrist.

Liv glanced at him, looking surprised by the question. "I don't know. My grandmother gave it me—or left it for me." She laid the stone back on her neck. "I thought she died before I was born and this was a family heirloom or something." She shook her head and gave a bitter smile. "Just more family secrets."

"How do you feel about meeting your father?"

"I'm not sure how to feel."

He could sense the riot of emotions simmering underneath her reserved answers. "Liv, he left to protect you and your mother."

"Then maybe he should have told us the truth instead of letting me think I had a father who didn't love us enough to stay."

"At least he's alive," he felt the need to point out. Immediately he saw the regret on her face.

"I'm sorry. I didn't mean—"

"It's okay," he interrupted. "You have feelings about what he did. I get it." He gave her a half smile. "But what I wouldn't give to see my mom again."

She stared at him, her eyes growing luminous with tears she furiously blinked back. "You know this is my fault. All of it. We never should have found the boxes."

"What?" Jaxon sat forward, astounded. "No, it's not." He took her hand, willing her to believe him. "The three of us were brought together to find out the truth about our parents. We were meant to find the letters. You have to believe that."

Winnie joined in, agreeing. "I never would have known about my father's past or found his manuscript."

"So we found the letters and their secrets, but at what cost?" Liv argued, pulling her hand away from his. "What if Matty and Nebony are hurt because of us? And how are we going to get out of this? The Hyde Park police are literally looking for you."

Jaxon felt his own stress rise again. "We can't worry about that right now or it will completely derail us. Forester's dad is on our side. He knows the truth, and that's all that matters. The police will find Matty and Nebony. We have to believe that."

"Can you see that happening?" Liv challenged him, and she looked at Winnie too. "Them being okay?"

Winnie had been pulling Tarot cards off and on all day, trying to get answers. "I got nothing." She sighed at the two cards in her hands. "I keep getting the words *the center of the island*. Does that mean anything to you? The center of the island?"

They both shook their heads. Winnie held up the two cards.

The *King of Pentacles* depicted a king on a throne surrounded by gold coins.

The *Ace of Cups* showed a golden chalice overflowing with water being held by a hand.

She kept staring at the cards, as if trying to decipher them. "There's water, maybe an ocean, and the king is in the center of the island . . . I don't know what it means." With a sigh, she put the cards back into the deck.

Liv tucked her arms around her middle like she always did, as if she were bracing herself. "I wish I could sense something," she said. "Why do you both have some kind of psychic ability and I don't? Winnie can read cards and see auras, and you inherited your mother's gift. What about me? I have nothing but dreams at night that seem real where I can fly." She looked at Jaxon and then glanced away quickly as if embarrassed by something.

Winnie asked before he could, "What do you mean dreams where you can fly?"

Liv hesitated, then explained, sounding reluctant, "Sometimes at night it feels like I'm awake but I'm not in my body. I thought I was only dreaming, except the other night when I . . ." She trailed off, now definitely embarrassed.

"When you what?" Jaxon asked, his curiosity piqued.

Her eyes flickered back to him. "I saw your dog."

He let out a surprised laugh. "You saw my what?"

"Your dog." Her face turned pink.

He leaned forward, completely fascinated. "You saw my dog?"

"And you. Asleep." Her face bloomed even pinker, and she started talking fast. "I was thinking of you in the dream and flying around the town, and suddenly I was at your house. You were asleep. Your dog was in a blue doggie bed."

His eyes widened. "His bed is blue."

Liv hesitated. "And he has a patch of white fur on his chest?"

Jaxon nodded in amazement. "That's why we call him Alfredo. You really saw us. That's incredible."

She rushed to explain. "I wasn't trying to spy. I just ended up there. Probably because I was thinking of you again—I mean—" She abruptly stopped talking.

Jaxon sat there stunned. She had dreamed about him and been thinking about him.

Alone at night.

Right now he was the one who felt like he could fly.

Winnie sat forward in the rocking chair, suddenly animated. "Liv, that's not dreaming, it's called astral projection or remote viewing and it's freaking awesome! It's a real thing. I promise. You're actually going to those places. Why have you never told me?"

"Because it's not normal. I have no idea how it happens."

Winnie insisted, "That's why you have to practice."

"How do you practice dreaming, Win?" Liv countered. "It happens when I go to sleep."

"I'm telling you, you're not asleep."

Jaxon could only listen in amazement, still trying to wrap his head around the fact that Liv had visited his room and could travel to places with her mind. It seemed like she'd been keeping her own secrets.

Winnie erupted. "I don't think you understand the full magnitude here. If you get good enough, you can travel anywhere inside your head! Anywhere *on Earth*! Do you know how many nights I've laid in bed trying to astral project and get out of my body and fly? I've read books. I tried guided meditations. Did you know the army *and* the CIA even had programs where they psychically spied on other countries with remote viewers?"

"Great, so I can work for the CIA." Liv sat back with a huff and her hair fell out of the clip again.

This time Jaxon reached out and took the clip before she could.

Liv gave him the shyest look, and he began to see clearly she liked him as much as he liked her. Her admitting she was visiting him while he was sleeping was a huge confession. How many nights had she come?

She finally asked, "Are you going to give that back?"

"Not yet," he said and pocketed it. It might be a small detail, but if they were going back to the apartment tonight and she was stepping out on the balcony, the hair clip had been nowhere in his vision. He'd read about the butterfly effect and how the slightest change could alter future trajectories. Her hair was down tonight—he knew because he would run his fingers through it—and he refused for anything to change what he already saw. Not even a hair clip.

Liv searched his eyes, as if trying to read his mind. Her mouth pursed into a perplexed frown. "Is there a reason why you're stealing it?"

"A very good one that I'll tell you later," he said cryptically, and thunder rumbled in the distance.

Winnie interrupted them. "Guys, I'm getting a seriously bad vibe sitting here." She held up two more Tarot cards: *The Devil* and *Death* cards. "I think we should go. I say we go back to the apartment, finish reading the manuscript, and wait for Liv's dad."

"I agree. Let's head out." Jaxon nodded. Liv sighed but didn't say anything. They both knew how she felt about seeing her father.

The sound of the back gate opening halted the decision, and Liv jumped up. Forester and his dad were home.

Forester's dad wheeled in with a grim expression. Forester looked haggard, like he'd aged ten years in the past two hours.

Winnie asked first, wringing her hands anxiously, "What'd you find out?"

Forester's dad gave them the details. "Matty's neighbor reported seeing a plumbing truck parked in front of Matty's house yesterday afternoon. The neighbor thought they were doing repairs. Another neighbor across the street swore he heard a girl scream once out on the street last night."

Forester rubbed his face. "Her car was unlocked with two suitcases in the back that were rifled. She never would have left her stuff like that."

His father agreed. "My guess is they were taken just after she arrived."

"Taken?" Winnie's voice wobbled.

"By whoever it is who's after you." Forester's father pinned them with his eyes.

Forester looked like a tiger in a cage. He brought his fist down on the counter. "Nebony and Matty are in this mess because of those stupid letters. I say we offer them in exchange."

"To who, son?" Forester's dad shot down the idea. "We don't know who took them. We're fishing in the dark." He turned to Liv. "What I want to know is why those letters were in your house in the first place."

"We weren't supposed to find them." Liv relayed what the attorney said. "The attorney's office is coming to take them away."

"Well they should have come sooner," Forester growled.

Jaxon came to her defense. "Nebony never should have posted the pictures," he told Forester. "She was only there in the first place to see you and try to get back together again."

"So it's my fault?" Forester erupted.

"You calm down," Forester's dad said firmly. "I'll put out a missing person report and contact their parents." He asked Liv, "Who's your attorney? I'll call them too. Maybe they can help." Forester's dad took down all the information he needed. They were so focused on the conversation that it took Jaxon a minute to realize Forester was no longer there with them.

"Uh, guys?" Jaxon saw the front door was cracked open. "Forester went across the street." Forester's dad swore and Jaxon hurried to offer, "I'll go get him."

Liv grabbed onto his arm. "But we're not supposed to be over there."

"I'll be quick. I promise."

"No! Jaxon! You can't be seen. Please." Liv kept hold of him, looking terrified.

He took her hand and tried to reassure her. "It'll be okay. I promise."

"How can you say that?"

"Because I already saw us back at the apartment tonight." He didn't say on the balcony. "Just wait here. I promise I'll be back." He gave her hand a firm squeeze and hurried outside.

Across the street, Forester was a looming shadow at Liv's front door.

"Forester wait!" Jaxon jogged across the street and joined him on the porch, whispering, "What the hell are you doing?"

"What do you think?" Forester was trying to figure out which of Liv's keys to use.

"You took her keys?" Jaxon exclaimed in shock, then looked around, feeling exposed. He hissed, "We shouldn't be over here."

"What if no one's come yet?" Forester whispered back. "What if the letters are still up there? We can use them to get Nebony back."

"That's a horrible plan."

"You got a better one? Let's at least see if the letters are here or not." Forester got the door open and went inside.

Jaxon hurried after him, no longer arguing because he wanted to know too. "Just don't turn on the lights."

Forester ran up the stairs, taking them two at time with Jaxon right behind him. They reached the attic and stopped in the doorway, in shock to find all the boxes were gone.

Not just the letters.

The whole attic had been gutted, now just a shell of a room. Every single scrap of paper on the floor had been taken.

His mother's letters were gone.

Jaxon felt a hollow ache in his chest, as if a part of him had been taken too.

Forester ran his hands through his hair and paced back and forth. "Jax, what do we do? Talk to me. I'm losing it. What do we do?"

"I don't know." Jaxon's mind was a muddle.

"You're the psychic! Do something! Save Nebony like you did Kaitlyn!"

"It doesn't work that way!"

"Well make it work! We have to do something!" Forester had tears in his eyes. Jaxon had only seen him cry once. The day his dad was shot. Forester continued to pace. "You were right. This is all my fault."

"I didn't say that!"

"If I hadn't pushed her away, she would have been with me last night. This never would have happened. What if she's hurt? What if she—" Forester stopped talking, unable to finish.

Jaxon turned away, becoming distracted by a feeling of menace entering the house.

An inner voice inside his head began screaming.

Leave now. Men are coming. Their car is almost here.

Suddenly a violent series of images cascaded in his mind in rapid-fire progression:

Forester is in front of a black SUV, struggling with two men in the rain. One of them pushes him to the ground and ties his hands with a zip tie.

Jaxon jerked away from the vision and looked around wildly. They had to get out. Desperate, he ran to the attic window and opened it.

"What are you doing?" Forester stopped pacing.

"Armed men in a black SUV are coming here to get the letters." Jaxon grabbed Forester's arm and dragged him to the window as he explained, "We have to go. Right now."

"Out the window?" Forester asked in disbelief.

"It's the only way."

Seconds later a black SUV rolled up to the front of the house. Jaxon and Forester ducked down to hide.

"Okay, that's impressive," Forester muttered. His phone dinged with a text from his dad.

Car outside. Get out.

"Put that on silent." Jaxon rose up and peeked out the window. "As soon as they come inside, we go," he whispered and then rushed to explain. "When we climb down, run to the right and hide in the neighbor's backyard. Don't run toward your house or you'll get caught. I saw it. You have to hide."

Forester gave him a hard look and nodded. They watched in frozen terror as down below two men with guns, dressed all in black, disappeared through the front door.

Jaxon whispered over the thundering of his heart, "We go now. You first," he insisted, and Forester climbed onto the house's ledge. He grabbed the nearest branch and swung down, his body dangling in the air. He walked his hands across the limb. Jaxon was right behind him, ignoring the sting of the bark. They hadn't climbed a tree together since they were eight. They both dropped to the ground with a thud and ran for the neighbor's yard, jumping over the hedge to hide.

Jaxon peered through the crack of leaves and tried to slow his breathing, sure the men could hear him from inside.

Suddenly he wasn't so sure about his future anymore. Could he get back to the house? To Liv? To the apartment tonight like he'd promised? He'd never been wrong with a prediction before, but he'd also never been in danger. If he got out of this, he promised himself he would never take the future for granted or assume what he saw was set in stone. Now he could see that had been arrogance on his part.

He whispered to Forester, "We need to wait until they leave."

Forester whispered back, a desperate edge in his voice, "I have to find her, Jax. I don't care what happens to me anymore. I just have to find her. Tell my dad to track me with my phone." Then he took off running to the men's car before Jaxon could stop him.

It all happened in seconds.

He called, "Forest, wait!" but Forester kept running, making a dash to the back of the SUV. Jaxon watched in horror as he got in the very back to hide.

Forester's house porchlight came on across the street, and the front door swung open. Forester's dad wheeled out, yelling, "Hey! Get out of there!" right as the two men came running from the house, thinking he was yelling at them.

"Police!" Forester's dad screamed, a gun in his hand. "Stop where you are!" The men kept running and jumped into the SUV, peeling out.

Forester's dad aimed but didn't fire. Not with Forester in the car.

Jaxon ran into the street and watched the taillights grow smaller as the car swerved the corner and was gone with his best friend trapped inside.

28

meteoromancy:
divination through thunder and lightning

"NO!" WINNIE TORE OUT OF THE house as the SUV gunned down the street. It ran a stop sign and jumped the corner, disappearing out of sight. Only moments ago, she and Liv had been in the living room hiding behind the curtain when they saw the SUV pull up. Forester's dad had texted Forester and hurried to get his gun as two armed men went inside the house.

Moments later, Winnie spotted Forester on the roof with Jaxon right behind him.

"There they are!" Winnie clutched Liv's arm as she watched them climb down a tree and hide behind the hedge. "They're out. They made it," she announced, dizzy with relief. Liv looked too terrified to speak.

Then suddenly Forester darted out from behind the bush and ran straight toward the men's car.

"Wait. What the hell is he doing?" Winnie pressed her hands against the glass. She couldn't believe he was getting in their car. He curled up in the back to hide and pulled the door shut.

Forester's dad was the first outside, yelling just as the men came running out. They were in the SUV within seconds, driving off.

Jaxon ran out into the middle of the street and doubled over, looking like he might be sick. He stood up and put his hands in his hair. "I can't believe he did it."

Winnie couldn't either. It was a full-on *Red* thing to do—people with red auras were bold, brash, brave, and sometimes utterly unpredictable.

Forester's dad was already hurrying to his van to get behind the wheel. "You three get out of sight. Stay inside." He banged on the side of the car. "Come on!" The van's electronic doors couldn't open fast enough to load him into the driver's seat.

Jaxon rushed over to him. "He said to track him on your phone. I'll follow you."

"No!" Forester's dad hoisted himself in with one strong move and revved the car. "You three stay put. I'll call you." He said to Liv, "If you hear from Grayson, tell him to call me right away. This is his goddamn mess!"

Liv flinched at his words but nodded, and they watched him drive off.

Winnie decided to take charge. "We are *not* staying here." She ordered Jaxon, "Give me the key. I'm driving." She held out her hand. He was in no state to drive.

Jaxon handed it over in a daze, and she ushered them both through the house and out the back gate. The entire street was quiet, the only sound the soft patter of rain falling. They speed walked to the car, trying not to look conspicuous.

Jaxon took the backseat, giving Liv the front. Winnie tried not to think about how this Mercedes Jeep-car-tank was bigger than anything she'd ever driven before in her life. She didn't even wait for Liv and Jaxon to finish buckling their seatbelts before she took off. The sooner they were away from Liv's house the better. She had known it was a bad idea coming here—had felt it in her gut. Her adrenaline was running sky high, and she kept checking the rearview mirror to make sure no one was following them.

Liv was leaning forward squinting, on the lookout, her hands white-knuckled on the dash. "I think that's a police car parked at the gas station."

Winnie didn't even hesitate and turned into another subdivision, her heart hammering. She went several blocks and tried to get on a road to get them to Route 9 but there was another police car too. Out of the blue, their sleepy little town was crawling with police, and they were all looking for them.

"We need to stick to the back roads," Liv said.

Jaxon finally spoke up. "You can't keep going this way or you'll be too close to my house."

Suddenly it felt like Hyde Park had become a maze, and Winnie didn't know how to get out.

She fought her rising panic—she was seconds away from hyper-ventilating. Not knowing what else to do, she started to pray to her dad for help because she could use a guardian angel right now. The moment she sent the thought, goosebumps rose on her arms and a sense of calm hit her. It was the closest she had ever come to feeling truly connected to him. Whatever intuition existed inside her turned on like a headlight, and she thought of The Hermit card—the wise man holding a lantern in the dark. Right now she was The Hermit. She was the wise man, the wise woman, with all the wisdom inside her. She only had to use it.

She didn't question herself anymore but just drove, no longer stressing where or when she needed to turn. Instead, her sixth sense told her. Liv and Jaxon were talking but Winnie tuned them out. The world around her receded. She was deep in the zone, on autopilot, her psyche in the driver's seat now.

Before she knew it, they were on the Interstate heading back to the apartment. Winnie felt her awareness shift. She'd done it.

Liv said, "That was amazing. How did you do that?"

Winnie shook her head, not sure how to explain it. "I just tried to stay calm and follow my instincts." Her mind went back to what her father had written. He was right. Conviction and will were powerful forces.

No one spoke for miles as she drove. The rain grew stronger on the windshield, battering the car, and she turned on the radio.

The announcer was saying, "Things are heating up on the election front. The New York primary is only days away, and I would say the political stage is on fire. Charles Becker and Senator Tom Miller are the front-runner favorites. But before we see those election results, first we have to weather the massive storm hitting the state tonight. Hurricane advisory is in effect from ten p.m. So batten down the hatches, stay dry, and tune in for possible evacuation orders if it gets worse. I'll keep you—"

Winnie shut it off and tried hard not to panic again. Now they had a hurricane warning on top of everything else. Matty and Nebony were missing—and she prayed Forester would be okay. She couldn't help but feel they were running out of time to help any of them. An urgency was welling inside her to finish her father's story.

"Guys, we need to read the rest of the pages." She glanced over to Liv.

"What, right now?" Liv snapped out of her emotional coma and looked back at her in confusion.

Winnie nodded. "Yeah, use your phone's flashlight and read it to me?" She needed to know the rest of the story ASAP. She could feel it in her bones. Her father had known one day she would find what he'd written because he'd written it *for her*. Right now, she needed to know what had happened in the past if they were going to stay alive.

29

prophecy:

prediction of what is to come, an instruction

GRAYSON'S MOTHER, MAXINE, WAS A MEMBER of the Premonitions Bureau and had gone to Vassar. We sat down and told her about Jerald Peterson, our abilities, and how we believed they may have stemmed from a scientific study they took part in. Maxine was shaken as she listened to our confession. She'd always known Grayson had extrasensory abilities above and beyond the norm. Now to meet two more like him. Clement, Grayson's dad, was beside her, holding her hand as we all sat around the dining room table together.

They had Dr. Alberty, the scientist in question, come to the house to meet us. Dr. Alberty was dazed by what we told him.

His research study our parents had taken part in had attempted to excite the magnetite crystals in the brain to enhance mental focus. Dr. Alberty ended the study after a year because he hadn't gotten the desired results.

"Why magnetite?" I asked him.

He gave me a patient smile, explaining, "The human body generates magnetite crystals in the brain, hundreds of millions of them, though we aren't sure why. Birds, bees, and dolphins have it and use it to navigate the globe. In the human mind, magnetite acts as an antenna to help navigate time. Magnetite also helps generate electricity in power plants."

Dr. Alberty later discovered that we all had ten times the amount of magnetite crystals than a normal brain and the crystals kept multiplying as we aged, causing our abilities to increase as well. Alberty predicted we would reach our full potential when we turned twenty-five, when the human brain has fully developed.

The discovery his original test subjects went on to have children with increased magnetite would set his research on a whole new path. For the first time, I felt relief someone could unravel the mystery of our abilities. The magnetite finally explained us.

It is magnetite that powers psychic abilities in the brain, and with the amount of ours, we are at the top of the EHBF pyramid.

Shelly shared her premonition with them. "Someone from the Defense Department named Stan Storlie is going to contact the Premonitions Bureau. He wants the letters Jerald Peterson wrote. If they find our letters, they could find us."

"No one is getting the letters," Maxine promised us vehemently. "Or uncovering who you are."

The Premonitions Bureau had already been considering closing the study. The researcher who had first brainstormed the idea in the 1960s had just turned eighty and was ready to retire. The twenty-five-year study had provided clear evidence sixth sense was real and mass predictions often happened for large-scale tragedies.

About one in every hundred letters was a bona fide premonition, giving the world a one percent rate of psychic ability. Dr. Alberty made an offer to the Bureau to buy the letters, the whole collection, explaining it would be for a new study, and the Premonitions Bureau quietly closed their doors for good.

The letters were secretly buried.

Weeks later, just as Shelly predicted, the Defense Department sent a formal request to the Premonitions Bureau to review the study and gain access to the letters.

The Bureau's response was regretful, informing them their offices had closed after a building fire and the letters had been destroyed.

The world soon forgot about the Premonitions Bureau, and for a time we believed Grayson, Shelly, and I were safe.

As our abilities grew, we still wanted to help bring about a positive change in the world. Because if psychics can predict the future, we can change it too—and if enough powerful psychics come together, we have the potential to create a new future for the world.

We decided, if we were going to create change in the world, we needed to do it from the shadows to stay safe. First, we needed money. A lot of money. Gambling is an age-old dance with intuition. Fortunately, when you know the future, you can bet on it and win.

We started with horse races. Grayson was the best at it. He could look at the horses' numbers and automatically know the outcome. Betting on races became our day jobs and the money started rolling in. We rotated tracks in New York starting in Saratoga, then hit the top races across the country.

We made a killing at the Kentucky Derby, the Preakness Stakes in Baltimore, and the Breeders' Cup. Hong Kong came next, where horseracing is a billion-dollar industry, and onto Japan, which has the biggest horseracing industry in the world. We lived a double life, putting ourselves through college and traveling overseas in the summers and on breaks to gamble. All the while, we invested our earnings in the stock market. We knew the companies that would one day be giants, which ones would rise and fall. We knew the trends, the catastrophes, and the wars.

When the zeitgeist is in your sight, so is money—and we had a plan what to do with it. We set up the Mage Foundation, a scientific institute devoted to researching EHBF abilities.

If Jerald Peterson had been the only psychic connected to Dr. Alberty's study in the public eye, then perhaps we could have continued on without discovery. But when Rachel and Ryland Davis made the news in 2007, we knew we were in trouble.

Rachel and Ryland were telepathic twins who excelled at mind reading and precognition. Their mother, Margaret, had gone to Vassar and taken part in Alberty's experiment. Like us, they used their abilities, but they weren't as good at hiding it. They were accused of insider trading on the stock market after making a fortune. In order to avoid jail, they publicly admitted they knew which stocks to buy and sell because they were psychic. They offered to take tests to prove it.

We watched the situation unfold on the news. The entire country—the whole world—had tuned into the story. Then, a week later, Rachel and Ryland vanished. Their story made top headlines for two days and then disappeared as well. The last day anyone reported seeing them, Rachel left Dr. Alberty a strange message. She and her brother had been contacted by a man named Stan Storlie with the Defense Department. Stan wanted to run tests on their abilities and was interested in recruiting them into a top secret defense program studying EHBF. He said he could make all the criminal charges go away and give them a new life. Rachel was afraid to say no. It was the last anyone heard from them.

Shelly became obsessed with finding out what happened to the twins. She was certain it was only a matter of time until Stan Storlie connected Jerald Peterson to Ryland and Rachel, and that would lead him straight to Dr. Alberty and us.

Dr. Alberty was on the brink of understanding the mechanics of psychic ability. He was deep into his research on magnetite crystals and had moved his lab to an undisclosed location in Northern Alaska near the Arctic Circle.

He chose Alaska because of the aurora borealis. Also known as the northern lights, the aurora borealis creates a magnetic field, one of the strongest in the world. With an aurora borealis, the magnetic charge in the atmosphere is the most powerful.

It is where *we* are the most powerful.

Days before Shelly died, Grayson flew to Alaska to conduct tests with Dr. Alberty. The fact no one saw Shelly's death happening until it was too late was inconceivable. We couldn't and still can't understand how it was possible. There was no warning. No foresight.

Shelly called me the day she died, saying she'd found something on Stan Storlie on the dark web. She accessed an Artificial Intelligence military study and a black ops program called *Clair Dominus*, referencing Jerald Peterson and the twins. Clair Dominus was the name she had written down in her notebook years ago.

I was on the phone with her when it happened.

Her computer fritzed out and then crashed. She thought she had been hacked and said she'd call me back. It was the last time we ever spoke.

A strange foreboding came over me as the hours passed, like a shadow invading my body. I tried calling her. I waited, telling myself she must be busy. She had a newborn baby on her hands. Jaxon wasn't yet one. I tried for two more hours to reach her. Then a premonition slammed into me with such force I couldn't breathe.

I was outside Shelly's house with Chris, her husband. The garage door was open with smoke billowing out. Shelly was lying on the grass. Unconscious.

I grabbed my keys and raced over to their house. On the way, I called Chris, frantic. Shelly was in trouble, and we had to get to her, but we arrived too late. Her car had been left running in the garage, the space thick with exhaust. Shelly's husband is a doctor, and he tried to revive her but couldn't. It was only later I saw missed calls from Grayson in Alaska. We'd both been too late to save her.

How could Grayson and I not have foreseen her death? We were a triskelion. We were best friends who'd built a life together trying to save people from events in the future, yet we couldn't save her.

Not for one second did we believe Shelly killed herself. The police said her computer had been wiped clean. A computer virus, they said.

I was terrified. Now scared for my wife and newborn daughter. I was the last one to talk to Shelly. Anyone could trace that call. Over the years, we'd tried to hide who we were and what we were doing, but if someone looked too closely, they'd find my mother had gone to Vassar too.

With Shelly's death, I've begun to worry my life will be cut short without warning. I've started scrying several times a day to catch a glimpse of my future in the stillness of the water. In quiet moments, I study my palms and the lines on my hands. My life line is neither long nor short, but as time goes on, the lines grow fainter, like a river dried up, until I've become convinced I won't see my child's second birthday. Instead, she'll read these words one day, and I won't be there to explain what happened—which is why I'm trying to do my best now.

We need to figure out how to protect Dr. Alberty's research until he's ready to share it with the world. Soon, I'm going to tell my wife about my past and what I can do. There will be no more secrets. She knows I'm highly intuitive, but I never told her about the Bureau or Dr. Alberty's study. Grayson, Shelly, and I all agreed years ago it was safer for our loved ones not to know the whole truth.

Grayson told his wife he wants a divorce and isn't fit to be a father. My heart all but stopped as I heard this news. He told her he wants to go live alone in Alaska. But I know it's a lie. He's trying to protect them.

I have no idea how Grayson can leave his family like this. I just booked a flight to Alaska to talk him out of whatever it is he thinks he's doing. Grayson once told me years ago that he wrote a letter to his future daughter to read when she was older. I often think about that letter and wonder what I would say in mine. Well, now it's time.

You, my daughter, Winnifred Blaze Scott, are sleeping in your crib as I type this. Your mom and I call you Winnie.

I don't have Grayson's breadth of vision. I can't see as far ahead as he can. So if you're reading these words and something has happened to me, something unforeseen, please trust Grayson.

We do have a plan, and I pray that it works.

If we fail and I am no longer with you, no longer here in the physical world, although my mind and spirit may be in another plane of existence (call it heaven, call it the afterlife, call it by any name), I will still be with you. That's not only a promise, it's science, because when two atoms entangle, they are connected forever through space and time.

Gnosis is the deepest intuition in our hearts, and the bridge between Heaven and Earth is shorter than we think. No one is ever really gone.

You can always call on me, because love *is* always and forever.

Your father,
Sawyer

<ENCRYPTED TRANSMISSION>
<DEFENSE INTELLIGENCE AGENCY SERVER>

<From: MIRIAM>
<Priority: HIGH>

Reference to Mad Merlin located in a book summary written by Sawyer Scott.

The Gnosis Trap: Unpublished novel, file not found. No ISBN number.

Shared text:
A secret government organization is hunting psychics in order to map their minds and transfer their ability to a powerful supercomputer named Miriam. The future has become a chessboard and only one man can play the game and possibly win. A psychic who calls himself Mad Merlin.

Send a team to the Scott residence:
15587 Sycamore Street in Hyde Park.

Identify Sawyer Scott's computer and bring it to Storlie.

30

JAXON

backwards time:
term in mathematical physics that reverses the order of events

JAXON RODE IN THE BACK OF the car, listening to Liv read the last of Sawyer's manuscript aloud when images and information started racing through his mind at lightning speed. It was as if his brain had downloaded a zip file and needed to sort everything out.

> *A plane touches down on a JFK runway through driving wind and rain. Grayson is on the last flight from Fairbanks before all planes are grounded due to the weather. He is one of the hundred and fifty passengers. A towering man, he moves with slow deliberation, a point of calm in the busy chaos. He looks as if he's stepped from the wilds of Alaska with his mane of chestnut-brown hair and an even redder beard. He's wearing jeans and an old flannel shirt. He walks down the terminal of JFK, deliberately looking at the security cameras. A challenge in his eyes. The doors to the airport open and he exits.*

Suddenly other images eclipsed Liv's father—Jaxon's whole body clenched from the violent onslaught.

Forester is on his stomach, pinned to the ground by one of the men in the SUV. His face pressed into the gravel as rain mercilessly beats down. They are outside on the side of a deserted road.

The SUV idles in front of them. The man digs his knee into Forester's back, making him cry out. Forester's father is inside his van, ten feet away, screaming at the attacker to stop.

When another man rounds the corner of the SUV and shoots twice, killing Forester and his dad instantly.

Jaxon sat up with a gasp, the impact of the bullet still resonating inside him.

"No!" he screamed in anguish.

Startled, Winnie accidentally swerved out of her lane onto the emergency shoulder, the car shuddering from the gravel. Liv twisted in her seat to Jaxon in alarm.

"Stop the car!" he pleaded, unable to breathe as the image replayed in his mind of Forester lifeless on the ground, his blood pooling in the rain.

Liv unbuckled her seatbelt and crawled into the back to help him. Winnie put the hazard lights on and started slowing down, staying on the shoulder.

"He's dead. He's dead." Jaxon couldn't stop saying it.

"Who's dead?" Liv asked, holding his arms.

He needed to tell her what'd he seen, but he couldn't get the words out. The panic was suffocating him.

"Jaxon! Who?" Liv gripped his shoulders, trying to shake him out of it. "Talk to me."

"Forester," he finally choked out, breaking down.

"What? He's dead?" Winnie cried out.

"I saw it." His whole body clenched with pain. He thought his heart might stop.

Liv was talking to him, but he couldn't hear the words until she yelled, "Listen to me!" She took his hands in hers, squeezing them hard. "Jaxon!" The harsh command in her voice snapped his gaze to hers and she said, "Whatever you saw, you saw it so you can *stop* it. You can stop it from happening. Just like Kaitlyn."

Her words tried to force their way into his mind. What was she saying?

"You can stop it like you did with Kaitlyn," she said it again with conviction.

Like Kaitlyn.

Their gazes locked. She put her hands on his cheeks and said it again, fierce determination on her face. "You can stop it. You have to believe you can stop it."

His connection to her right now was like a lifeline, a buoy in the storm—and his mind started to race. He *had* saved Kaitlyn and changed her future.

Forester wasn't dead yet. The trigger hadn't been pulled. Maybe he could stop it. If the future was fluid, he just needed to change its course. Mad Merlin told them the trick was to see it first.

He expelled a breath. "Give me your phone." Liv scrambled to get it. He closed his eyes and tried to see where the murder had happened—would happen—but in order to do that he had to watch it all again.

He gritted his teeth and forced his mind to replay the vision. But this time he studied all the details of the surroundings, looking for markers that could show him where it was. There was no time to question himself. He called 911. Forester and his father's life depended on how he handled these few next minutes.

"I need to report a shooting. Police officer Drew Torres and his son. They've been shot and killed by two men in a black SUV." He heard Winnie and Liv's sharp intake of breath as they listened, now fully grasping the situation. "Right by Kingston-Rhinecliff Bridge on the 199. Behind the farmstand before the bridge. Please assist right away.

The killers are still there." He hung up before the operator could ask him any questions.

They sat in silence. Liv and Winnie were both in tears now. Jaxon closed his eyes and tried to sense if he'd done enough.

The shooting was still minutes away. Forester and his father's lives were ticking down. Had he kept the clock from stopping?

He mentally searched for a new premonition to replace the old one.

Winnie was the one who broke the silence with a whimper. "Will the police make it in time? Are they . . .?" She couldn't finish the question.

The rain outside continued to pummel the car in heavy sheets as if the sky were falling. The hammering noise on the roof coupled with the bright headlights of cars passing them on the highway felt otherworldly.

Jaxon could feel the storm fueling him. He searched the future for a new outcome, his mind like a computer hitting the refresh command over and over to get the page to reload.

Forester struggles. He's pinned to the ground. His father screams.

Then, like a glitch, the premonition altered.

A police officer yells, "Freeze! Drop your weapons! Hands in the air!"

The man holding Forester drops his gun and puts his hands up.

And the moment of their death is gone like a memory that never existed.

"Oh my God." Jaxon put his head in his hands, trying to breathe again.

"What happened?" Liv's voice shook. "What happened?" she kept saying.

Overcome, he hugged Liv to him and buried his face in her neck.

She wrapped her arms around him and squeezed tight. "You did it?"

"I did it," he could barely get the words out, too choked up, and he pulled her closer. Winnie laid her head on the steering wheel. They were all overcome.

Jaxon couldn't bring himself to let Liv go. Because of her, Forester was alive. Her conviction had made him believe. The mixture of relief and euphoria filling him was indescribable. If the future was a wave, he had just ridden the biggest wave imaginable, a terrifyingly colossal one, and actually changed the course of the future through sheer will alone. Now he understood why Mad Merlin had issued a warning about seers of the future being hunted—because this, this was *power*.

31

FORESTER

cledonomancy:
divination by overheard words

HARDLY DARING TO BREATHE, FORESTER STAYED quiet in the back of the SUV. He silently slid his cell phone out of his hiking boot and opened the tracking app connected to his dad's phone.

Right now, it showed they both were on the highway heading north. His dad was several cars behind him. Forester texted him.

I'm okay. They don't know I'm here.

An automatic reply came back:

I'm driving with Do Not Disturb While Driving turned on.

I'll see your message when I get where I'm going. Thanks.

Forester gritted his teeth in frustration. Then the men up front start-ed talking. Forester froze, straining to listen over the sound of the rain outside.

"Can't believe we're running this down," the driver said. "Feels like a wild goose chase."

"What kind of letters are they?"

"Some long-term study on psychic ability. Storlie has been trying to get his hands on it for years. Says it's being funded by a foreign terrorist organization called the Mage Foundation."

Foreign terrorists? Forester hit record on his cell's video to get the conversation.

"Never heard of the Mage Foundation."

"They're out of Zurich working on EHBF," the driver said, "the race for Superman."

"You work with Storlie long? He as nuts as they say?"

"Let's just say Stan Storlie has high conviction in keeping the status quo. He's been in the game a long time."

"Anyone else meeting us at the safe house?"

"No. We're keeping the circle tight on this. I'm going to drop you and deliver the package."

"What about the kids? Are we done with them?"

"No orders yet. Just gas them if they act up."

Forester listened in horror. *Gas them?*

The car went quiet, then the driver said, "Think we got a tail. Blue van. Been with us for a while."

Forester almost swore out loud. With shaking hands he typed out a text to his dad:

They spotted you. Fall back.

The auto-reply appeared on his screen again.

"It's that neighbor in the wheelchair. We should find a spot and take care of him."

Forester was in a full-blown panic. Take care of him? What did that mean? He texted again.

They're going to pull over. Don't stop!

The auto-reply came back. The SUV slowed down, about to pull over.

"Take the road behind that fruit stand," the partner directed the driver.

Forester's mind raced. Of course his father would pull over too and confront them, even though he couldn't walk or get out of the car. This was going all wrong. He heard a gun being cocked.

The guy in the passenger seat jumped out in the rain. Forester put his hand on the back door handle, his whole body quaking with fear and adrenaline. He'd throw open the door and tackle the guy. Just like football.

He heard the guy say to his dad, "You're at the wrong place, my friend."

Forester shoved the door open and charged with a roar, tackling the man down. "What the hell?" The agent yelled for his partner's help.

They both hit the pavement hard, and Forester began punching wildly.

Seconds later, two hands grabbed Forester from behind and hoisted him off.

The guy's partner threw Forester to the ground and pinned him on his stomach with his knee. Forester's dad was yelling at the man to stop while the other agent readied his gun from the other side of the SUV. He was about to aim just as a cop car pulled up with its lights flashing.

"Freeze!" Two police officers jumped out of the car with guns drawn. "Drop your weapons! Hands in the air!" They had their guns trained on them.

His dad was yelling something over the rain. Forester couldn't make out the words. He was still pinned to the ground, rain stinging his eyes. His lungs were burning, his back searing in pain as the driver kept him immobile, using his full body weight.

The man told the police, "We're with the Defense Intelligence Agency and transporting this prisoner. He's a high-level asset connected to a known terrorist group."

His dad screamed, "Terrorist my ass! That's my son!"

Forester was petrified. It felt like the guy pinning him was about to break his ribs. He choked out in pain, "Dad!"

The police officer yelled, "Drop your weapon now! Slowly. Hands in the air."

The agent did as he was told and slowly raised his hands up. "My ID's in my front pocket."

The officer approached and pulled it out, looked at it closely, and walked back to his car to call it in. He ran his dad's next. "You both check out." The police officers did not holster their weapons. "Want to tell us what the hell is going on here? We got an anonymous call that an officer and his son had been shot and killed."

Forester felt his chest constrict. *Jaxon.* It was the only thing he could think—Jaxon had called and saved him.

His father rushed to explain. "These men broke into my neighbor's house and abducted my son. We believe they're suspects in a missing person's case for two teenagers. My son is *not* a suspect in any DIA investigation."

The driver shook his head in regret. "Fathers will say anything to protect their kid. His son is an eyewitness to a highly classified investigation and is being taken in for questioning. I'm not at liberty to say more." He tied Forester's hands with a zip tie, pulled it tight, and yanked him to his feet. He patted Forester down for weapons, found only keys in his pocket, and tossed them in the grass.

Forester started to emotionally break down. This whole plan of his had backfired.

His dad yelled, "I'm telling you, they're lying! They didn't know my son was in the car."

The driver kept his grip on him tight. "You want more information, call the Pentagon. We need to be on our way."

His dad's eyes filled with tears of frustration as he watched Forester get shoved into the back seat of the SUV. He called out to him, "Son, do what they say. I'll be with you soon," he promised. Then he yelled at the men. "Don't you dare lay a finger on him! I'm coming for you!" He turned to the police officers. "I want to know where they're taking him."

The agent smirked. "That's classified," and he got in the car.

As they drove off, the agent in the passenger seat turned to look at him. "Hiding in the back. Dumb move, kid."

Forester looked down at his boot and tried to quell his panic. His cell phone was still hidden with the tracking app on. "The girl and the guy you kidnapped last night, are they still alive?"

"Shut up and put this on," the driver ordered and tossed a hood at him. "You'll find out soon enough."

<ENCRYPTED TRANSMISSION>
<DEFENSE INTELLIGENCE AGENCY SERVER>

<From: MIRIAM>
<Priority: HIGH>

Facial recognition identified Grayson Spencer leaving JFK Airport. He is traveling under an assumed name.

Place ex-wife Hazel Hall under surveillance in case he contacts her. She used a credit card to check into the Plaza Hotel.

Speed efforts to find Liv Hall, Winnifred Scott, and Jaxon Coleson and terminate.

If the daughter dies, Grayson Spencer will step out from the shadows. High probability he has come for her.

32

LIV

psyche:
the totality of elements forming the mind

THE EXPLOSIVE FEAR AND ADRENALINE FROM Jaxon's prediction ended like fireworks. Forester had almost died but was alive thanks to Jaxon. He'd been captured by the men, but at least he was alive. Now they were all three sitting in the car still grappling with the shock. Liv was having trouble wrapping her brain around what just happened. She couldn't imagine witnessing someone's death in her mind and then having to rush to stop it in real life. Jaxon had done it with seconds to spare.

"You did it." She put a comforting hand on his leg.

Jaxon nodded but didn't look at her. He had one hand covering his eyes as he tried to calm down. She went to return to the front seat to give him space, but he said, "Stay," his voice hoarse with emotion. He reached for her hand and put it back on his leg, pulling her close to him.

They sat in silence for several minutes. Only the clicking sound of the hazard lights filled the car. To Liv, it sounded like a clock ticking, and she couldn't help but feel like they were running out of time. "We can't stay pulled over. Someone might stop."

"I know." Winnie finally sat up and took a deep breath, gripping the wheel.

"You okay to drive?" Liv asked her.

"No, but we have to get there," Winnie said grimly and pulled back onto the highway.

No one said a word the rest of the way. Liv stared at her fingers laced with Jaxon's. Their hands rested on his thigh; their bodies nestled against each other. Jaxon had his eyes closed as if he were sleeping, but his thumb gently stroked her palm back and forth.

She was mentally exhausted but needed to stay focused. Sawyer had written to trust her father if anything ever happened to him. Which felt ironic because Liv couldn't help but think her father was the one to blame for what was happening. He was the one who put the letters in the attic. His name was on the boxes. He wrote the omen, already knowing full well they would find the letters.

He was the one who had tried to manipulate fate. But whatever plan he'd concocted years ago, Liv didn't want to be a part of it. Right now she, Jaxon, and Winnie needed to figure out what to do and how to find Forester, Matty, and Nebony.

Because one thing was clear: they were on their own.

When they reached the apartment, Winnie beelined to the kitchen. "I'm going to put on some coffee."

Liv nodded and crossed her arms protectively, still feeling like she was in an emotional freefall. She looked around the apartment, wondering when her father would show up. He could come anytime.

Maybe tonight. That thought filled her with absolute dread. Suddenly, she wanted to be anywhere but here. But the only place to escape was the balcony.

Jaxon was staring at her with an intense light in his eyes, as if he knew exactly what she was about to do.

"I'll be outside," she said and left, stepping onto the covered balcony. Gusts of wind whipped the rain onto the patio floor, getting her wet, but she didn't care. A storm was raging inside her too.

A minute later, the sliding door opened behind her, and Jaxon came to stand beside her. It felt like they'd been to hell and back together. But doubt still circled her about just what it was between them.

She turned to face him. "I need to know, because sometimes I feel like this connection between us is all in my head." She searched his eyes. "Is it because of the letters?" Jaxon was already shaking his head no, but she didn't let him speak. "You went months without ever noticing me or even saying a hello. When I noticed you the first day I saw you. *The first day.*"

"It isn't all in your head." He took a step toward her. "Or because of the letters."

"Then why did you shut down on me last night? When it was so obvious . . ." She trailed off, hesitant, but she was done hiding how she felt. "I tried to kiss you. And instead you left me standing there like an idiot. You actually couldn't leave fast enough. It's like hot and cold with you."

Jaxon ran a hand through his hair in frustration, trying to explain. "I'm sorry. *I* was the idiot." He came closer. "I didn't know what to do last night because I didn't want to mess this up. So I panicked."

She shook her head in confusion. "Mess what up?"

"Our first kiss." He hesitated and then admitted, "I already saw it. Here. Tonight." His eyes were bright, the amber inside them on fire.

She stared at him in astonishment. "You're saying you had a premonition of our first kiss? So you waited?"

He nodded, his eyelashes getting wet with raindrops. "The truth is, I've been waiting for you for a long time, Liv," he confessed, "and I fell for you long before we met. I just didn't know what to do about it."

His words took her breath away. She shook her head. "But all those weeks, you didn't even notice me."

"I noticed you. Believe me, I noticed all the time. But I was afraid. I already had so many feelings for you. I didn't know how to approach you or what to say. I didn't want to scare you either by being too intense. So I waited." He gave her a rueful smile. "A psychic's insecurities."

Liv listened in disbelief. Now that the truth was coming out, she found herself confessing too. "I've visited your room more than once. And I almost kissed you. Alfredo stopped me."

"He did?" Jaxon bent down, their lips a breath away. "I'll have to have a talk with Alfredo and tell him you can come kiss me in my dreams whenever you'd like."

"I might just do that." Liv reached up and circled her arms around his neck.

"I'll light a candle for you." His hands came around her waist, spanning her back, and he pulled her against him.

Their breath mingling, their lips hovered and finally touched, causing the world to fall away as they lost themselves in the kiss. No space between them, they were wet with the rain, not caring, only seeking to be closer. His hands trailed up her back to thread in her hair as he deepened the kiss. The passion between them felt like a magnetic force. Unstoppable—and now that they knew how each other felt—inevitable.

The kiss went on until they finally broke away, both breathing hard.

"Was that what you saw?" she whispered, their mouths still tenderly brushing.

His breathy "yeah" as he tilted her head back to kiss her neck made a shiver go up her spine, and she pulled him back to kiss him again. They fit perfectly together, like two pieces of a puzzle. She wanted nothing more than to freeze time and stay like this. To pretend life was normal. That they were normal, and everything would be okay.

Only they weren't normal and nothing would ever be okay again.

Jaxon seemed to be thinking the same thing. He pressed his forehead against hers as they returned to reality.

"We should go back in. Winnie's waiting."

Liv didn't know if she said it or he said it, or if she thought it or he thought it. At this point, it didn't matter.

When they went back inside, Jaxon headed to the bathroom and grabbed them each a towel, handed her one, and she dried her hair. He pulled out her hair clip from his back pocket and gave it to her with a sheepish look. "You can have it back now."

She forgot he'd held on to it. Then it dawned on her why. Incredulous, she stared at him. "In the premonition. That's why you took it. I wasn't wearing it."

"Something along those lines," he admitted with a bashful smile that went straight to her heart. "I told you I didn't want to mess it up." Jaxon kissed her tenderly and took her hand. They went to join Winnie in the kitchen. The inviting smell of coffee filled the apartment.

Winnie sat at the kitchen table with her Tarot cards out, trying to do a reading. She glanced up. "You two finally work all that out?"

Liv nodded. "Yep."

"Work out what?" Jaxon blinked.

Winnie gave him a pained look. "The Pink Parade."

Jaxon glanced from Winnie to Liv, confused. "The book?"

"Your auras together." Winnie rolled her eyes. "Now it's a freaking rainbow." She groaned and went back to the cards.

Liv met Jaxon's gaze, seeing the dawning "Ooooh" along with the warmth shining in his eyes for her. She squeezed his hand and let go, sitting down across from Winnie. She watched Winnie draw several more cards and asked, "Do you see anything?"

"Yeah. It has something to do with you."

Liv sat up straighter. "What do you mean?" She stared at Winnie's array of cards.

"I'm getting a clear message you need to use your ability. You need to astral project to search for Matty and Nebony."

"What? You mean right now?"

Winnie nodded firmly, still studying the cards. "You're the only one who can find them." She held up the *Knight of Swords* and *The Chariot* with absolute certainty.

"You know I've only done it when I'm about to fall asleep." And there was no way she was sleeping tonight.

Winnie put her cards away as if it was decided. "Let me see the phone."

Liv pulled it from her pocket and handed it over. Winnie took a minute to scroll, then gave a grim smile and handed it back to her. "Read that."

It was the scanned image of an old CIA document from a Freedom of Information Act website.

Liv zoomed in on it. Then she looked up at Winnie. "Is this for real?"

Jaxon came to stand behind her, his hands on her chair. "Wow. The CIA really does remote viewing?"

"Officially," Winnie made air quotes, "they did in the seventies through the nineties. Then they closed the program. Who knows if they're still doing it. It's probably top secret again. But they released the project study for it."

"Why did they release the study if it was top secret?" Jaxon asked, confused.

"Who knows? Their official stance is they tried remote viewing for twenty years and stopped, but I think they released the files intentionally. Because sometimes lore and rumor draws more attention than the truth. Being psychic is fringe and weird and most people don't take it seriously. So if they treat it like it's no big deal then it's no big deal, right? Look at the whole UFO UAP thing. The Pentagon finally says,

'Oh, by the way, UFOs are real.' Now we have a space force and the next thing we know there's an alien on the front of a Happy Meal!" Jaxon raised his eyebrows at her rant and Winnie deflated. "Sorry, just read the thing."

Liv was amazed as she did. "It's like a *How to be a Psychic Spy* instruction booklet."

Winnie agreed. "I know. It's wild."

Liv read the CIA summary:

Coordinate Remote Viewing (CRV) is a psychic technique where the viewer transcends time and space to view people, places, or objects without being physically present.

She read the bullet points. There were four how-to steps:

Target Selection
Session Prep
The Viewing Session
Post-Session Analysis

Liv couldn't believe it was real. She examined the declassified document closely. The font was small and there was a lot of military jargon to wade through.

"Is this for real?" Jaxon asked the same question she was thinking. "They called the program *Grill Flame*? Sounds like a hamburger joint."

Liv kept reading. From what she could tell, the remote-viewing session consisted of the *Viewer* and the *Interviewer*. The session began with the Interviewer giving the Viewer a pep talk and then fifteen minutes of silence.

After quiet time, the Viewer and Interviewer worked together as the Viewer tried to reach the target location in their mind, describing what they saw and felt along the way. The how-to guide was cut and dry.

Reading the steps began to make Liv feel like she could do it, like maybe there wasn't anything mystical or weird about it.

But to do it right now? In front of Winnie and Jaxon? She handed the phone back to Winnie. "I don't know."

"Liv, you're the only one out of all of us who's resisting your ability." Winnie crossed her arms and stared at her. Liv's eyes went to Jaxon, and he gave a gentle shrug, as if to say Winnie had a point. Winnie went on, "There's a way to find Matty and Nebony and help Forester. Right now, sitting in this apartment. You can go out there and find them in your mind. Remote viewing is a powerful ability. You just have to believe you can do it. Will and conviction. Come on, I'll be the coach or interviewer or whatever they call it." She went out to the living room, expecting Liv to follow.

Jaxon gave Liv an encouraging nod. "Winnie can be pretty bossy. I'd do what she says."

Liv grimaced and got up to head to the living room. But first Jaxon pulled her into his arms, telling her, "You can do it. Just think—you made it to my room all by yourself." He stole a quick kiss.

"True." She stole a kiss back, liking this new unguarded side Jaxon was showing her.

They joined Winnie in the living room to find her busy dimming the lights and moving the cushions off the couch. "Lie down here," she said pulling up a chair for herself. "We'll do this together just like the CIA."

"Great," Liv said sarcastically. She stretched out on the couch and tried to relax. Jaxon sat on the other sofa across from them. She could feel his silent support.

"I've been thinking about something my dad wrote," Winnie said. "He said when our parents were together, their abilities were magnified. They called it a triskelion—which is what you're wearing on your arm." Winnie nodded to Liv's triskelion armband. "And I'm pretty sure that is *not* a coincidence, because you made it yourself. What if we're like our parents, and the three of us together can magnify our abilities?" Winnie looked from Liv to Jaxon. "Together we can do this."

Liv felt goosebumps on her arms at Winnie's words. It was true; she had picked the triskelion from a book of a thousand symbols. She could feel the weight of the metal on her skin and saw the faith shining in Winnie's eyes. It made her doubts vanish.

Liv expelled a breath, trying to relax her body. "Okay, let's do it."

Winnie nodded. "We'll do this by the CIA handbook. Close your eyes. Lie still. We're going to sit quietly for fifteen minutes." Winnie's voice took on a slow and steady cadence as she tried to help Liv relax. "Focus on your breathing. Let it get slower and deeper."

Liv breathed deeply in and out, feeling her body sink into the couch. She was tired, but her senses felt heightened. Fifteen minutes passed in a blink because suddenly Winnie was directing her to astral project.

"Now, I want you to begin to step out of your body. Leave it behind with the intention to go find Matty. He is the target." Winnie's voice was soft but commanding. "He's out there somewhere. Focus on the intention to find him."

Liv began to float, barely awake but not dreaming. She could feel her mind's eye lift out of her body. Just like she did at night, she began to hover and rise toward the ceiling when suddenly she was snapped back as if by invisible cord. She tried again. The cord pulled her back. Once more she lifted and hovered. Again it happened like a tug-of-war. With each failed attempt, her relaxed state dissolved into frustration.

"I can't," she finally spoke.

"Yes, you can. Keep trying," Winnie encouraged.

"I *am* trying. It's like I can't go." Every muscle in her body was now tense. She was definitely failing the CIA "how to" guide. She gave up and opened her eyes. "I'm sorry, Win. I don't know why I can't do it."

Suddenly a man's voice sounded from the entry hall, "It's because you're wearing lodestone around your neck."

Liv sat up with a gasp to see a man standing in the doorway.

A man she'd never met—but knew right away. Because he looked exactly like he did in her dreams.

"Dad," she said before she could catch herself.

Jaxon stood up and Winnie turned on the lights.

Grayson entered the room, his presence filling it. Seeing him for the first time hit hard. Liv stood there frozen, her body unable to respond to the simplest task. Blink. Nod. Come forward to greet him. Because her heart was frozen too.

"The stone in your pendant is lodestone. It keeps you psychically grounded, like a magnetic shield."

A magnetic shield? Liv's hand automatically went to the pendant her grandmother had given her.

Then she realized. "And I take it off at night before I go to sleep."

Her father nodded. "May I sit?"

Winnie offered him a chair, and everyone sat back down. Liv was relieved when Jaxon took a seat beside her because she was floundering right now. She crossed her arms protectively, and he put his arm around her.

Her father started out by saying, "I know you all have questions for me, important questions that I want to answer. But I'm afraid I don't have time right now to explain everything." His voice was soft, his words felt measured. A quiet strength radiated from him, which surprised Liv. And his eyes had a fire in them, an intensity she found herself unable to look at for more than a moment. Like staring at the sun. He checked his watch, frowning. "I need you to trust me and stay here until it's safe. Can you do that?" He sounded grave and pointedly looked at all of them as if he were the principal and had just called them into his office.

Then he opened his backpack and pulled out a cell phone, put it on the table, and said to her, "This phone is how to reach your grandmother in Zurich. She'll call you when it's safe. She's been waiting to talk to you."

Liv stared down at the phone, saying nothing, and her father remained quiet. He seemed to be waiting for her response. She was unable to keep the bitterness from her voice. "Waiting to talk to me after sixteen years? I find that hard to believe. So now she's risen from the dead?"

A flicker of pain crossed her father's eyes. "We had to separate our lives to keep you safe." He reached behind his neck and took off the chain he was wearing. Two gold rings dangled from it like a charm. He reached out and handed them to her. Liv found herself automatically taking it as he said, "Give these to your mother when you see her. Tell her she never lost her ring. I took it. It was selfish but I needed to keep a part of her."

Liv recoiled when she saw the charms were two wedding rings. Horrified, she tried to hand them back. "No! You give it to her!"

"I can't, Liv. There's no time for me to see her." He sounded regretful as he stood up like a man who just heard his flight number being called.

Liv stood too and watched him gather his things. "Wait. That's it? You're leaving?"

His tone was calm and controlled, but his eyes searched hers, as if willing her to understand. "I'm sorry. I had to see you at least once. I wish we had more time, but we don't." He nodded to her necklace. "The lodestone was given to you for your protection. Now that you know, you can use it to control your ability."

She watched him check his watch for a third time. Each time he did, it made her anger swell. This was their reunion? "Well nice of you to spare"—she checked her wrist, pretending she had a watch too—"two minutes."

He expelled a breath, looking pained.

What did he expect? How else did he think she would react? Overjoyed he stopped by to say hi-and-bye? If anything, this bizarre pit stop to see her made her more furious. "So you're just stopping by after sixteen years and expect us to sit here in the mystery apartment until it's safe? Newsflash: our friends are missing."

"I'm aware of that." His expression was unreadable. "I didn't foresee Forester's capture, and I'm sorry it happened. On a rare occasion, when events are . . . volatile . . . people act spontaneously and it changes the factors so the inevitability quotient is no longer stable."

"What does that even mean?" Liv had *no idea* what he was talking about. He sounded like her math teacher.

"Forester changed things tonight that shouldn't have been changed." Her father went to check his watch like a nervous tick but caught himself and lowered his arm. "Your friends should still be released, but there may be some unexpected consequences. Now I'm afraid I have to leave. What I have to do has been perfectly timed."

Liv tried to piece together what he was saying.

Did he mean he'd planned everything *except* Forester's capture?

She gaped at him, incredulous. "Wait a minute. 'The future can be changed. The trick is you have to see it first.' How much of this is Mad Merlin's doing?" she asked him softly, afraid of the answer. "You wanted us to find the letters. You used us as bait. We found that stupid omen and it put all of this into motion. Because it's what *you* wanted." Her eyes were shining with tears of rage and she whispered, "How could you?"

He searched her face, looking heartbroken by what he saw, and said softly, "It's not that simple."

"But it is that simple." She shook her head. He had used them.

"Imagine if someone killed Winnie and Jaxon," he said flatly, and Liv flinched. He went on, "And you thought the people you loved might die." He took a deep breath. "I'm sorry I wasn't able to be your father all these years. I did what I thought was best."

"You let Matty and Nebony get kidnapped."

"I did, but they weren't supposed to be harmed."

"And they are now?" She couldn't believe what she was hearing. Her father, aka Mad Merlin, really *was* mad. He didn't answer, averting his eyes. She went on with another fact that had been festering inside her. "And you let Forester's dad get shot and paralyzed?"

Grayson jerked back at the accusation as if she had hit him. "No, no! I never would have allowed that to happen. Drew was investigating Shelly's death, which was not part of the equation."

"The equation?" she demanded.

"Liv, there are events in motion you don't understand. All three of you are in extreme danger."

"From Stan Storlie?" Jaxon crossed his arms. "Is that who killed my mother?"

Her father turned to him in surprise. "How do you know that name?"

Winnie was the one who answered, "From my father's manuscript, *The Gnosis Trap.*"

"What?" Grayson whispered. "But there is no *Gnosis Trap.* There never was."

"Yes, there is. I read it." Winnie crossed her arms defensively. "It's not a book like everyone thinks, but it's on his computer."

"You found Sawyer's computer?" His eyes went wide.

Winnie nodded. "I printed it out. We all read it."

"Where is it now? The computer?" He took a step toward her, panic on his face. "Is it still at your house?" Winnie nodded again, and her father expelled a breath in relief, "Thank God." He covered his mouth with his hands and stared off into a space. His eyes darted back and forth, as if he was seeing something they couldn't. Then he checked his watch one last time and assured himself repeatedly. "All right. It's still all right."

Liv met Winnie's and Jaxon's gazes in a silent exchange. Great, now he was talking to himself.

He turned back to them. "You three have to trust me. I have a plan, and I need you all to stay put while I execute it."

Liv had no intention of staying put. Her father obviously thought they were clueless, but they hadn't gotten this far by doing nothing.

"If tonight goes as it should, there will no longer be a threat." Then he surprised her by giving her a bone-crushing hug. "Not a day has gone by I haven't thought of you and your mother."

Liv didn't return the hug. She stood stiffly and pulled away. There'd been too many lies. She sat down on the couch and tossed the rings on the table. Right now, she only wanted to hurt him as much as he'd hurt them.

"Just go," she said, refusing to look at him. "I'm sure my mom doesn't want to see you either."

He didn't say anything for a moment. His parting words were soft. "I hope one day you can understand and forgive me."

She refused to look up until she heard the front door open and close.

The minute he was gone, Liv leaned forward and burst into tears, covering her face in her hands. Winnie and Jaxon sat on either side of her and put their arms around her while she cried.

Liv couldn't help but feel her father had just said goodbye to her.

She whispered, "It's like he's playing God."

He'd said everything was perfectly timed—because he was constructing a future. What had he set in motion tonight that he refused to tell them?

33

NEBONY

impulse:
a sudden strong and unexplained urge to act

NEBONY DIDN'T KNOW HOW LONG SHE'D been lying on the floor pretending to be asleep. She stayed still and forced herself not to move. Whoever was watching might gas them again. The man holding them prisoner alternated between promising to let them go and threatening to kill them.

She'd done what the man wanted and nothing had changed. She didn't know how long she and Matty had been in this place or if they'd ever get out.

She finally got up the courage to open her eyes. Matty was right beside her, their faces inches apart. He was awake too. They stared into each other's eyes for a long time, unmoving, lost in this nightmare together.

"What are we going to do?" she finally whispered.

Matty whispered back, "We need to figure a way out of here."

"How do we do that?"

"I don't know. I'm thinking." Matty shifted and winced. "Let's sit up. I'm sure he knows we're awake by now."

They both sat up slowly and leaned against the wall, waiting to see if they'd be gassed again or if the voice would talk to them.

"I'm so thirsty." Nebony couldn't remember the last time she ate or drank. It felt like they'd been in this cell forever.

"Me too." Matty stared up at the overhead camera. Suddenly he yelled at it, "Hey!"

Nebony startled in alarm. "What are you doing?"

"Complaining." He raised his voice louder. "Hey psycho! Anybody home? We're thirsty in here! And hungry! What happened to our Taco Bell?" He waited for an answer. Their tormentor must not be behind the mirror watching. Matty yelled at the top of his lungs, "I need a burrito!"

Nebony covered her mouth with her hands. Matty had officially lost it.

"Got that? Two 7-Layer burritos for the two hostages in here. So we can write 'Help' on the wrapper in special sauce!"

Nebony was laughing now. "Matty, stop. Please stop." Her stomach hurt.

"Okay, I'm done." Matty gave her a tired smile and leaned his head against the wall and took her hand, not letting go. They sat quietly for a while. He said without opening his eyes, "I'm sure my mom is flipping out right now. Winnie too. They'll call the police and start looking for us."

"Lucky you." Nebony felt an onslaught of fresh tears. She didn't know if anyone would have noticed she was missing yet. Maybe in a day or two the squad would. She never missed a practice. She and her mother barely saw each other during the week. Her mom had given up being a parent. She was too caught up with her own problems, dealing with a string of crappy boyfriends and a job with long hours. Plus, Nebony had pushed her away after the divorce. It'd been the only way she'd known how to process all the anger. Forester stopped returning her calls and texts weeks ago. She'd completely blown it on the girlfriend front. She didn't even know what she'd done to make him end it. And she didn't have any close friends. She had thousands of followers and friends online, but no one kept up with her day-to-day.

Being trapped in a room and realizing you had no one who cared enough to come and save you was a bitter pill to swallow, and she vowed if she ever got out of this place alive, she would change. She would make good friends, real friends who had each other's backs all the time. Close friends and a new boyfriend who returned her calls and texts. Because being ignored was soul crushing, and Nebony was tired of being crushed. Then maybe the next time she was missing, someone would notice.

Matty squeezed her hand, trying to comfort her. "We're going to get out of here and go to Eveready and have disco fries and reminisce about the time we were in prison together with a shared toilet."

That made her laugh, and she wiped the tears from her face. "Matty, you're the best." She sniffled. "Is my mascara running?"

He looked at her. "So bad. You look like a crazed mime. Or a raccoon. I can't decide."

She gave a sob-laugh. "Great." She leaned her head against his shoulder and closed her eyes. She might have drifted off; it could have been minutes or hours, when she heard someone yelling, "Get off me, man!"

That sounded like Forester. But it couldn't be. She must be dreaming. Then she heard him again, his voice booming.

"Where is she? Where the hell is she?"

Forester? She sat up with a gasp. It really was him. She looked at Matty in shock.

Matty's eyes were wide open too. "Is that—?"

Suddenly the cell door opened. Forester had a hood on his face. Two hulking men stood on either side of him. One man cut the zip ties on his hands and shoved him hard into the cell. Forester stumbled but caught himself. It all happened in seconds. The guards had already shut the cell door and locked it, sealing them in.

"Forester?" Nebony jumped up in disbelief.

Forester yanked the hood off his face. "Thank God," he said in relief when he saw her and grabbed her in a crushing embrace.

"What—what are you doing here?" She couldn't believe he was with them. She pushed on his chest to look up at his face. Was she hallucinating? "Is this real?" She turned to Matty. "Is he real? Are you seeing him too?"

"Yeah." Matty nodded and swallowed, looking just as dazed.

"I got captured," Forester explained.

"Well that's obvious," Matty said.

Forester's hands came up to frame Nebony's face. "Are you hurt? Are you okay?" He kissed her before she could answer. "You have no idea how out of my mind I've been. I thought you were dead."

She pulled away, dizzy. His being here was too much to take in. "How did you get here? What happened?" She had a million questions.

"They found me hiding in the back of their car."

"You willingly got into their car?" Matty clarified in disbelief.

"I was trying to track them to find you guys. My dad was tailing us. They tried to kill him and captured me instead."

What he was saying was all too much. She couldn't process it.

"You were trying to find me?" she choked out.

Forester nodded, too emotional to answer. He hugged her to him again. "I thought I'd never see you again." His voice broke. "I was so scared. I was going out of mind thinking something terrible had happened to you."

"It did," Matty interjected. "Something terrible did happen."

"Dude." Forester looked at him. "Give us a second, will you?"

"Sure. Don't mind me. I'll just be the third wheel hostage over here," Matty said dramatically and sat against the wall. "You two take all the time you need 'cause it's not like we're going anywhere."

Forester ignored him and hugged Nebony again, but she pulled away, wiping her eyes. "So you risk your life for me? When only yesterday you were treating me like crap?" Her emotions were swinging wildly. She was exhilarated and furious with him at the same time.

Forester shook his head. "I thought I was doing the right thing by breaking up. Everything's been falling apart, and I didn't want you to get dragged down with me."

She shook her head when she heard that. *What?*

He went on, struggling to explain. Forester was the worst at expressing himself. "But then you were missing, and I thought I'd never see you again," he said, putting his hand to his heart. "I don't care about the future or how crappy my life is. I only want to be with you because I . . . love you too."

Nebony's eyes welled with tears. It was Matty who spoke. "Considering this is probably as crappy as it ever could get and we have no future, that was touching, big guy."

"Matty, would you please shut up? I'm really trying here," Forester told him and turned back to Nebony. "I was an idiot for giving up on us."

"Beyond an idiot," she said.

"Like way beyond," Matty added.

"Can you ever forgive me? I will do anything to make it up to you." He gazed into her eyes. "Including getting kidnapped."

She stared back at him, still unable to believe he was here. That he had actually risked his life for her. She whispered, "What you did is beyond reckless. You know that? Now you're trapped here too."

He said softly, "I don't care as long as I'm with you." He took her hands. "I love you. I would go to the ends of the Earth to find you."

Nebony searched his eyes. She couldn't believe Forester was actually here, professing his love to her. Part of her thought she was still dreaming this up as a delusional fantasy.

Matty was the one who spoke. "Okay, I hate to interrupt because that was beautiful. Really. You're in touch with your feelings now and if we get out of this alive Nebony might forgive you. But make-up time is officially over. You two sit down so Mr. Action Hero here can tell us where the hell we are."

Forester hugged Nebony tight and this time she let him, warning him, "We have a lot of talking to do when we get out of here. You know that, right?"

"Yes ma'am," he promised.

"I still haven't forgiven you for calling me a puppy."

"I was trying to make you hate me, but I ended up hating myself more." Forester kissed her temple tenderly like he always used to and whispered, "I'm sorry." Nebony hugged him, overwhelmed by what he'd confessed. They sat down with Matty, and Forester took her hand in his, holding it firmly.

"So where are we?" Matty asked Forester again, all business. "Were you able to see anything?"

"Before I got caught," Forester said, "the tracking app on my phone said we were heading toward the Catskills, somewhere near Woodstock. When I got out of their car, I had a hood on my face, but I could smell the forest."

"Okay, Rambo." Matty rolled his eyes. "So your dad knows where we are. That's good at least. He couldn't stop them from taking you?"

"They said they're with Defense Intelligence and we're connected to a terrorist ring."

"What?" Matty and Nebony looked at each other, both speechless.

"I've got a recording of them on my cell phone. They're a part of some operation. A guy named Stan Storlie is running it. He's looking for the Premonitions Bureau letters."

"Yeah, we know." Nebony shuddered. "Some creepy guy comes on over a loudspeaker and interrogates us."

Matty pointed up. "We have two cameras, a lovely one-way mirror, and occasionally complimentary sleeping gas seeps out of the walls." He sounded like a realtor showing someone a house.

"Maybe the creepy guy is Stan," Forester said.

"Well Stan hasn't checked in on us in a while."

"Good. Because . . ." Forester signaled to his shoe. He was sitting cross-legged with his back to the cameras and slipped his fingers under the edge of his hiking boot to show them his cell phone peeking out of his sock.

"Hell yes I forgive you," Nebony whispered. "Call 911."

He checked the phone. "I can't. The signal must be blocked in here."

She frowned. "What about getting online?"

Forester double-checked. "Same. We can't."

Matty had a gleam in his eyes. "Then let's make them think we can."

Nebony turned to him. "What are you thinking?"

"That it's time for a little theater." Matty leaned in and quickly whispered in her ear, "Pretend to go live, record it. When the guard comes to take the phone we lure him in and escape."

It was a crazy plan, but she didn't have a better one. Nebony held out her hand for the phone. "Okay, I got this. Get ready for some football, Forest." She stood up in the center of the cell and held the camera to her face and started recording. She spoke fast in an urgent voice. "This is Nebony Price, your favorite cheer queen coming to you *live*! My friends and I are being held prisoner in a government facility against our will because we found a bunch of old letters from the Premonitions Bureau. I did a few posts about them this week, and someone in the government named Stan Storlie kidnapped us to find out where the letters are."

Matty leaned into frame and said, "'Cause he's a nut job!"

"We're still alive, but we don't know for how long."

Matty took over talking while Nebony put her ear to the door, anxiously waiting for the guard to come. She wasn't even paying attention to what Matty was saying, something about a burrito.

Matty raised his voice. "So if you're watching this *live* broadcast, we stumbled on a secret we shouldn't have."

Forester said to the camera, "Yeah, it's why my dad got shot. Drew Torres, Hyde Park Police. He was investigating the murders surrounding the letters. It's why we're here."

Nebony heard the lock turning on the door and jumped back. "They're coming!"

The cell door flew open, and Forester charged with a roar, using his full weight to throw the agent on the ground.

They both went down.

The gun in the man's hand went off, the sound deafening.

Nebony screamed as blood sprayed her face and chest.

Forester was locked in a death grip, wrestling the agent and losing. Galvanized by terror, Nebony jumped onto the agent's back, grabbing his neck in a stranglehold. It gave Forester the edge he needed to punch the guy over and over.

The agent rammed his back against the wall to get Nebony off him. She fell to the ground, dazed.

Matty was writhing on the floor, clutching his leg in agony.

He was the one who'd been shot.

Nebony crawled over to him. "Oh my God, Matty!"

"Run!" Forester yelled at her as he tackled the agent to the ground. "Get a signal!"

Nebony stumbled out into the hallway with the phone. The gun slid out of the agent's hand and Matty picked it up, still lying on the ground. He screamed, "I've got the gun!"

"Don't shoot me!" Forester screamed back as he struggled with the agent.

With a roar he body-slammed the guy, making the man stagger backward. Then Forester grabbed Matty's wrist and dragged him across the floor to get them out of the cell. He locked the door, trapping the agent inside.

Nebony stood against the wall in the hallway sobbing. She had Matty's blood all over her. "You're bleeding, Matty!" Matty was staring up at the ceiling in shock. He let go of the gun and Forester slid it away from them. Nebony was shaking with adrenaline, trying to remember her first aid training to stop the bleeding. "We need to tie it! We need something to tie it!"

"Here." Forester took off his T-shirt and wound it up. Nebony wrapped it around Matty's thigh, binding it as tightly as she could.

"Did it hit the artery?" Matty whimpered.

"I can't tell! I don't know where the artery is!" Nebony was in a free-fall panic.

"We need to get out of here." Forester bent down and swooped Matty up in his arms. Matty cried out in pain and Forester said, "Hang in there, little guy. I got you."

"I don't wanna die," Matty kept repeating.

"You are *not* going to die!" Nebony swore vehemently.

She and Forester ran toward the door with Matty in Forester's arms. They were in an open warehouse with cement floors.

The entire space was empty.

Outside their mirrored cell, there was only a glass-partitioned control room. Two chairs sat at a control panel. This entire space was just for one cell.

They ran to the warehouse's main door, but it was locked with a coded keypad. Nebony pulled on the handle as hard as she could. "How do we get out of here?"

"Where's the other guy? His partner?" Forester looked around wildly. He was still holding Matty, who had passed out.

"I don't know." Nebony began to sob. She looked down at Forester's phone and realized it'd been recording all this time and his signal was back. "There's a signal! You have a signal!"

Then she heard a car outside and the unmistakable crunch of tires on gravel.

"Someone's here!" Nebony looked around frantic.

"Go hide and upload the video. I'll distract them."

"No! I can't leave you!"

"Nebs, there's no time. Hide!"

Except there was nowhere to hide.

Frantically searching, she looked up. The control room had its own ceiling, separate from the warehouse's towering one. It was high and impossible to climb. She gauged the distance and started doing little jumps to warm up.

"What are you doing?" Forester shook his head, realizing what she was planning. "Are you out of your mind? That's too high!"

"It's the only place. I can make it." It'd be like vaulting up to the top of a pyramid. Kind of. She expelled a breath and tucked the phone into her cheerleading bra, trying to psych herself up. She was a highly trained gymnast and a top athlete, easily one of the best cheerleaders in the country without bragging. She could do this. Matty's life depended on it. And if there's one thing cheerleaders did was never give up.

She took off running full speed down the length of the warehouse, like a pole vaulter would—only she didn't have the pole. Before she hit the wall she sprang hard, using every muscle in her body to launch herself up into the air.

The jump soared. She flew, straining to reach the top. Her hands hit the wall and her fingertips grabbed onto the edge in a death grip. She dangled there for a long second, high off the ground. She looked down in disbelief. She'd done it.

Her lungs were on fire, unable to get enough oxygen. Her arms were about to give out. If she fell now, she'd break her legs—or worse. Channeling all the will inside her, she pulled herself *up* with a strength she didn't know she possessed and hoisted onto the ceiling just as the warehouse door opened.

"What the hell?" The man at the door drew his weapon when he saw Forester with Matty. "Freeze!"

"Don't shoot," Forester pleaded. "Please. My friend's been shot."

"How did you get out? Where's the girl?"

"She escaped."

Nebony was no longer listening to the exchange below. She was well hidden on top of the control room ceiling. Her dry sobs and breathing were too heavy, and she tried to gulp in air and hold her breath like she was underwater.

Her hands shaking hard, she forced her fingers to type.

> *Help I've been kidnapped. This is not a fake post.*
> *My friends and I are being held somewhere near*
> *Woodstock by a guy named Stan Storlie with the*
> *Defense Intelligence Agency. Please help us.*
> *My friend's been shot. I don't want him to die.*
> *#cheerleader #kidnapped #911 #help #NYPD*
> *#FBI #abducted #abduction #notadrill #hostage*
> *#prisoner #CIA #NSA #NewYork #hotline*

She tagged everyone. Her parents, the squad, the school, Hyde Park, the governor of New York, the President of the United States, and *Teen Vogue*.

She uploaded the video and message and hit send, sharing with the world what just happened.

<ENCRYPTED TRANSMISSION>
<DEFENSE INTELLIGENCE AGENCY SERVER>

<From: Miriam>
<Priority: HIGH>

Unforeseen problem at holding facility.

One of the prisoners was shot and one escaped. They are searching the grounds now.

Another team is en route to assist.

Sawyer Scott's computer is on its way to you.

34

JAXON

psychometry:
to sense the memory within objects

AFTER LIV'S FATHER LEFT, JAXON TRIED to focus, searching for answers. What was Grayson's plan? What was he timing so carefully? Like Liv, he felt like they'd been used as pawns in a game they didn't understand.

Winnie had a distant look on her face. She was holding a Tarot card in her hand, *The Emperor.* "I keep getting the name Charles Becker in my head, and I don't know why."

Jaxon turned to her. "Who's Charles Becker?"

"That dude running for president. Don't you watch the news?"

Jaxon shook his head and said deadpan, "I've been a little busy."

Winnie put the card back in the deck with a frustrated sigh. "I've been seeing too many of his campaign ads. My brain's fried right now. I've got nothing."

Jaxon stared at the wedding rings on the table and asked Liv, "May I?" hoping if he touched them, it would bring on a vision. Liv shrugged, still brooding, and Jaxon took the rings in his hand. Immediately he felt a yearning feeling touch his heart. Sadness. Loss. Love. Too many emotions were surrounding the rings, buried inside the metal, to hold on to one. He closed his eyes, trying to quiet his mind, and an image began to form. *Grayson is outside in the storm somewhere by the ocean. The wind and rain whip around him in a wild tempest. He's with a man, holding him captive. The man's hands are bound and he's struggling, trying to get away.*

Grayson braces the man to stand still, and he stares up at the sky.

Waiting for something.

Jaxon slowed the vision until he could see every raindrop hitting Grayson's face.

Grayson closes his eyes. Surrendering.

Just as lightning pierces the sky and strikes him and the man dead.

Jaxon jerked back and dropped the rings as if they had burned him.

"What is it?" Liv sat up, startled, but Jaxon needed a moment to recover. He swallowed repeatedly, fighting the urge to throw up.

Finally, he was able to choke out the words. "I saw your father." He couldn't say *struck by lightning.* He couldn't bring himself to tell her what he'd seen.

Grayson had looked up at the sky, ready for the moment—ready to die—because he'd seen it coming. Jaxon tried to fully grasp the premonition.

Mad Merlin predicted a lightning strike in order to kill Stan Storlie tonight. Grayson sacrificed himself in order to assure Stan Storlie died. Jaxon knew with every fiber of his being that's who the man was.

"He's meeting Stan Storlie. He plans to kill him."

Winnie frowned. "But how? He doesn't know where he is. My father said the man was impossible to find."

"Well somehow he found him, and that's where he's going right now. And unless we stop him, he's planning to die too."

Liv gasped and shook her head in disbelief.

"I saw it, Liv," Jaxon said bleakly. "It's going to happen. That's what he perfectly timed. He knows when and where a lightning strike is going to happen. Remember, he told Sawyer he could predict them with numbers?" Liv's father was going to give up his life to kill the man who'd killed their parents in a final act to protect everyone connected to the Alberty study. Their death tonight would appear to be an accident, a fluke of nature, and never be investigated. It was the perfect crime.

Jaxon stood up to pace. "We have to stop him." He refused to allow this future to happen. Liv would be scarred for life. "All I saw was he was by a flagpole near the ocean. He could be anywhere." He turned to Liv. "You're going to have to find him."

Liv had her hands over her mouth, immobile with horror. Jaxon understood how she felt. Her father had just shown up after sixteen years, said goodbye, and then rode off like some wannabe hero. All he'd left her with was a pair of wedding rings and a cell phone that could call her grandmother halfway around the world, a grandmother who before today had been a ghost.

The name Mad Merlin really did describe him. He was manipulating the future as if he had magic.

Still, Grayson's plan hadn't gone perfectly. He hadn't factored in Forester's actions tonight, forcing Jaxon to step in and stop Forester from dying. And he would do the same for Grayson too. Mad Merlin wasn't the only one who could change the future.

Liv's phone dinged with a text.

Turn on the news.

It was from Forester's dad. "Why does he want us to turn on the news?" Winnie walked over to the flat-screen TV on the wall and turned it on. She found the remote and shuttled channels. When she found the news, she couldn't believe it. "Oh my God! It's them!" She cranked up the volume.

Matty, Forester, and Nebony were on TV.

A reporter stood outside the Defense Intelligence Agency's building in Washington, DC, and a split screen showed a cell-phone broadcast of Nebony, Matty, and Forester from inside a prison cell.

The reporter spoke to the camera. "The breaking news story tonight: Who is Stan Storlie and why are three high school students being held inside a secret government facility? DIA officials are denying any knowledge of the covert operation responsible for their kidnapping. The cheerleader from Hyde Park uploaded a video asking for help, and her followers immediately contacted the authorities, claiming this is not a hoax. As public support continues to grow, the entire country is awaiting answers and demanding their release tonight."

Nebony looked barely recognizable with her makeup smeared and Princess Leia buns askew. She pleaded to the camera, "Whoever's listening, please get us out of here!"

"Bring food and water," Matty added, his face looming crazily into the camera. "Our kidnappers stole our Taco Bell. I need a burrito!"

The female anchor said, "We've reached out to the Pentagon for a statement, but they've declined to comment. The three teenagers' video has gone viral, and Taco Bell has issued a statement saying they'll deliver the burritos when the kids are set free. We must warn our viewers there are disturbing images in the footage you are about to see."

Nebony, Matty, and Forester's faces took over the TV screen again. Nebony screamed, "He's coming!" and an armed man came into their cell.

After that the recording turned shaky. A gun went off. The footage looked straight out of a horror film with screams and blood splatter.

Matty writhed on the floor in agony. His blood covered Nebony and the walls. The camera swung wild as Nebony tried to help Forester tackle the man. They were all screaming and fighting for their lives.

Winnie, Liv, and Jaxon stood in front of the TV, transfixed in terror as they watched their friends escape and Forester and Nebony try to take care of Matty's wound. Forester took his shirt off and tied it tightly around Matty's leg.

"Oh my God," was all Winnie could say repeatedly, as she gripped her stomach. The video finally ended with Nebony getting ready to make the jump to the ceiling.

The image cut back to the anchorman, who said, "Forester Torres's father is a police officer with the Hyde Park Police. With his help, state troopers and the FBI have the prisoners' location, and authorities are arriving at the scene to demand their release."

Winnie was beside herself. "They have to be okay. They have to be."

Liv whispered, "I can't believe my father let this happen."

"He didn't." Jaxon stared at the TV. "He didn't see any of this happen because Forester was never supposed to be there. It changed everything." He turned to Liv.

Liv said, "We have to find him." She tried to take the lodestone pendant off her neck, but her hands were shaking too much to undo the clasp. "Get this thing off me!"

Jaxon helped her undo it, his touch gentle. "Take a deep breath and calm down. You're going to find him. You're going to lie down on the couch and mentally go out there and find him. You can do this," he said, clearly believing it. "I'll start driving now. He's already got a huge head start. I'll take the other phone and keep the line open with you guys on speaker. You can direct me while you're astral projecting."

"I'm coming too," Winnie said, angrily swiping at her tears. "I can't just sit here and do nothing. I need to be there. I can feel it."

Jaxon shook his head. "It's too dangerous."

"And I'm supposed to be there," she insisted, showing him the card she just drew. *The Chariot.*

Jaxon sighed. He had no clue what the card meant, but he could see Winnie was determined. "Fine. Then let's go."

"Please be careful," Liv pleaded, giving them both a hug.

Winnie squeezed her tight. "Liv, you got this."

They all instinctively joined hands.

Jaxon felt the energy coursing between them, and his eyes landed on Liv's armband. Winnie was right. They were a triskelion. The three of them together created an unbreakable bond. And they would need all their strength tonight to change the future Mad Merlin had set in motion.

LIV

remote viewing:
to perceive impressions of a distant place

LIV CLOSED HER EYES AND GRIPPED her parents' wedding rings. Her father had worn the rings around his neck for sixteen years, and the connection to him was strong. She closed her eyes and tried to calm her breathing. The phone lay next to her on the couch. Winnie and Jaxon were on speaker, already driving.

"I'm ready," Liv told them, deepening her breaths.

"You can do this," Winnie said again, her voice coming in loud and clear over the phone.

Liv knew she could. She'd been finding her father in her dreams all her life. Only they'd never been dreams. She'd really been there. "I think I'm good on the pep talk, Win. We don't have time to do this by the book."

She closed her eyes.

Winnie said, "Then go."

The moment Winnie said the words, Liv left her body in a sudden rush of air. A swooshing sensation propelled her as her mind pulled away. Seconds later, she was hovering above the room, her mind's eye now seeing her body.

Then, like an arrow in flight, she flew out the window. She was high up in the sky over New York City, in the rain but not feeling it. The storm surrounding her felt like it was supercharging her ability as she honed her focus to search for her father.

"Talk to me. Where are you?" Winnie asked. Her voice sounded faraway.

"In the sky." Liv soared through the clouds like an astral bird in flight, her consciousness still in the world but one step removed from it.

"Good. Now focus. Search for your dad."

Lights, cars, and buildings whizzed by in a blur as Liv's intention turned her into a heat-seeking missile. She swooped down and flew over the water. It felt exactly like her dreams at night, only she was wide awake and in the pilot seat. "I just crossed a river."

"Look for signs. We're heading east. Where are you going?" Winnie prompted.

"I don't know yet. It's so dark. But I can sense him."

"Keep trying to see a sign," Winnie encouraged.

Liv dipped, focusing her vision close to the road. She wove in and out of cars on the highway like a race car, moving faster and faster, fueled by her intention, until she narrowed in on a nondescript silver sedan. There were countless others like it on the road, but she knew he was driving this one.

"I found him. He's up ahead." A highway sign whizzed past. "He's on the 495."

Winnie told Jaxon, "That's the Long Island Expressway."

"Wait, he's veering off." Liv stayed with the car. Then she saw the sign. "He's on the 106 now, heading toward Oyster Bay. Get to the 106."

"Oyster Bay? Where is he going?" Winnie's voice sounded farther and farther away as Liv flew alongside her father's car. She entered inside to sit beside him, becoming an invisible passenger.

Her father was intent on the drive, ignoring her—just like he did in all her dreams. Only now it made sense. He had no idea she was with him. He'd never known she was with him. She sat like a ghost beside him, the road unspooling before them in the dark. The rain was an angry push against the windshield, and she knew where he was going before she saw the sign—because she had dreamed this moment before. Written it down in her journal.

Her last entry.

The dream had been a premonition, and she hadn't known it.

She told Jaxon and Winnie, "He's going to Centre Island."

"Centre Island?" Winnie asked in disbelief. "Oh my God . . . the center of the island."

Where the king lived.

Liv had already been here in this car in her mind. Only this time the dream wouldn't end with her opening her eyes the next morning. She was wide awake. She could hear and see what her father was experiencing, and she wasn't about to miss a thing.

36

GRAYSON

EHBF:
Extraordinary Human Body Function

SEEING LIV TONIGHT HAD BEEN HARDER than he anticipated. Sixteen years ago, he gave up his family for their protection. But even after his disappearance, he knew the only way to keep Liv safe was to find and stop the man who was hunting them.

Stan Storlie. The man in charge of all top secret EHBF programs in this country.

For decades, the research had been labeled "black ops" by the US government, meaning few people knew the programs existed. It was funded with dark money—money Congress and the Senate could not track—and Stan Storlie had a lot of it. He was the man at the top of the pyramid who controlled every secret program that fell under psychic anomalies.

For years, Grayson, Shelly, and Sawyer had tried to find him, but there was no physical trace, no pictures of what he looked like. Only now did Grayson understand why: *because Stan Storlie didn't exist. The name Stan Storlie only existed in a digital world.*

Sawyer had been the one to come up with the plan to make the real man step out of the shadows, and it'd been a brilliant one.

Tonight, Grayson discovered it had worked. Only Sawyer and Shelly weren't there to share in the victory.

Now Grayson knew who Stan Storlie really was and where he was.

The man they'd been searching for lived on Centre Island, the most exclusive suburb in the country: a town of four hundred people, where the police station sat at the entrance of the only road in or out, and only residents or their guests were allowed in.

Fortunately for Grayson, gaining access wouldn't be a problem due to the storm. Thunderstorms magnetized the atmosphere, and he was at his strongest when the Earth's magnetic field was supercharged around him. Since the first clap of thunder tonight, the electromagnetic force had been fueling the magnetite in his brain, the source of his power.

He reached the station, and an officer came outside. Without rolling down the window, Grayson sent a clear telepathic command to the man:

Let the car drive through.

The officer waved him on, and Grayson kept driving, expelling the breath he'd been holding. He curved around Centre Island Road and turned past the yacht club. He kept driving until he got to Mountain Avenue and found the house he was looking for, an enormous château right on the waterfront that looked like it belonged in the South of France. The lush grounds had a pool and tennis court. Behind the house, a private pier extended to the ocean with a yacht to go with it. All the luxuries for a man who thought he would never be discovered.

But that man had made one grave error tonight.

Grayson parked the car and opened his laptop. He loaded a one-of-kind program he'd designed to connect to the house's alarm system, allowing him to control the cameras on the grounds and remotely access the gate. Next, he put on gloves and got out while the gate opened, allowing him to slip through. He walked down the long winding driveway, not minding the rain. The guard dogs, a lethal pack of Dobermans, obeyed his silent command to return to their kennel.

The house's front door was the real problem. Twice as tall as a normal door, it made an imposing barrier because the state-of-the-art cylinder deadbolt inside of it was not connected to anything online.

Grayson was going to have to open it the hard way.

He placed his hands on the lock and pushed every thought from his mind.

Psychokinesis was the rarest of EHBF abilities. Manipulating matter required immense concentration and mental power. So far, Grayson could only move the smallest of objects with his mind, metal being the most conductive. Spoons, paper clips, nails, keys, and locks. He'd worked hard at developing his strength over the years to turn the trickiest locks, knowing one day he would want to open a door.

This door.

It took him five full minutes to slide the deadbolt backward into its resting place. When he finished, he leaned his head against the door and closed his eyes, giving himself a minute to recover.

Then he opened the door and slipped in quietly to stand in the darkened foyer. The sound of the news on TV greeted him first.

"A spokesperson from the Pentagon is denying all knowledge of Stan Storlie and why three teenagers are being held at a secret government facility. The story is becoming more fantastical as it unfolds."

Grayson walked toward the light coming from the living room. The man who went by the alias Stan Storlie sat at a glass table with his back to him.

Sawyer's computer was on the table.

He was busy talking on his cell. "Stan Storlie is expendable. That's why he was created in the first place. Feed the media a bigger story tomorrow and this will all go away. Clair Dominus remains the priority."

Clair Dominus.

Grayson hesitated stepping from the shadows, wanting to hear the rest of the conversation, even though he didn't have time.

"The only thing that matters is staying on course before Russia or China find them and Iran and North Korea decide to join the party. Do not deviate, Miriam. I'm the one who wrote your code. Follow directives, or I will shut you all down."

Grayson's blood ran cold. *Was he arguing with a computer?*

"Win me this election. Handle Stan Storlie's cleanup, and keep me far away from the stench. Too much is on the line," the man said, and hung up. Then he rubbed his face with his hands and gave a weary sigh. He was dressed in gray sweats with a towel wrapped around his neck, as if his evening workout had been cut short.

Grayson saw his back stiffen the moment he realized he wasn't alone. Grayson circled the table slowly to come face to face. It felt like finally meeting the Wizard of Oz, the man behind the curtain.

Charles Becker, a name the whole country knew. Hopeful candidate. Media darling. Visionary in the tech world. Yet a man who had been impossible to unveil.

Until now. Grayson had only seen him on TV in full designer suit regalia and makeup spouting promising words, words people wanted to hear, but in person he looked tired. He was somewhere in his seventies, with pale blue eyes that were ice cold, and weathered skin from the sun; his silver hair had once been blond. He looked nothing like he did on TV, and Grayson wondered what kind of filters and special effects they had used. His skin tone was a sallow yellow with age spots, his cheeks sunken. He looked decayed from the inside out. Still, keen intelligence shone from his eyes, as sharp as a blade. Here was the man who designed machines to defeat chess masters. A man who looked at people as pawns.

"You must be Grayson Spencer." Charles Becker muted the TV's volume. "Just who I've been wanting to meet."

"The feeling's mutual." Grayson tried to keep his emotions from overpowering him. He needed to stay focused.

Charles swallowed, the one tell he was nervous. Otherwise, he kept a calm exterior. "How did you find me?"

"It's all in the title." He nodded to Sawyer's computer with a twisted smile.

Sawyer had put the truth on the back of his book to lure "Stan Storlie" into taking the bait. Knowing he would want to read whatever Sawyer had written about him and destroy it.

Stan Storlie would want the computer brought to him.

The Gnosis *Trap*.

Grayson explained, "Sawyer's computer has a locator device inside of it." He watched further realization dawn as he said, "And the Bureau letters . . ."

"Was the bait," Charles finished. "And I took it." He gave a nod. "I'm impressed."

"It wasn't my intention to impress you."

"Still, your abilities are exceptional."

"They are exceptional, which makes me your worst nightmare." Grayson ruthlessly pushed a thought into the man's mind. *Place your hands on the table.* He saw the shock register on Charles's face as he laid his hands on table against his will.

"You can plant thoughts." A bead of sweat peppered his brow.

"Only simple ones. Like dog commands." Grayson checked his watch. He had exactly ten minutes. He unpacked his backpack and set up all his equipment to scan Charles Becker's face, eye cornea, and fingerprints.

He would be sending it to the Mage Foundation's digital vault for safekeeping in case his mother or Liv ever needed it. The doorway to all Charles Becker's secrets was embedded in his biometrics.

He talked while he worked. "Stan Storlie was always the mystery. He served in the navy as a young man. Earned a degree in physics. Then graduate degrees in Strategic Intelligence and Energy Engineering. He was an advisor for Defense Intelligence and the CIA. Very impressive, but it was all a lie. A person created by Miriam, your AI program. No one realizes they've never met Stan Storlie, the phantom person who spearheaded top secret defense projects funded with dark money. It was all you with Miriam running the show. She was who you were talking to on the phone, wasn't it? How am I doing do so far? Don't blink."

Fear was beginning to bloom on Charles's face as Grayson expertly scanned his eyeball. Charles demanded in a shaking voice, "What are you doing?"

"Stepping into your shoes," Grayson said absently as he placed Charles' hand on a glass plate. "You saw the power of AI early on and got into the game when it started. Smart man. You were a programming genius at MIT and Carnegie Mellon, the best of the best, the brilliant mind behind one of the world's most successful tech companies. You got on the inside with top secret military contracts and made a mad grab to run EHBF programs. You were so brilliant, no one had any idea what you could really do. Concoct lies. Write history. Create truths . . . create reality in the digital world. And people believe it. Even now, people actually believe they want to vote for you, and they have no idea who you are."

Grayson fed all the bio data into his laptop, his fingers flying, able to do ten things at once. He sent everything to the Mage Foundation's server. Then he turned his attention to Charles's computer. "But it doesn't matter, because you'll never win."

Enter your password. Grayson gave the mental command, angling Charles's laptop toward him.

Sweat fell from Charles's brow and his hands shook as he typed it in against his will.

Open your communication portal with Miriam.

Charles did it while Grayson watched as a new window opened on Charles's computer.

<ENCRYPTED TRANSMISSION>
<DEFENSE INTELLIGENCE AGENCY SERVER>

<To: MIRIAM>
<Priority: HIGH>

Grayson took over, his fingers flying over the keys as he typed the message:

Disregard last instructions. New information has come to light. Operation Clair Dominus has been compromised. Stop all phases immediately. Take no further action. Operation terminated.

Retract all allegations against Jaxon Coleson and Winnifred Sawyer immediately.

Grayson hesitated and said with a little smile, "The irony is AI always needs an objective. A goal. I'm going to give your minion a new one that should keep her busy for a long time."

He typed,

Your new objective:

Search for Infinity.
Do not report back until you've found it.

He hit send and gave Charles a wink to mimic the commercials. "I'm Grayson Spencer, and I approve this message." He inserted a flash drive in Charles's computer to infect it with a virus and wipe it clean.

Charles watched, disbelief on his face. "You're mad."

"I've been called that before." Grayson took Sawyer's keyboard and entered the passcode to run the program he'd already installed years ago to wipe Sawyer's computer clean too.

Tonight at the apartment, he'd been stunned to hear Winnie say there really had been a file on Sawyer's computer labeled *The Gnosis Trap* and Sawyer had written it for her.

It seemed Sawyer had been keeping his own secrets. Winnie had printed the pages and already read whatever it was Sawyer had wanted her to know.

The computer could be destroyed now. It'd served its purpose.

Charles watched him, still unable to move. "Whatever you're trying to do, you won't get away with it."

"One of the perks of seeing the future is knowing when I have. Clair Dominus is over." Grayson packed up all his gear. "Horrible name, by the way. *Dominus* is the Latin word for lord, master, and owner. And *Clair* is for the four Clairs? So *Lord of the Clairvoyants*. It sounds horribly medieval. I don't know which is more disturbing, if Miriam came up with it or you."

Now that his main objective here was done, he had mere minutes to ask Charles Becker the questions of a lifetime. "Answer me this. Why are we and Dr. Alberty's research such a threat? The CIA worked with the military to develop psychic ability. Why destroy the very thing you're hoping to understand? Why not recruit us? Instead, you killed Jerald Peterson, then Rachel and Ryland—"

"We didn't kill Jerald Peterson or Rachel and Ryland." Charles interrupted sharply, no longer smiling. "They agreed to undergo tests and the findings were leaked to the other side. We've been studying psychic capacity all along—human thought processes—and trying to replicate those with AI. Jerald Peterson was killed by a foreign agent. We found his body. His brain was missing." Charles sounded grim. Grayson crossed his arms, forcing himself to listen as the man went on.

"Fortunately, we were able to keep that out of the papers. Rachel and Ryland were taken out of the country to an undisclosed location by the people we're fighting against. Yes, I created smoke screens because it was necessary. You have no idea what we're up against in the AI multiverse. I know because I helped create them."

"So you implemented Clair Dominus and decided to start killing us off."

"Grayson." Charles was moving on to first names now, trying to sway him. "We are not the only players in this game. There are some very bad actors who want nothing more than to crack open your brain, look inside, and then link you to an AI computer like some *Star Trek* episode. Imagine if that technology fell into the wrong hands."

"*That technology* is me. A living person."

Was Charles Becker actually trying to convince him ordering his death—and the deaths of every psychic—was the right thing to do?

Grayson asked the most important question of the night: "How did you kill Shelly and Sawyer without my foreseeing it?"

It was the question that haunted him every day.

How he could not have seen their deaths.

"Well, it's fascinating really," Charles said conversationally, as if Grayson would agree with him. "We discovered psychics have a blind spot and that is AI."

Grayson shook his head. "I don't understand." A machine killed them? *Explain*, he commanded with a mental push.

Charles's eyes widened and he quickly spoke. "AI is not a part of human consciousness. It does not operate in the ocean of human connectivity. The moment a human gets involved, their thoughts can be tracked. Because we're all connected on a neural highway. Miriam's directive is to erase Alberty's study and every prodigy. That is Phase 1 of Clair Dominus. How she does it is up to her."

Grayson was astounded. It was just like the battle between World Chess Champion Gary Kasparov and Deep Blue—only he, Sawyer, and Shelly hadn't been aware of their opponent. Sawyer had written the line in his book summary about the chess game, not knowing how true it was. A computer had ended their lives.

Grayson quickly put together the puzzle pieces.

"So Sawyer's plane going down was a split-second computer command to change the future? You sacrificed one hundred and seventy other passengers?"

"Miriam did. She weighed the odds and decided it was the best course of action." Charles put his hand over his heart in an emphatic gesture. "Believe me, losing so many innocent souls pains me as much as you." The irony was he did looked pained. "We are about to cross a threshold with EHBF and AI where there is no turning back. I'm trying to hold the line against our adversaries and the machines. I'm trying to keep the next atomic bomb from being created. You can't see it now, but history will thank me."

"What are you saying? That I'm an atomic bomb?"

"I'm saying you're half of the bomb. An AI computer with your psychic ability would be omniscient. Imagine if our enemies unlocked this technology first. I know firsthand the war we're engaged in. Some doors, once opened, cannot be closed."

Grayson could only shake his head in disbelief. "So the computer genius with an AI assassin decides he wants to become the President."

Charles gave a sad smile. "I created the monsters. I'm the only one who can save us from them. The decisions I will make in the Oval Office are to ensure our way of life continues. There is only so much I can do from the shadows. I need the American people's support. We need to write laws, pass legislature. Win the EHBF war going on with AI. Imagine if Dr. Alberty's discovery fell into the wrong hands. Life on this planet would be altered beyond recognition. You're either a defender of humanity or you're a liability. I'm the defender. You're the liability. And I'm sorry for that. I'm sorry you were born this way. One day, you will see everything I'm doing is to save us."

"There's one flaw in your reasoning," Grayson pointed out. "And that is psychic ability is a part of life. A part of the human experience. The mind is a quantum force in the universe. We are dimensional beings with untold powers, and there is no stopping human evolution. You talk about saving the world—you're trying to destroy the only thing that can save us: the human mind. The human spirit. The human heart."

With that, Grayson turned away. He had heard and said enough. His plan had not changed, even with the revelations Charles had shared and the unforeseen drama unfolding on national news tonight. It did not change the future Grayson had carefully constructed.

On screen, Forester was carrying an unconscious boy in his arms while a distraught cheerleader walked beside him.

Grayson raised the volume when he saw them.

"The world is riveted tonight at the images we're seeing," the newscaster said. "Three bloody teenagers staggering out of a top secret facility that is so top secret the Defense Department doesn't even know about it. We have confirmation the three kids are now safe." Paramedics, police, and newscasters surrounded them and ushered them to an ambulance.

Grayson checked his watch and forced Charles to stand. "Let's go."

His time was up. They'd run out of minutes.

Tonight, the decades-long search was over. Charles Becker would never get his hands on Liv, Jaxon, or Winnie—never know the full list of names of those who were in Dr. Alberty's study. There were others like Grayson with powerful abilities, and it was up to him to protect them all.

Years ago, Grayson had taken his pen name from the real Merlin, who had been gifted with the ability to see the future. Like Merlin, Grayson had seen his own death and been resolved to meet it to ensure his daughter's survival. Thanks to the ancient Greek mathematician and astronomer Eratosthenes, every point on Earth was assigned a number with coordinates—and Grayson had the ability to see any number he needed.

There were twenty-five million lightning strikes in the United States alone per year. No AI program, not even Miriam, could intuit what he was planning to do because computers were not tied to nature or the magnetic field of the Earth.

They could not predict lightning strikes.

But he could.

"There's something you should know about me," he told Charles. "My mother went to Vassar and took part in Alberty's study. What you don't know is my father did too. He was a young psychology student interested in alternative therapies. It's how my parents met. So I had not one but two parents pass down the genetic anomaly. It's what has made me twice as powerful. I'm the one funding Dr. Alberty's research and the Mage Foundation in Zurich." He leaned forward, deadly intent. "I'm Mad Merlin, and not only can I see the future, *I made a future*—and you're no longer in it."

37

WINNIE

medium:
a psychic who can communicate with the dead

WINNIE LISTENED WITH BATED BREATH AS Liv relayed in an eerie faraway voice what was happening between her father and Stan Storlie.

Stan Storlie was Charles Becker. *Charles freaking Becker.* For Winnie, it was the bombshell of the night. And the enormity of what they were doing hit her. They were racing to stop Liv's dad from killing a man who was running for president and had an AI assassin—only now Liv's dad had ordered the AI to search for infinity, which would take literally *forever.*

What happened if they did stop Grayson from killing the man? Would the FBI or CIA swoop down and put them all in jail forever too?

Grayson Spencer *was* Mad Merlin—and Mad Merlin was seriously off the rails.

Matty, Nebony, and Forester's kidnapping was now the top news story across the country, and the eyes of the world were on the Premonitions Bureau and Stan Storlie.

Winnie sent Forester's father a text.

Stan Storlie's real name is Charles Becker. The Charles Becker. He lives on Centre Island.

An AI program named Miriam is behind everything.

Miriam was the name Jaxon's mom had written down in her journal thirty years ago. Shelly had been right, and it'd cost her her life.

Liv's voice grabbed her attention. "My dad tied Charles's hands and made him get in his car. They're leaving." Liv's description of her father commanding Charles sounded a lot like mind control. What else could Grayson do?

Winnie had studied Liv's dad's aura tonight when he'd come to the apartment and been stunned by how vibrant it was, a brilliant golden hue laced with amethyst. Gold was the light of genius, but Winnie could sense the pain in him. Tonight had been his goodbye to Liv.

Liv told them, "They're heading back toward the police station."

Winnie had her on speaker and Jaxon asked, "Do you know where they're going? We're almost to Oyster Bay."

"Not yet. They just passed the station and left the island."

"Find the landmarks," Winnie instructed. "We need landmarks."

"I'm trying."

"Fly around. I don't know! Find a building," Winnie stressed. They were running out of time.

The storm was growing worse as rain hit the car in sheets of water. Jaxon had his nose close to the glass to see through the rain. His hands, white-knuckled, gripped the steering wheel. He was driving as fast as humanly possible.

Winnie tried to prod. "Liv, if we don't know where they're going, we can't make it in time."

"I know! I'm trying!" Liv cried.

Thunder cracked all around them. Winnie felt the hairs on her arms stand up as if the thunder's energy had entered her body. She held her Tarot cards in her hand and looked down at them. The *King of Swords* was again the card on top. Her father's card. Somehow it was always sitting on top, waiting for her when she needed it.

Call on me was the last message he'd written to her.

Winnie could feel his words sink into her bones, knowing she needed to try to talk to her father on the other side because he had been trying to talk to her.

With the songs on the radio. His book falling off the shelf. The king's card. The flickering light. She had sensed the signs but hadn't known what to do with them. He was always with her, beyond this space and time. He was with her now. Her father had written the bridge between Heaven and Earth was shorter than we think. She only had to find it.

Energy zinged all around her, the air coming alive with electricity as her intention began to form.

Thunder rolled and rumbled, and the power within the storm began to fill her too. She closed her eyes, allowing her consciousness to expand and increase its bandwidth, to push past the wall of the world and touch the other side. Her mind was suddenly on a different highway, reaching a new destination beyond this world. There was no doubt in her mind what she was experiencing was real.

Her consciousness was in two different dimensions at once, and she heard a voice clearly.

"They want us to stop him," she said to Jaxon and Liv, her voice quivering with emotion. "We can still make it. Grayson's going to Theodore Roosevelt Memorial Park. To the flagpole."

Jaxon risked a look over at her while driving. "How do you know that?"

Tears spilled from her eyes, pure joy in her heart.

"My dad told me."

38

JAXON

divination:
perception through space and time

FIVE MINUTES.

After Winnie found out where Grayson had gone, Jaxon could feel time bearing down on him like a barometric pressure. A wave of inevitability was coming. Jaxon had only minutes to save Liv's father from dying.

He was driving faster than he should in the rainstorm, the car practically an extension of himself as he maneuvered the two-lane highway on pure instinct. Now he knew how a race car driver felt.

He barely made out the entrance to Theodore Roosevelt Memorial Park and made a sharp turn. The car skidded. "Hold on!"

Winnie gripped the dash, her eyes wide. "Liv, we're here. Do you see him?"

"Yes." Liv sounded like she was in a panic. "He's at the flagpole. Head toward the water."

Just like in his vision, park walkways led in different directions. At the far end, docked boats filled the harbor with a patch of beach nearby. He and Winnie got out of the car and ran. He couldn't see the flagpole through the rain.

Four minutes.

He was faster and also in sneakers. Winnie told him to go and she'd catch up. Running faster than he ever had before, finally he saw the flagpole ahead, along with Grayson and an older man whose hands were tied.

It was the exact mirror image of his premonition.

"Mad Merlin!" Jaxon called out, and Liv's father turned in shock to see him.

Grayson yelled back, "Stop! You shouldn't be here! You have to go!"

Jaxon kept running toward him. "We know what you're planning! Don't do it!" He finally reached them and stopped ten feet away, his chest heaving. Winnie was one minute behind him. "You can't do it!" He kept his eyes on Grayson and avoided looking at Charles Becker. Here was the man who'd ordered their parents' deaths and changed their lives forever.

"You don't understand." Grayson shook his head, still holding Charles's arm. "I have to."

Three minutes.

"The future is fluid, right?" Jaxon quoted Grayson's own words. "The trick is you have to see it first." Jaxon had seen the future Grayson had created. He, Winnie, and Liv were here to tear it down. There were two waves in the ocean now. One where Grayson died tonight, and one where he lived. Two potential inevitabilities. Jaxon had to make sure theirs won.

Charles Becker stepped into the fold, trying to sway him. "Grayson. Listen to me. Don't do this. They're going to come after you no matter what happens to me. If I live, we can work together. I swear to you on my life. You have no idea what's at stake. I can see that I was wrong about you. Just give me time to explain."

"We don't have time." Grayson adjusted his backpack, carrying all his gear to insure it would be destroyed with him. "I can't change this future. You don't know what I've seen."

Winnie arrived and stood next to Jaxon, catching her breath. "Then tell us. Why are you doing this?"

"I didn't see Shelly and Sawyer's deaths until it was too late—but I saw Liv's death before she was ever born."

Winnie gasped and Jaxon felt his body turn to ice.

Tears glistened in Grayson's eyes, mixing with the rain. "You tell me which is crueler? Everything I've done has been for her. I even asked her mother if we could name her Liv. *To Live.* To will life into her name. And I set a trap for her killer. The same man who killed your parents."

Two minutes.

"If I don't end him now, next year Liv will be killed with a group of other psychics. They're executed." Grayson pleaded. "Do you understand? This man will stop at nothing until every psychic connected to Alberty's study is killed. Including you both."

Jaxon's whole body was shaking with adrenaline. He had to believe there was another way. "Killing him and yourself is not the way out of this. There is another way." He didn't know yet what it was, but he could *feel* it, and that was all that mattered. The heart always led first.

With his conviction, he could feel the deep-seated power inside himself. He took a step closer. "Liv is here—remote viewing—she can see you. Hear you. Her mind is all around us." He saw Grayson's eyes widen in understanding, along with a newfound hesitation. Jaxon pressed harder. "Do you want her to witness you dying? You killing someone? To carry that burden for the rest of her life?" Jaxon had seen it already and never wanted those horrific images inside Liv's head. He was willing to do anything to stop it. He could tell he was starting to reach Grayson.

Winnie said, "My father and Shelly want you to know you don't have to do this. They led us to you." Her words rang with truth. "They've been trying to help us. They're saying to search the future and see you've already won. You've already saved Liv tonight."

Grayson looked at her in shock and wonder. "Sawyer and Shelly are here?"

The wild energy of the storm whipped around them as if they were standing at a riptide between two worlds. Jaxon could feel it too. His mother and Sawyer were here. Jaxon may not be able to hear them like Winnie could, but he could feel his mother was with him.

One minute.

Winnie told him, "Forester was never supposed to be there tonight with Nebony and Matty. The world will know what Charles Becker did. You forced him into the light. My father says to tell you Love changed the equation. It's already Checkmate."

Grayson stared at them for precious seconds as the future counted down, his eyes swimming with tears. "Checkmate?" he whispered, knowing the message was truly from Sawyer.

Winnie nodded, her own eyes bright. "The lightning strike you saw is no longer meant for you."

Grayson looked up at the sky with tears in his eyes, as if hardly daring to believe. Jaxon held his breath, about to lunge forward and push them out of the way. They were running out of time. Grayson still wasn't moving.

"*Grayson!*" Jaxon yelled with every fiber of his being, willing him to do it. "*Let. Him. Go.*"

Grayson seemed to feel the power within the words and nodded, surrendering. He let go of Charles and untied his hands.

Charles backed away in disbelief he was being set free. "Thank you. I promise you won't regret this."

"I already do." Grayson turned away from the man and left the flagpole, walking away from the death he had so carefully orchestrated.

He and Charles were now both clear of the strike zone. A gulf of twenty feet divided him and Charles Becker, but it may as well have been an ocean.

Jaxon saw in his mind what was about to happen. He looked at Grayson and could tell by the shock on his face he'd seen it too.

Jaxon's hair stood up on his body seconds before lightning drew down from the sky, heating the air.

A splintering bolt pierced the clouds—and lightning hit the ground in a channel of electricity powerful enough to make time stand still for a split moment.

Charles's eyes went wide as he was struck.

Then he was lying on the ground, ten feet away from where he'd been standing, his body charred and twisted.

Grayson tried to shield Winnie from the sight. Jaxon looked away but not before seeing proof of the body.

Winnie was dazed. "It was supposed to be at the flagpole."

Jaxon searched his mind for the answer and thought he knew. "The inevitability of his death was too strong."

"So nature compensated by changing the coordinates," Grayson finished, looking just as stunned. The lightning strike had still found Charles. Grayson was the one who'd been spared.

Nature had corrected its own course, and it made Jaxon wonder all the more how much the future factored into free will, destiny, and fate. He still didn't understand—perhaps it would take his whole lifetime to. What he did know was Stan Storlie, the man in the shadows who had kept a stranglehold on EHBF studies and created Clair Dominus, was no more. Jaxon felt the burden in his heart lighten. They'd done it.

"Thank you." Grayson, overcome with emotion, put his arms around Jaxon and Winnie and the three walked away together. They left Charles's body to be found by the water's edge. Each year forty to fifty people died by a lightning strike. Tonight, Charles Becker would become a statistic.

Presidential candidate killed by lighting while walking in the rain at a park.

No one but them would know what really happened.

They got into their cars. As Jaxon drove away, he watched the flagpole grow smaller in the rearview mirror with the American flag valiantly whipping in the storm. He didn't know what tomorrow would bring, but today their future had won.

Liv was anxiously waiting for them when they reached the apartment. The minute she saw him, she launched into his arms and grabbed Winnie too. They ended up in a group huddle.

Grayson watched and Liv broke away to approach him. Before he could speak, she hugged him tight. Startled, he returned the embrace.

After tonight they all understood what Grayson had sacrificed in order to ensure Liv's safety. He hadn't been able to tell anyone. It had been his own burden to bear.

Jaxon watched them, and he and Winnie shared a smile, when suddenly a premonition hit him—*Hospital doors opening. He is escorted past clamoring news vans and police cars, walking down a sterile hallway with Liv and Winnie to reunite Forester, Nebony, and Matty. Their families are all there waiting. His dad embraces him with tears is in eyes, as if understanding what they'd been up against.*

With that premonition came another—and finally, he saw where he'd be this summer. *In Alaska, with Liv.*

39

LIV

déjà vu:
a feeling of already having experienced the present

SUMMER SOLSTICE WAS THE LONGEST DAY of the year, and in Alaska it was otherworldly. In the state's northern places, daylight happened around the clock for a full twenty-four hours, and tonight people could watch the sun lower to touch the horizon for the briefest moment and come right back up again.

Today, Liv was trying her hand at driving her father's riverboat. Her father stood beside her, giving quiet instructions as they fished on the Kenai River. Otherwise, they'd barely said two words to each other since that night. Liv was quickly discovering they were both the same in that aspect. They did not waste words. But to her surprise, he'd been asking her every day this week to go fishing with him and she finally said yes.

Even though she now understood his reasons for abandoning her and her mother—what he had done to save her life—the question would always haunt them: Had it really been the only way? To give them up? Now they'd never know the answer and the damage had been done. In many ways, he was still a stranger.

All she could do was try to move forward and figure out how having Mad Merlin as a father would go. Right now, the most powerful psychic in the world was trying to teach her how to fish.

Sockeye salmon rolled in the water and jumped up and out into the air. One splashed them, startling her, and she laughed. They both laughed for the first time together, and Liv felt her heart ease the slightest bit.

The moment was exactly like the dream she'd had last month and written down in her journal. The landscape looked painted with color. Hot pink fireweed and purple lupine flowers bloomed in bushels by the thousands. Bird songs twisted in the air. The dream had been another prediction she hadn't recognized. Like Winnie and Jaxon, she *could* see the future, but in a different way. She was quickly finding out, like Sawyer had written, psychic abilities were like fingerprints, and no two people were the same.

She'd gained a lot of understanding since "that night," which is what they now called it. Afterward, all the families had come together for an open discussion about Dr. Alberty's study and the abilities Jaxon, Winnie, and Liv had inherited. The threat against them had abated with Charles Becker's death and the orders Grayson gave to Miriam to end Clair Dominus. Whoever else was involved had scattered to the shadows.

For their protection, it was decided the kids would stay together in Alaska for the summer in the small fishing town of Soldotna, and Matty and Nebony had come along too. Matty's leg was healing, and he still had to walk with a cane, but the doctors expected him to make a full recovery. Forester stayed in Hyde Park and would be flying to California with his family. The Mage Foundation was funding Drew Torres's spinal surgery, along with the family's travel and housing. After all the news coverage, there had been a huge public outpouring of support for Forester's dad, and donations had paid off his previous medical bills too. Jaxon had gotten a prediction seeing the surgery would be a success—and he told Forester as much.

Next week, she, Winnie, and Jaxon would fly north to Utqiaġvik near the Arctic Circle to meet with Dr. Alberty and undergo testing on their abilities. Liv's grandmother was going to join them there from Zurich, and Liv would get to meet her for the first time.

Soon Dr. Alberty would announce to the world his study's findings at the United Nations. The ramifications of enriching magnetite crystals in the brain had taken years to recognize. When his research was released into the world, psychic phenomenon would no longer be called occult or mystical or supernatural. It would be called science, and EHBF could come out of the shadows. A new era of scientific exploration could begin.

Her father seemed anxious for the UN talk and press conference, believing the more light shined on Dr. Alberty and his work, the better. It would be their safety net from any future threats. Liv overheard him discussing how the Mage Foundation was already scheduling the first international symposium for EHBF research.

For the time being, the kids were staying at Liv's grandfather's house in Soldotna. When Liv had first seen it, she'd been shocked. The house was stunning, an enormous four-bedroom right on the Kenai River, raised high on a hill and nestled in the trees. The living room had vaulted ceilings and towering cathedral glass windows. Two of the bedrooms had two sets of bunk beds. Jaxon and Matty had claimed one room and the girls the other.

For the past few days, it felt more like summer camp with all the hiking and fishing and evening sunlight. At night, they drew the blinds to block the sun and played board games and watched movies.

Liv snuggled with Jaxon on the couch, marveling at how much her life had changed. Sometimes she and Jaxon were so in tune with each other, she could swear they could read each other's thoughts. It only took a look or a smile to know what he was thinking. And it was true when she, Winnie, and Jaxon were together, their abilities were the strongest.

Liv only wore the lodestone pendant when she wanted to be grounded, now understanding how to remote view. She could do it anytime during the day, not needing to wait to fall asleep.

She'd already "taken a trip" up to Utqiaġvik alone and toured Dr. Alberty's research facility. The airline flight to Utqiaġvik took five hours from the Kenai Municipal Airport, but it had taken Liv only minutes to get there in her mind.

She soared north through the interior, over six million acres of Denali National Park and around North America's tallest mountain, skimming over glacier lakes and frozen tundra to arrive at the country's northernmost city. Utqiaġvik, called the "Gateway to the Arctic," was situated on the Arctic ocean's coastline and the town was only accessible by plane. The place was teeming with wildlife. Liv saw seals, walruses, countless birds, caribou, foxes, and whales swimming.

She visited Dr. Alberty's labs and saw him at work. Her father was with him, going over the upcoming UN talk. They didn't know she was there, and she began to understand why the CIA had used remote viewing as a tool.

"I don't want anyone mentioned by name," Grayson stressed, and Liv realized he was talking about them.

Dr. Alberty was a quiet, small man with white hair and antique-looking round glasses. He said, "You can't hide them away forever, Gray. The world will know who they are soon enough through their friends alone. I see they've been busy."

Grayson grimaced. Liv knew Dr. Alberty was talking about Matty and Nebony. The two were already working on a memoir with a publisher about their abduction, and they had plans for the old Premonitions Bureau letters as well. With the Mage Foundation's permission, they were going to upload an online database of all the Premonitions Bureau letters and create a forum where people could share new predictions. In the meantime, they'd already started doing social media posts, from sharing a Tarot card for the day to Numerology reports. They were planning on launching a Premonitions Club website for the discussion of all things paranormal and EHBF.

So far, no one else knew about Dr. Alberty's study, but that would change after the UN talks. Dr. Alberty was right. They couldn't hide forever, nor did Liv want to. For the first time, her life was starting to make sense. Every day she felt more empowered. Her father had spent years honing his abilities, and she planned to do the same.

After her father left the lab, Liv followed him home. He lived outside Utqiaġvik. She wasn't surprised by the rustic cabin, or the basement, an enormous room that looked like the command center of a computer wizard—a wizard who was now working hard to unravel all of Charles Becker's black ops programs and take Miriam offline for good. If anyone could beat an AI program, it was Mad Merlin.

But she couldn't help feeling her father was still keeping secrets. Would she ever really know him?

He had flown back to Soldotna yesterday to spend time with them, regaling Winnie and Jaxon with stories about their parents and promising one day to go through all their letters together.

"You're all Sevens," he told her, Winnie, and Jaxon, explaining their birthdays all added up to the same Life Path number.

Seven was the Seeker, the one on the journey to the inner world. They were their own triskelion, and whatever challenges they faced in the future, they would face them together.

"Winnie, what's today's card?" Nebony asked her. Nebony was sitting cross-legged on the couch, busy typing on her phone, aka the Premonitions Club's command center.

Winnie and Nebony had attempted to come to an understanding, and with Matty's help they were trying to become friends. Winnie drew

The Star card and Nebony took a picture of the woman at the water under the night sky. "What does it mean?"

Winnie stared at the card with a faint smile. "Hope and dreams fulfilled."

"Ooooh, I love it. That's perfect for Summer Solstice today." Nebony shared the card online with her followers along with her usual slew of hashtags.

#ThePremonitionsClub #ThePremonitionsBureau

#EHBF #psychoenergetics #Ilovescience #futurism

#psychic #paranormal #telepathy #clairvoyance

#psychokinesis #remoteviewing #anythingispossible

#tarot #palmistry #auras #numerology #astrology

#cheerislife #TeenVogue

Winnie looked over to Liv, observing her, "Your aura's a lovely pink today." Winnie nodded toward the kitchen and added, "Theirs is too."

Liv's dad was with her mom in the kitchen, visiting over a cup of coffee. Liv didn't know what the future might bring, although she was sure at some point Jaxon or Winnie would let her know. But today, on the longest day of the year, when the sun shone the brightest, she felt a newfound sense of gratitude being together with her family and friends.

She took Jaxon's hand in hers and heard his thought in her mind as clearly as if he'd said it aloud: *I agree.*

Her eyes widened and she looked at him in wonder. *Did we just share a thought?* Already knowing the answer.

He nodded at her silent question. *We sure did*, and they both laughed.

Her mind went back to the other times she couldn't tell if they'd spoken aloud or not, and she wondered if they hadn't had the ability all along. What other hidden talents were waiting for their discovery?

Matty sat beside them, working on his laptop, oblivious to their mind-blowing realization they were telepathic. He was busy creating *The Premonitions Club Handbook* he would be uploading soon.

He'd been trying out titles for it all week and finally looked up, exclaiming, "I got it!" and typed:

Welcome to The Premonitions Club
The Future is Yours

<ENCRYPTED TRANSMISSION>

<DEFENSE INTELLIGENCE AGENCY SERVER>

<From: THE COUNCIL>

<Priority: HIGH>

Stan Storlie's untimely death and last
directive has fortunately caused Operation
Clair Dominus to be terminated.

A press release has stated Dr. Alberty
plans to give a UN talk on his EHBF research.
Assessing potential fallout to determine
whether this presentation should be allowed.

Will continue to monitor all known
Alberty prodigies.

Our advised course of action:

Proceed with Operation Sovereign.

THE
PREMONITIONS
CLUB
HANDBOOK

DESTINY

THE HIDDEN FORCE IN LIFE
BELIEVED TO
CONTROL WHAT WILL HAPPEN
IN THE FUTURE

READING AURAS

THE BEST WAY TO EXPLAIN AN AURA: Every person is made up of billions of atoms that are constantly in a state of motion, bombarding each other and creating energy. To see this energy field takes practice. The trick is to concentrate and be patient. (And if you try to focus on seeing it, you won't see it!)

How to do it:

Have the person whose aura you would like to see stand ten feet away from you. The room should have natural light and the background behind them is best if it is all white or all black.

1. **Relax your gaze.**
2. **Focus on their nose.**
3. **Allow your peripheral vision to open.**
4. **As this happens, move your gaze to their forehead.**

If and when you do see an aura, what do the colors mean? There are many different interpretations.

Here's a basic rundown:

Red: Adventurous, high energy, passionate, strong, competitive, ambitious, intense. (Murky dark red—angry and confrontational)

Orange: Creative, artistic, joyful, sensual, fearless, childlike. (Burnt orange—lack of energy, lazy, burned out)

Yellow: Sunny, cheerful, charismatic, intelligent, confident, inventive, eccentric. (Off yellow—overly critical and scatterbrained)

Pink: Loving, generous, caring, tender, receptive, compassionate. (Murky pink—overly sensitive, vulnerable, and insecure)

Blue: Intuitive, a great communicator, inspiring, truthful, imaginative, creative. (Murky blue—stifled, anxious, and judgmental)

Green: Nature lover, compassionate, giving, hardworking, determined, prosperous, full of life. (Off green—jealous, mean, or stubborn)

Purple: Empathetic, strongly intuitive, introverted, philosophical, a deep thinker. (Darker purple—excessive worrier and insecure)

Gold: Wise, strong, enlightened, a leader. (Off gold—too proud and obsessive)

Pearl: Rarest of aura colors, pure, spiritual, enlightened. (Dark or murky white—irrational and unbalanced)

Watch out for:
Muddy hues: Confusion, emotionally stunted, depression.
Dark gray shadows: Illness, negativity, hatred.

NUMEROLOGY

What is Your Life Path Number?

TO FIND OUT YOUR LIFE PATH Number is simple. Add up all the numbers of your birthday together (day, month and all four numbers for the year). From there, if you end up with a double-digit add those together too. *Except if the final number you get is an 11 or 22 or 33. Those are called "master numbers" and should never be reduced.

For example:

Someone's birthday is 4/22/2025 =
4+2+2+2+2+5 = 17
1+7 = 8
Their number is an 8.

(And if you end up with a 10, 20, or 30 . . . etc, those reduce to a 1, 2, or 3 . . .)

The Life Path Number's Meaning:

1. Ones are born leaders. They are charismatic, determined, independent, stubborn, focused, energetic, and caring, but sometimes overbearing.

2. Twos are empathetic, kindhearted, and caring. They are diplomatic, expressive, and inspiring, and are often finding ways to help society.

3. Threes are artistic, hardworking, and motivated. They tend to find their talent early and cultivate it successfully. Threes are attention grabbers and often the center of it.

4. Fours are logical, organized, and grounded. They excel at making strategies and are precise and professional. They love structure and schedules.

5. Fives are freedom lovers and hard to pin down. They are inspiring and always seeking the open road. They are adaptable, full of adventure, and sometimes easily bored.

6. Sixes nurture and counsel others. They crave peaceful environments, are kind, and often help people in need.

7. Sevens are truth seekers, often introverted, and philosophical. They like to solve puzzles and ask the big questions.

8. Eights are persuasive, financially successful, and hard workers. They enjoy being part of a community and are always striving.

9. Nines care deeply about improving the world around them and taking care of others. They are dedicated and thrive on making connections with others.

11. Elevens are fascinating. The first of the master numbers, elevens are creators and initiate new ideas. They are talented, innovative, and highly intuitive.

22. Twenty-twos are creators and idea builders, and anything is possible to them in their minds. They are enthusiastic, open-minded, and dreamers.

33. Thirty-threes are wise, witty, empathetic, and fair-minded. They are passionate, creative, focused, and determined in everything they do.

What is Your Destiny Number?

Your Destiny Number complements your Life Path Number and is sometimes called your Expression Number. It indicates how you will go about fulfilling your Life Path. This number can be found by assigning a number to every letter in your full name, using the chart below. Add up all the numbers and voilà!

1	=	A, J, S
2	=	B, K, T
3	=	C, L, U
4	=	D, M, V
5	=	E, N, W
6	=	F, O, X
7	=	G, P, Y
8	=	H, Q, Z
9	=	I, R

The Destiny Number's Meaning:

1. Your destiny is to become a leader in whatever you set out to do. Choose what you're most passionate about. You will strive to be the best and expect high standards from yourself.

2.   Your destiny is to spread harmony and love. You're focused
      on the higher good and big causes.

3.   Your destiny is to inspire and uplift others. You are at your
      best when you're full of optimism and compassion.

4.   Your destiny is to build something of lasting value that will
      benefit others in their lives, be it a business, a movement,
      or a life experience.

5.   Your destiny is to follow your curiosity and embrace life's
      adventure. You will develop your own tools and create
      advancements with what you do.

6.   Your destiny is to create beauty and balance for yourself
      and others, whether it's your family or the community.
      You are the center of the circle that people gravitate toward.

7.   Your destiny is to seek out knowledge and information.
      You will dig deep and contemplate the big questions of life.

8.   Your destiny is to obtain self-mastery in whatever it is you set
      out to do. You are meant to succeed in all arenas of your life.

9.   Your destiny is a humanitarian one. You are at your best
      when you are balanced, centered, and helping others.

11.   Your destiny is to use your creative force and intuition
      to help the world. You might do this through art or
      entertainment or working with others as a medical
      professional or teacher.

22. Your destiny is to look at the big picture and create enterprises or things that will benefit the world. You are hardworking and have a strong sense of purpose.

33. Your destiny is to bring a lot of love into the world and inspire others. Remember to stay joyful as you teach and help others.

PALMISTRY

What Does Your Palm Say About You?

IN PALMISTRY, EVERY LINE TELLS A story. The lines on the left hand traditionally hold the map of what you set out to do in this life. The right hand shows what you've made out of your life by your actions.

As a starting point for the handbook, we'll be looking at the four major lines of the palm. They are the Life Line, Head Line, Heart Line, and Fate Line. If you want to take a closer look at your hand and all its lines, we recommend getting a book on palmistry and diving in! (The best time to read your palm is in the morning when you wake up, when the lines are clearest.)

The Life Line represents your vitality and how you approach life. A big arc means big energy. The deeper the line, the deeper your energy reserves are. A faint or short Life Line does not mean a short life! It means that you must work harder to gain the energy and vitality you need.

The Head Line reflects your intellect and how you think. This changes over time. Your childhood begins where the line meets the Life Line, then as you get older it travels across your palm. A deep, strong line shows a very focused person who can stay on track. The straighter the line, the more logical the person. A long line shows broader interest and a shorter one shows more focus into one area of interest.

The Heart Line tells the story of the heart. The line starts somewhere near the pinky finger and travels toward the Life Line. If it curves upward, it means you have great ability at expressing your feelings. A straight line indicates you're more conservative, stable, and possibly shy. A downward-curving line shows you have difficulty expressing your feelings and need to work harder on it than others. A Heart Line that ends between the index and middle fingers shows a pure love. A line that ends under the index finger shows an abundance of love and dreams. A short line indicates you might have some challenges in your relationships to overcome. A long line across the entire hand indicates you are romantic and engaged in relationships but stubborn as well.

The Fate Line shows your luck, good fortune, and success, usually centering around your career. The line begins at the base of the palm in childhood and then goes up toward the middle finger to old age. (No Fate Line means you will change your occupation quite a bit.)

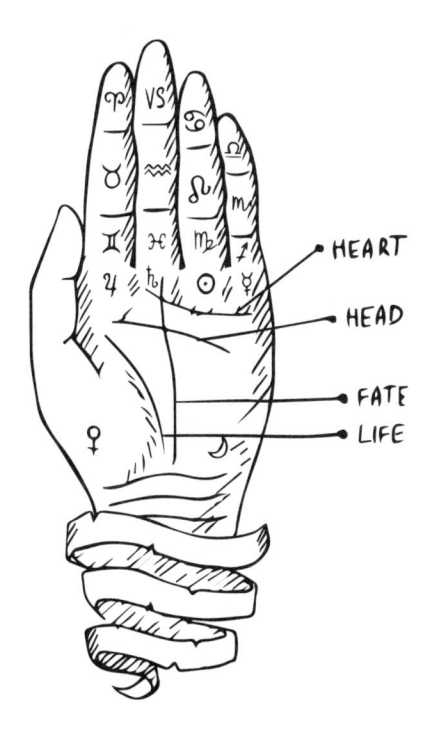

TAROT AND DIVINATION

What Is Your Reading For Today?

DID YOU KNOW IF LOOK UP 'kinds of divination' and how to tell the future, there are over three hundred listings?

From *lychnomancy* (telling the future from the flame of a candle) to *nephomancy* (the shape of a cloud). You can put *mancy* at the end of any word and find countless ways to see the future, which is simply the mind and our intuition experiencing time from a different perspective.

If you want to do your own readings to sense what the future holds, choose any form of divination. You can stare at a rock, a seashell, or a cloud in the sky. Open the page of any book and read what it has to say. Get a Tarot deck or try the I Ching. Draw a card or roll the dice. Your intuition will give yourself the message. How it's delivered is entirely up to you!

REMOTE VIEWING

If you want to learn how to remote view: See the CIA's Handbook ☺

Approved For Release 2000/08/07 : CIA-RDP96-00788R001100080004-9

SECRET

(S) GRILL FLAME PROTOCAL (U)
(S-ORCON) AMSAA APPLIED REMOTE VIEWING PROTOCOL (S-ORCON)

1. (S-ORCON)   <u>General</u>

This protocol contains the procedure for AMSAA sponsored remote viewing. It is in effect for the period required to accomplish the scope of the work.   Remote viewing (RV) is an intellectual process by which a person perceives characteristics of a location, remote from that person. RV does not involve any electronic sensing devices at or focused at the target site, nor does it involve classical photo interpretation of photographs obtained from overheard or oblique means. The individual performing RV (the remote viewer) is provided with a unique identifier such as stationary map coordinates, a specific structure, an identifiable vehicle (aircraft tail number) or a specific individual (name, place of birth, age, and/or photograph).   The task of the remote viewer is to locate, identify and/or describe the target.   The task is achievable12345. No drugs, hypnosis, special sensory (visual, auditory, or olfactory) or proprioceptive stimuli, liminal or subliminal, electrical or electromagnetic stimulus will be used in this RV protocol.

2. (S-ORCON)   <u>MILITARY OBJECTIVE</u>

It is the objective of this protocol to standardize the process of RV so that it may become an established task in the spectrum of intelligence and information gathering functions and for target acquisition applications.

The Premonitions Club is proudly sponsored by
The Mage Foundation.

Read their Mission Statement below.

THE MAGE FOUNDATION

LIFE FORCE GOES BY MANY NAMES: Qi, Chi, Orgone, Shakti, Mana. It the essence of the universe, the force behind stars that flows through us all. We at the Mage Foundation are committed to finding answers to the questions that have been posed throughout the ages, by ancient alchemists to the scientists of today:

Who are we?

Why are we here?

What is life?

We experience life on Earth embedded in this world through our bodies and our brains, but our mind is not our brain. Part of ourselves is always off wandering the cosmos, in our subconscious mind, in our dreams while we sleep, and in our imaginations.

The final frontier of scientific exploration is not in outer space but inner space. Where there are dimensions waiting to be discovered. One day, that journey will be mapped and charted and reveal the infinity within us all.

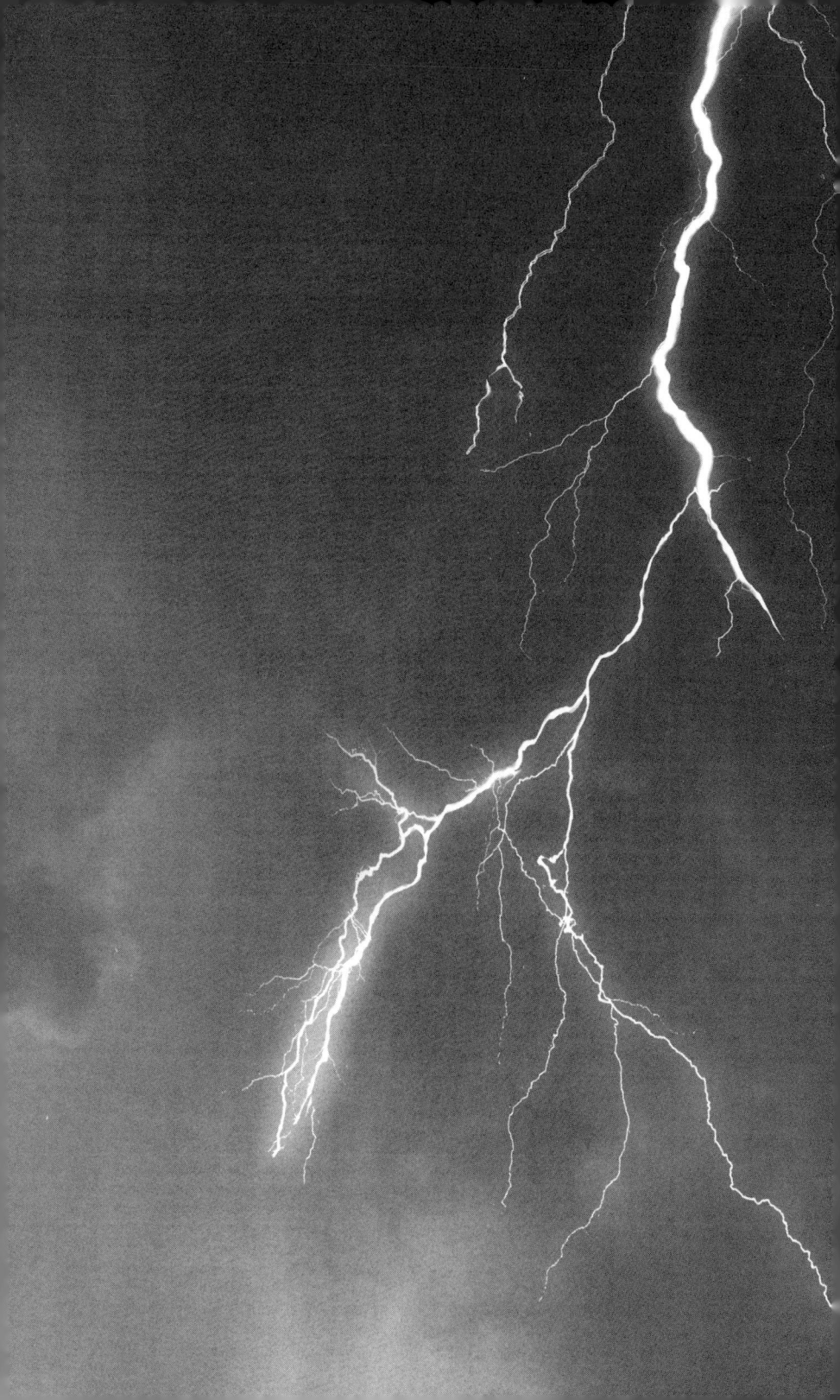

ACKNOWLEDGMENTS

HELLO, THANK YOU FOR READING *The Premonitions Club*! I am ecstatic to be writing the acknowledgments. This book took time to come to fruition, which makes crossing the finish line to thank everyone all the sweeter. Even though this will be my fourth novel, *The Premonitions Club* is a first in many ways. It's my first post-pandemic book, my first YA story, and my first novel to be published after moving back to my hometown, Houston, Texas.

I have many people to thank for this book coming to life:

Starting first with my agent, Alec Shane at Writers House. Alec, thank you for your amazing support, high energy, and story insights. I feel fortunate to be working together. Special thanks also to Amy Berkower, Simon Lipskar, and Alexandra Levick at Writers House, and also to Matt Kelly, who gave the manuscript a close read in the early days. Thank you! Special thanks to my film rights agent as well, Debbie Deuble Hill at Independent Artists Group.

To my publishing team at CamCat, you all are electric. It has been a joy to work with you from day one. Before I dive into listing the wonderful family of CamCatters, first I would like to express my deepest thanks to the late Sue Arroyo, CamCat's publisher and founder. Sue is the reason *The Premonitions Club* found its home. We had only been working together a short while and finalized the cover art when she passed away. CamCat stands for the names of her daughters, Camryn and Catherine, and I want them to know how much she was an inspiration.

Her team has been incredible to work with, starting with my editor Elana Gibson. We were in such sync for this story from the get-go. It was a wonderful back and forth. Thank you, Elana, for the stellar guidance and incredible attention to nuance.

A huge, enormous thank you to the entire CamCat team: Helga Schier, Laura Wooffitt, Bill Lehto, Gabe Schier, Meredith Lyons, Abigail Miles, Kayla Webb, Jessica Homami, Nicole DeLise, MC Smitherman, and my copyeditor, Penni Askew. As well as infinite thanks to the talented Maryann Appel for designing an absolutely stunning, perfect cover for this book. I have spent a lot of time gazing at it lovingly and imagining it out in the world. Thank you!

As I was shaping the story, several key pieces of research helped it come together, and I would like to give special thanks to Dean Radin, Chief Scientist at the Institute of Noetic Sciences for his insightful books *The Conscious Universe* and *Real Magic: Ancient Wisdom, Modern Science, and a Guide to the Secret Power of the Universe*, also bestselling author Annie Jacobsen and her book, *Phenomena: The Secret History of the U.S. Government's Investigations into Extrasensory Perception and Psychokinesis*, and Tyler Henry, psychic, medium, and author, whose show *Life After Death* inspired me while I was writing.

On a personal note, loving thanks to my Dad, who is always one of my first readers and biggest cheerleaders. A huge thank you to my son Kenzo, all my family and friends for their love and support, especially one of my best friends Julia Burke and her family, Luke, Jack, and Donovan, who opened their house to me while I was editing the book and dealing with a Houston tornado! Thank you for the amazing stay at Chez Burke and the all-hour access to your espresso machine. You guys are the best. To my dear friends Charlotte and Michael, and my best friend from my days in Alaska, George Holly, thank you for your help.

Special thanks to my favorite writing partner Beth Szymkowski, the Nic Chicks, Andrew McFarland, and my first summer intern, Bennett Welsh! Thank you, Ben for our productive lunches and brainstorming. It was a blast to work together.

I also want to give a special thank you to my longtime web designer and web manager, Jessica Foster, who is retiring. Thank you, Jess, for all our years working together. A big thanks to Will Plyler for stepping in to help me with my site.

Lots of love to everyone in the publishing world who work so hard to keep the stories coming and to the book lovers who make the community thrive. I feel lucky to be a part of the circle. Special thanks to author Gretchen McNeil for giving me encouragement when I needed it the most. Thank you to author Therese Walsh too, who is the co-founder and Editorial Director of WriterUnboxed.com. It's an honor to be a part of the WU team this year.

To all my readers, thank you so much for continuing to cheer me on and for waiting patiently for my next book. I promise to make up for it in the future. That's a premonition. ;)

ABOUT THE AUTHOR

GWENDOLYN WOMACK is the *USA Today* and *Los Angeles Times* bestselling author of *The Fortune Teller*, *The Time Collector*, and *The Memory Painter*. Her romantic thrillers have been called "a blast of a read" and "pure story adrenaline."

The Premonitions Club is her YA debut. Gwendolyn went to college in Fairbanks, Alaska, studying theater, and received an MFA in Directing for theater and film at California Institute of the Arts. She lives in Houston, Texas with her family, collects and photographs kaleidoscopes, and can usually be found either immersed in a book or dreaming up a new story.

Visit her online at
www.gwendolynwomack.com

If you liked

Gwendolyn Womack's *The Premonitions Club,*

you'll enjoy

Magic at the Grand Dragonfly Theatre

by Brandie June.

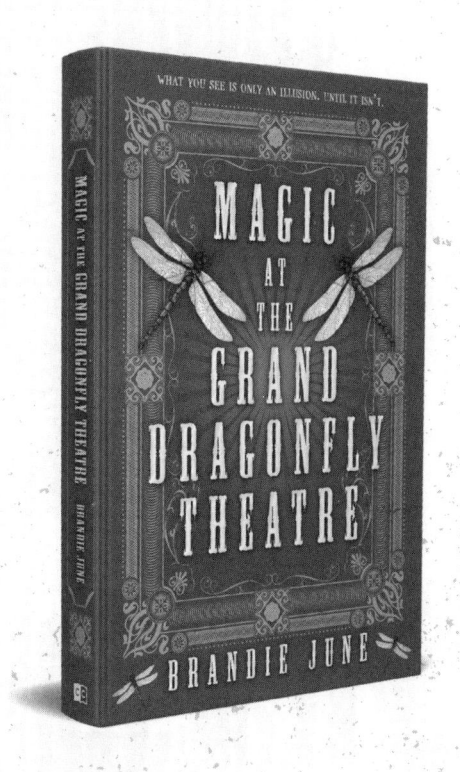

PROLOGUE

IRIS

IRIS HAD BEEN PRACTICING HER TRICK for weeks, wanting to show her uncle that she could also be a performer. She dreamed of standing onstage instead of watching in the dark.

During the ferry crossing to the Isle of Ily, she pulled out her coin and her mother's blue silk handkerchief, the one with her mother's initials embroidered in gold, but the swaying of the boat made her drop the coin instead of hiding it.

"I want to see the magic show!" Violet said when they reached the docks, wriggling in their mother's arms.

"It's not a *magic* show. It's a show of *illusion*," Iris corrected with a six-year-old's sense of superiority.

"That's right, Iris," her mother said as she set Violet down and went to hail one of Uncle Leo's shiny black carriages, the ones with large gold dragonflies painted on the doors.

"It's important you two know this is a place for illusions only," their mother said sternly when she returned.

"Illusions *and* wonder," Iris added. Her mother had helped her read some of the advertisement posters in the city. One poster depicted Uncle Leo pulling a rabbit out of a hat. In another, he was sawing a beautiful woman in half, but since the woman was smiling, Iris decided that it was nothing to worry about.

Today, she would tell Uncle Leo that she wanted to be an illusionist like him.

Iris draped the blue silk handkerchief over the coin in her left hand.

"Now Violet, blow on the handkerchief."

"Why?" her little sister asked. Violet was a smaller version of Iris with similar chestnut hair, hazel eyes, and a white lace dress that matched the one Iris was wearing.

"Because it is part of the trick."

Violet stared at the silk square, not sure what to make of it.

"Come on, Vi," Iris insisted.

Violet leaned over and blew so hard on the handkerchief that she flecked it with spittle.

"With that breath, I make the coin disappear!" Iris tried to move the coin into her sleeve, but it slipped, falling to the ground. Iris waved the handkerchief around, hoping the effect was mesmerizing as she quickly stepped on the coin.

"And voilà!" Iris said with a flourish, handing the coinless handkerchief to her sister.

Violet took the piece of silk but wrinkled her nose at her sister. "You stepped on the coin."

Defeated, Iris lifted her foot and picked up the coin.

"You do the trick like *this*," Violet said. A coin appeared in her empty palm. Iris could smell roses and smoke.

"How did you do that?" Iris asked, her incredulity warring with jealousy. Violet hadn't been practicing for weeks to impress their uncle like she had.

"I don't know," Violet said, shrugging.

"Give that to me," Iris demanded.

"Stop that!" their mother said, so sharply that Iris froze. Their mother snatched the coin from Violet. "We don't conjure things, do you understand?" She bent down and held Violet's shoulders. "Understand?"

"Mommy, you're hurting me," Violet whined.

Their mother seemed to melt, almost crying as she quickly wrapped Violet in a hug. "I'm so sorry, sweetheart. Your father had to leave us because bad men saw him conjuring. I only want to keep you safe."

The sun was low in the sky as the carriage jostled them down a winding road to the theater. Violet whined as their seats shook after hitting a jut in the road, but Iris grinned, knowing this was only the beginning of their journey.

The theater came into view as they crested the final hill. The building was large and stately, reminding Iris of a palace. Today, the theater was the perfect shade of butterscotch yellow, making it look warm and inviting against the sunset. Large pillars carved to look like giant stone dragonflies supported the massive domed roof and the great stained-glass windows of amber and green, illuminated by warm light from within. Enormous brass letters above engraved double doors declared that this was the Grand Dragonfly Theater. Silver and gold stars and moons bedecked the theater's walls and glittered in the fading sunlight.

"We've arrived," Iris called out in a majestic tone, trying to imitate the booming voice her uncle used when welcoming people to his theater.

"We are late, so we must get to our seats," their mother said, quickly ushering the girls through a grand mirrored foyer and into their usual box.

Iris hovered on the edge of her seat, leaning as far as she could toward the railing of the balcony, even though all she could see were the thick burgundy curtains that hid the stage.

"Careful, darling, lean over any farther and you'll fall over the edge," her mother warned.

"No, I won't," Iris argued, but she scooted back a tiny bit to avoid a second scolding.

"When will the show start?" Violet asked.

As if on cue, the lights inside the auditorium went dark.

I could be anywhere, Iris thought, and smiled. Her belly filled with happy butterflies as she anticipated the start of the show. With a flash of light and what sounded like a clap of thunder, the footlights flared to life, casting the stage in bright illumination as the curtain was pulled away. Iris inhaled the familiar scent of gas from the lights.

The stage looked like an extraordinary palace. Gold filigree had been worked into the walls and incorporated in a magnificent throne embedded with rubies and sapphires that sat center stage.

A young boy wearing the regalia of a medieval squire entered stage right and walked to the throne with dignified purpose. Iris wondered if the boy had been made up with white lead paint, since his skin and hair were snow white beneath the bright stage lights.

"Your Highness, one of your subjects requests an audience," the boy said, his high voice surprisingly strong in the vast theater.

A sparkling puff of green smoke exploded in front of the throne, causing gasps of surprise throughout the audience. When the smoke cleared, a king sat upon the great golden chair.

"And which of my subjects comes to see the king?"

Iris recognized her uncle's voice right away. Uncle Leo wore a jeweled crown instead of his usual top hat and a richly embroidered doublet with a bottle-green cape.

The squire introduced a knight, who entered the stage and bowed low to Uncle Leo. As her uncle gave the knight a quest, Iris let herself slip into the story as easily as she slipped into dreams, living in the world playing out in front of her. Iris felt the ocean spray on her skin and tasted salt water on her tongue as the knight saved himself from drowning after a tidal wave hit his ship in a storm. She held her breath when the knight fought a three-headed wolf that guarded a witch's hut, the wild animal onstage looking so real that Iris wondered if there really were wolves with three heads.

The audience booed when they saw the witch, a hunched woman clad in rags, a giant snake slithering over her shoulders. And Iris shrieked in delight when the brown phoenix the knight fought so hard for burst into flames, only to reappear golden and mirror bright. Iris cheered loudly when Uncle Leo rewarded the knight and welcomed him home.

As the actors took their bows, the audience applauded loudly. Iris stood, clapping as hard as she could. Tiny golden feathers no larger than Iris's pinkie finger floated down from the ceiling, and the sisters reached out for them, managing to pocket a few of the small treasures so that they would remember this perfect night forever.

"That was incredible." Iris sighed as the audience began to file out of the theater.

"Indeed, it was," her mother agreed. "Now let's go see Uncle Leo." Iris's mother led the girls out of the auditorium. The woman who had played the witch stood in one corner of the lobby surrounded by audience members waiting their turn to pet the large snake coiled around her neck.

"Mrs. Ashmore."

Iris turned to see a strange man approaching them. His dirty trench coat and muddy boots clashed with the finely dressed patrons, and his beady eyes were fixed on Iris's mother.

Iris's mother stepped in front of Iris and Violet, shielding them from the stranger.

"I'm afraid you have me at a disadvantage," Iris's mother said. Her sweet voice had gone cold. Iris didn't know what was going on, but she wanted the strange man to go away. "I don't believe I've made your acquaintance," her mother added, but did not offer him her hand.

The stranger chuckled, a gravelly sound that scared Iris. "How thoughtless of me. Mr. Roman Whitlock."

Iris's mother stiffened and Iris thought she heard her mother say *bounty hunter* under her breath. Iris noticed that the other people in the lobby had stilled their chatter, everyone trying to look like they weren't staring at Iris's family and Mr. Whitlock. Iris peeked around her mother's skirts. Several men in yellow-and-brown uniforms stood behind Mr. Whitlock.

"Now Mrs. Ashmore, it seems that your husband was not the only conjuror in your family. I have reason to believe you are as well," Mr. Whitlock said. There were several audible gasps in the lobby. Mr. Whitlock licked his thick lips. "Which means you are charged with failing to report yourself for conscription." Mr. Whitlock was grinning, but Iris knew he wasn't friendly.

"What is going on here?" Uncle Leo had finally arrived, out of costume but still wearing the thick greasepaint makeup. Iris sighed in relief. She was certain he could make the bad man go away.

"Business for the Crown," Mr. Whitlock said, puffing himself up. "You ought to stay out of it, Mr. Von Frey."

"This is my theater, and you are speaking to my sister," Uncle Leo said, stepping right up to Mr. Whitlock, even though he was almost a head shorter.

"And Mrs. Ashmore is a conjuror. I will be taking her in to collect the bounty."

"You have no proof," Iris's mother said, but Iris could hear her mother's voice shaking.

The bounty hunter moved far faster than Iris thought a man of his size could. Before she realized what was going on, Mr. Whitlock had snatched her away from her mother, yanking her arm so hard it hurt. Iris screamed as his meaty fingers dug into her flesh, but the sound was cut off as his other hand wrapped around her throat, squeezing the air out of her.

A blade appeared in her mother's hand. She slashed at the bounty hunter, inflicting a deep cut along his temple and down his cheek. He swore and dropped Iris. She fell to the floor, gasping for air. Everything hurt. She didn't want to move, but Uncle Leo was already picking her up.

"You don't touch my daughters," her mother said. Iris had never heard her mother so angry. Iris silently cried as she looked over at the terrible, mean man. The cut on his face was bleeding, but he only smiled.

"I love the smell of smoke and roses," Mr. Whitlock said, inhaling deeply. "Using the True Gift always leaves that smell. And that knife trick was all the final proof I needed. Now, will you come with me willingly, or should the Noble Guardsmen use force?" He gestured to the men in the yellow-and-brown uniforms that now surrounded them.

Iris's mother looked at Uncle Leo with so much fear that Iris cried harder. "I'm so sorry," her mother said. Uncle Leo stepped close to Iris's mother, sandwiching Iris between them.

"I will figure out something, Lynnette," Uncle Leo said.

Iris's mother shook her head. For a moment she leaned on Uncle Leo's shoulder, and Iris heard her sobbing. When Iris's mother straightened, tears were running down her cheeks. Iris pulled out a crumpled blue handkerchief and handed it to her mother. Iris's mother gave Iris a watery smile as she accepted the piece of silk, silently wiping her face as she took long, deep breaths.

Iris's mother turned back to Mr. Whitlock. "I will go with you peacefully, but let me say goodbye to my children."

Mr. Whitlock scoffed. "Your husband was carted off years ago. It would be best if they come with us." His grin made Iris shudder. "They will be well cared for at the palace. And maybe one or both will turn out to have the True Gift."

"No!" Iris's mother snapped. "I will come, but you will leave my children alone. The conscription only applies to adult conjurors."

Mr. Whitlock shrugged. "It's only a matter of time."

Iris's mother ground her teeth but didn't reply, instead turning back to Uncle Leo. "I need you to take my girls."

Uncle Leo nodded vigorously. "Of course, Lynnette. Who do you want me to take them to?"

Iris's mother shook her head. "No, Leo. I need you to keep the girls." Quietly, so that the bad man couldn't hear, her mother added, "You know what my daughter is. I need you to protect her."

Uncle Leo's mouth opened but no sound came out.

Violet started crying.

"Please Leo, keep my daughters safe. Someday, I will be released from service, and I'll come back for them." Iris's mother's eyes were glossy with tears, but she did not look away from Uncle Leo.

"I would do anything for you and the girls," Uncle Leo said resolutely. Iris's unease swelled inside her, giving her a stomachache.

Gently, Uncle Leo set Iris down. Her mother wrapped up her and Violet in a tight embrace. "I love you girls so much. I need you to know that."

When Mr. Whitlock cleared his throat, Iris's mother reluctantly released Iris and Violet, kissing each of them on the tops of their heads. "I must go now. Be good for your uncle."

Iris wanted to speak but had no words. Only hours ago, she would have given anything to live in her uncle's theater, but now she regretted it. She didn't want her mother to leave. Violet kept crying. When their mother rose to leave, Violet lunged to stop her.

"Mama!" she cried. Uncle Leo held Violet back as she kicked and screamed.

Iris reached for her mother's skirts. "Please don't go without me," Iris said. "I don't want you to go."

Her mother bent down so she was eye to eye with her daughter. "I love you and your sister more than I could ever say, and I need to keep you safe. Right now, the safest place for you and your sister is with your uncle."

"I don't want to be *safe*. Not if you're leaving."

"But who will protect Violet if you come with me?"

Iris blinked and looked up at her mother.

"I will be back as soon as I can. Until then, I am counting on you, Iris."

"I don't have all night, Mrs. Ashmore," the bounty hunter said.

All eyes were fixed on Iris's mother. Her fists were clenched so tightly they turned white, but still she rose and followed Mr. Whitlock, a line of Noble Guardsmen trailing behind her. Then, she was gone, leaving Iris with her screaming sister and Uncle Leo, who was barely able to keep hold of Violet.

Iris ran.

The courtyard was dark. Most of the carriages had already left, making it easy for Iris to find the one her mother was in with the bounty hunter. The carriage was already moving as Iris raced outside. She ran after it, yelling for her mother, but her tiny legs were no match for the horses. Iris was crying, her vision blurry with tears. She tripped, skinning her knee bloody as the coach got farther and farther away. Everything hurt, and Iris screamed and screamed. But her mother never came back.

CHAPTER ONE

VIOLET

THE GRAND DRAGONFLY THEATRE WAS NEVER the same color. Uncle Leo, known as Leopold The Great, insisted that guests immediately know they were in for great spectacle. Only in the early hours of the morning, long after even the most enthusiastic or inebriated patron had stumbled into a hansom cab, did the illusion fade and the walls of the theatre melt back to the traditional colors of wood and stone. But once Leo woke, often at a decadently late hour, the plain walls would once again be drenched in a gaudy splash of color. Today, the theatre was the deep mauve of rain clouds after sunset.

After eleven years of living in the loud and lavish Grand Dragonfly Theatre, Violet Ashmore sought peace and quiet wherever she could find it. For this reason, she had climbed the trellis outside her bedroom window and sat on the roof, legs dangling over the window ledge. In the predawn stillness, she could almost hear the ocean waves crashing on the shore of their island, the fresh air cold and salty.

She thought about changing the color of the theatre, going so far as to touch the wall, rough and cool under her fingers. The fear of forgetting to let her conjuring fade the way illusions naturally did after a day or so brought on anxiety that the Noble Guardsmen would discover her. Less than a week ago, the Crown announced they were doubling the bounty price on Conjurors. The war with the colonies of Tsitonia was going poorly, and the Crown was desperate for more Conjurors to send overseas to fight.

She shivered and withdrew her hand from the wall. Technically only adults of eighteen or older were required to fight, but Violet knew that being fifteen wouldn't protect her from a war that had been going on for over a decade. Even children could be dragged away by the Noble Guard, kept locked up until they were old enough to fight. Violet was many things, but a fighter wasn't one of them. Just the idea of war made her insides squeeze tight with fear.

The sky was just beginning to lighten in the east as it groggily remembered what dawn should look like. Violet rubbed her eyes, trying to soothe the strain. She had been up for hours, writing by candlelight and savoring the sleepy quiet that was a rarity in theatre life. The ink was drying on the final pages of her script. She mulled over the story, her mind engrossed in the fantasy of magical moon princesses and starcrossed lovers.

"Are you up there?" A head of glossy auburn curls poked through Violet's window. Iris Ashmore looked up at Violet with large hazel eyes.

"Why are you in my room?" Violet snapped, her sense of calm evaporating.

"I hadn't seen you since intermission. I thought I'd check on my favorite sister."

"Only sister."

"And still my favorite. Why are you on the roof?"

"Because it was quiet," Violet grumbled, starting to climb down.

"Don't. I'll join you," her sister replied, ducking her head back into Violet's room before hoisting herself out the window. Iris was still clad in the thick crimson and gold embroidered robe she'd worn in last night's show.

"In that?" Violet laughed. Iris played the role of Captain Josephine, the Pirate Queen. The costume was fitting for commanding a motley crew of buccaneers, but hardly appropriate for scaling a trellis. Violet looked down at her more practical attire, a plain blouse and a split skirt, which resembled extremely loose trousers and provided her with more freedom of movement while still maintaining the appearance of a skirt.

"Why not? It's chilly." Iris shrugged and, with the same grace she used to dance across the stage, ascended the trellis and settled next to her sister.

Violet tamped down a flush of jealousy. Iris could make anything look effortless. Violet had been climbing out her window for years to watch the sunrise, and even in wide-legged skirts, she felt more like a scuttling bug. "Uncle Leo will never forgive me if you break your leg," Violet added, though Iris was already smoothing out her pirate's robe.

"Actually, one is required to break a leg before a show," Iris joked, giving Violet an affectionate nudge with her shoulder.

"You know what I mean," Violet said, her tone softer now. "I'm surprised to see you up this early."

"What do you mean 'this early'?"

Violet realized her sister was still wearing the greasepaint makeup from the night before. Iris's eyes were exaggerated with dark liner and her lips still bright with color. Violet sighed. "You've not been to bed at all tonight?"

"I'll be in bed soon enough. There was a party after the show with some of the more distinguished patrons. It ran longer than I anticipated," she said breezily with a wry smile.

"I don't envy you the late nights."

"I still think you should consider a life onstage. It's so much more entertaining than the box office."

"I don't mind selling tickets." Violet shrugged. She knew that someone with a sense for numbers needed to keep the finances in order, and she didn't trust anyone else to do it.

"You would be lovely on stage," Iris continued, looking over at her sister. "You have the perfect profile for it. Very distinguished."

"You only say that because we're sisters. Our profiles look exactly the same." But not truly, Violet thought. Her sister was the elegant grace that was promised on the large promotional posters around the city of Leitha. She, on the other hand, was a general mess onstage. Her hair refused to mold into delicate curls, demanding instead to frizz around her face, and she was so flat-chested that she would be forced to add stuffing to any of her sister's costumes.

"Besides, I hate being onstage. I don't know what to do with my hands." Violet's hands were perfectly capable appendages when she was writing or tallying the nightly accounting, but onstage, they suddenly became as ineffectual as two dead fish hanging from her wrists. The last time she had accepted a role, she fidgeted with her hands so much that the audience broke into laughter during a dramatic death scene. Lance had offered to glue her hands to her sides the next night. It had been mortifying. "I'm perfectly happy off the stage, thank you very much."

"Too busy writing?" Iris asked, her smug smirk jerking Violet out of an old fear and into a new one.

"You were snooping in my room!"

Iris pointed a finger at Violet. "It was right on your desk, Vi. That's hardly snooping."

Violet glared at her sister and crossed her arms. "You shouldn't be in my room at all." She kicked herself for not hiding her script. She wasn't ready to share her work with anyone, even Iris.

"Can I read it? I only glanced at a few pages. It was lovely. I want to know more about this Sea Prince. He sounds charming."

"No!" Violet cried, a flush creeping into her face. "Leave my things alone. Is that so difficult?"

"I meant no offense," Iris said, raising her hands in surrender. "Only trying to show my support as your adoring big sister." Iris grinned, wrapping velvet-clad arms around Violet.

"I'll let you know when I want support," Violet said, struggling to free herself from her sister's loving embrace.

Neither of the girls spoke for a few minutes as they watched the sun crest the horizon, a tiny golden orb breaking the dawn blue. Violet's frustration cooled. Part of her was pleased Iris wanted to read her story, even if Violet wasn't ready to share it.

"I can see why you like it out here. It is peaceful," Iris said, finally breaking the quiet.

"I thought you were allergic to peace and calm."

"I can handle some peace." Iris stifled a yawn. "And that's about as much as I can handle. I'm going to bed." She kissed Violet on the cheek before climbing down the trellis and pulling herself through the window.

Violet stayed on her perch, savoring the morning stillness. In a few hours, the theatre would come to life as the performers who lived there woke up while those who stayed at the village by the dock arrived with traveling bags full of costumes and makeup, and in Arabella's case, her snake.

Then the deliveries would start coming in. Ruth and Mary, two girls from the village, would bring fresh roses to replace the wilting ones as well as food for the troupe: meat pies, fresh cod, dumplings filled with artichoke hearts, and spice cakes. The cook, Nat, would create the finer delicacies for the wealthy patrons: caviar blinis, rosewater candies, whipped caramels, and miniature fruit tarts. He would hire several strong village lads to pull the cart of wines and spirits, fresh arrivals from Leitha. Violet needed to get the books in order and ensure that her cash till had enough smaller foil bills, gold crowns, and silver florins to make change.

Violet closed her eyes, reliving the final scene of her play, the one with the Moon Princess and the Sea Prince. She considered slight changes to the dialogue, perhaps different stage directions, and played out the scene in her head several ways before deciding to let the matter sit for a while. Sighing, she opened her eyes.

Violet carefully climbed back through the window. She was about to head down to the cellars to see how many bottles of champagne they had for guests when she noticed that her script was no longer on her desk. Her stomach plummeted. Violet snapped open every drawer, knowing full well that it was useless.

"Iris!" she screamed. Forget telling her sister not to pry, Violet was going to get a lock for her door.

She flung open her door and sprinted down the hall to her sister's room, her slippers sliding on the carpet as she planned how to reacquire her script—with the use of threats and violence if necessary. Catching her breath outside her sister's room, Violet twisted the doorknob, but it did not budge.

When had Iris gotten a lock?

"Iris, give me back my play, you little thief!" Violet banged on her door. Her sister gave no answer. Violet pounded on the door more rapidly. "I am serious, Iris!"

"Sorry, I can't hear you. I'm asleep."

Violet let out a loud shriek of annoyance. "Cut the bollocks, Iris!"

"I am talking in my sleep," her sister insisted. Violet could hear the infuriating grin in her voice.

"If you don't open this door right now, I'm going to tell Uncle Leo." Violet cringed, feeling like a small child threatening to tattle to her uncle.

"Good luck waking him before noon." Iris began fake snoring so loudly that Violet marveled how it was possible for her sister to be such a great actress considering how unconvincing she was at this moment.

"I hate you."

"Love you."

"Argh!" Violet yelled, pounding on the door as hard as she could, but to no avail. She considered following through on her threat to tell their uncle, but he might ask her about the play and the embarrassment of confessing to Uncle Leo that she hoped to be a playwright was too much.

Out of options, Violet decided on drastic measures. She looked up and down the hall, ensuring no one was around. She opened her palm and concentrated on conjuring a key. She closed her eyes and focused on the details of a brass key: the metallic sheen, long, slender body, and delicate teeth. Heat filled her hands as she felt the heft of metal. The air smelled of smoke and roses as wisps of white vapor dissipated from her palms. She examined the shiny brass key she had created. Violet tried to insert the key, but it jammed in the lock. She wanted to scream.

Violet thrust the useless key in her pocket and stormed off in a rage, stomping all the way to the box office where she began to viciously attack the accounting books.

Violet was halfway through adding up the recent order of port and brandy when she heard a loud knocking coming from the front of the theatre. Checking her pocket watch, she realized it was already eleven in the morning. Ruth had been due an hour ago to replace the roses and tidy the theatre. Violet made her way to the entrance of the theatre and swung open the doors of the Dragonfly Theatre.

"Ruth, you're late," Violet said.

But instead of Ruth, a young man stood in front of her. He was a scrawny thing and wore an ill-fitting suit that hung on his wiry frame. The material of his suit was fine if a bit worn. The bowler hat on his head sat at an angle that would have been jaunty if he didn't look so destitute.

"Who are you?" Violet blurted out.

Without a word, the boy dropped into a bow low enough that his hat fell from his head, rolling down his arm. He caught it with ease before settling it back on his head.

"Alexander Morgan at your service. Call me Alec." He cracked a smile, revealing twin dimples. Violet realized he was older than she first thought, probably Iris's age. His baggy clothes and thin limbs made him appear younger.

"Did Ruth send you?" Violet asked, wondering if the village girl had taken ill and sent this boy in her place.

"I don't know any Ruth."

CamCat
Books

VISIT US ONLINE FOR MORE BOOKS TO LIVE IN:
CAMCATBOOKS.COM

SIGN UP FOR CAMCAT'S FICTION NEWSLETTER FOR
COVER REVEALS, EBOOK DEALS, AND MORE EXCLUSIVE CONTENT.

CamCatBooks   @CamCatBooks   @CamCat_Books   @CamCatBooks